Across All
Time

Across All
Time

M. J. CROOK

authorHOUSE®

AuthorHouse™
1663 Liberty Drive
Bloomington, IN 47403
www.authorhouse.com
Phone: 1-800-839-8640

Published by AuthorHouse 12/02/2014

ISBN: 978-1-4969-5640-8 (sc)
ISBN: 978-1-4969-5639-2 (e)

Library of Congress Control Number: 2014921304

Chapter 1

She didn't really enjoy the company of most of the people she worked with, she thought to herself as she sat at her desk. Many of the people she knew from work were a bunch of Ninnies. They traveled only in circles that contained people who thought like themselves. In other words, meaning that they lived only for their own gratification. They seemed to lack any compassion for anyone other then themselves. So why in the world would she want to spend time with them?

Tina Taylor was a woman that cared about other people, even if they didn't reciprocate. She enjoyed being with people that were real and true to themselves and others. There were very few such people around, or so it seemed.

Tina was the Personnel Supervisor at Hart Personnel Development Corporation. She was a cute brunette with green eyes, with a personality that only very few actually got to see. She was a very shapely five foot five woman with a mind of her own. So on the job she appeared stern and almost unapproachable. She had had to develop this façade to stop the many requests for dates from the male employees. Now they seemed to shy away from her for fear she might get them in to trouble if they flirted with her. Little by little, the men who had pulled that stunt when she first started working with Hart

Development had moved on to other positions, and weren't around to share with the new males how friendly she actually could be.

As far as the job itself went, Tina enjoyed what she was doing. She understood 'the people business', and was effective in it. She could 'read' a person fairly accurately upon first meeting them. She was rarely wrong. But it did happen occasionally.

Mackensey Shaw, or Mac as everyone called her, was her closest friend. They had roomed together during college and after. And Mac worked for Hart Development too. Only she was in the insurance department.

Mac was a sleek five foot eight blond, with hazel eyes. She drew men around her wherever she went. It seemed they just needed to be near her whenever she came into a room. Fellow employees would leave their seats to welcome her with a hug. Strangers asked to be introduced to her. And, of course, she carried all of this with confidence. She had grown accustomed to arriving at her desk to find flowers or candy, or even invitations for drinks or dinner awaiting her. She was very popular with the guys.

The women in the business envied Mac. Sometimes they would approach her to ask for her suggestions as to dealing with a problem in their personal relationships. They had learned that even though Mac was confident, she was very approachable. And when her suggestions worked, Mac won another comrade in arms.

Tina's newest employee was giving her a few problems. Susan Garth was Tina's boss's niece. She had been brought in as a favor to Susan's mother, being sister to Daniel Thorpe, Tina's boss. Susan was to learn discipline, which she hadn't ever learned from her parents, as well as learning the art of getting along with people. Somehow all she had been successful in learning so far from her family was the knack of yelling at the help and expecting to have her morning cup of coffee brought to her as soon as she arrived at her desk.

Tina could be a very patient person when she needed to be, but this young woman made Tina want to slap her. She was rude to the other employees, yet cried to Tina the minute anyone said something back to her that hurt her feelings. Susan considered herself a sensitive caring person, the last thing from the actual truth.

Today Tina was planning on placing Susan with an employee that would be visiting various departments within the building. As the experienced employee would visit with each department head she was to get feedback on possible problem employees that might need retraining in some area of their people skills. As the information came back to Tina of the needs in each department she would schedule a workshop, covering that needed area of expertise and inform that department head as to the time and location so those employees, along with one or two others from the same department, could attend on paid status. That way the employees gained needed training without being singled out, and the company gained as well. It seemed to be a very workable way to prevent in-house staff problems. In the past two years, Tina had received high compliments from her boss as to the level of employee evaluation improvements.

Tina sipped at her cup of coffee as she watched the employees enter their respective offices, get their morning cup of coffee and head toward their desks to begin their day's duties. Tina liked getting in early. She believed that by just watching she could learn much about her fellow employees. She noticed the 'early birds' that came in long before they were required to be at their desks. And those individuals she allowed more breathing room in things such as arriving a couple of minutes late back from lunch. The people that arrived barely in time to clock in without being considered late, she watched to see how long they lingered over getting that cup of coffee, or how long they would stand at a fellow employee's desk talking about the club they visited the night before. After a couple of those she would invite the employee into her office and close the door. She would remind the employee that they were expected to be busy at their desk immediately after the time clock said they were officially 'on-duty'. She would let them know she would be scrutinizing their work and that she expected only their best from their efforts. And, naturally, she made sure the employee was aware that this meeting was being documented and going into their file and would be re-considered at their next evaluation. Usually they would consider Tina to be the 'bad guy' for a few days, and then the individual would buckle down and get back to doing what they were hired to do. But once in a while they didn't, and that was when another workshop would be scheduled for specified personnel to attend.

Most employees figured out the system pretty quickly and realized that the workshops were truly for the employees benefit and future employment security, and they went along with it. It seemed everyone gained from this approach. Morale flourished and so did satisfaction throughout the field.

Hart Personnel Development Corporation supplied experienced capable employees to many of the large corporations both within the city and the surrounding areas. With the basic people skills taught by Tina's staff, an employee that had learned the techniques of people management and leadership could easily slip into any managerial position no matter what the product that their future employee was manufacturing, because that individual had learned how to delegate effectively until they had the opportunity to learn their new employers service or knowledge of the produced items. Again Tina was correct in her idea that leadership began with people and knowing how to work effectively with them.

The eight o'clock buzzer sounded, shaking Tina out of her reverie. She looked around to see that everyone was busy at their posts, except for Susan. Her chair sat empty and there wasn't any sign of her arrival as yet.

Tina's eyes traveled toward the time clock and saw only one card still on the left side of the clock It was a little way down in the line, which was arranged in alphabetical order. Tina figured it was Susan's card.

Suddenly she heard a voice coming from the area of the elevators and looking up spotted Susan and another young woman exiting one of the elevators. The other woman looked around and realized they were late and hurried off to another office. Tina noticed her so she would be able to recognize her when she later in the morning cruised through the other offices. She would inform the woman's supervisor that this young lady needed a verbal reminder of how important it was to arrive at work on time. Then she waited until Susan had paused at two different desks to talk to the individuals there, then drifted over to the time clock and clocked in. Both of the individuals Susan had spoken with glanced up and were aware that Tina was watching, so they discouraged Susan from remaining to talk. It was all right if Susan got in hot water for being late to work, but they didn't want any part of it.

Susan glanced up and got the impression that she was being watched, so she stepped quickly to her desk. As she was putting her purse in one of the drawers in the bottom of her desk she glanced up to see Ms. Taylor standing beside her.

"Good morning Ms. Taylor. Is there something I can do for you?" she stated, hopeful that her tone would discourage any harassment.

"Good morning. Are you aware of what time it is, Ms. Garth?" Tina asked calmly.

"Of course! It's time to start work for the day. Why do you ask?" Susan was beginning to suspect she wasn't going to get away with her tardiness today.

"Would you step into my office, please. We need to talk." Tina requested, knowing Susan would realize it was an order.

"Certainly!" Susan stood up straight after closing the desk drawer and followed Ms. Taylor into her office.

As Tina approached the door to her office she extended her hand, palm up, moving her right hand away from her body toward her office, inviting Susan to go in first. As they passed through the portal Tina closed the door and said, "Please take a seat."

Tina walked around her desk and sat down. "As a new employee here at Hart, are you settling in? Do you like working here?" she asked.

"Yes, I guess I'm settled in. I'm not sure just what you mean by that. And yes, I hope to learn a lot while I'm here. Not that I plan on staying in just one department during my stay. As soon as I learn all I need here, I plan on moving on."

"If your goals are learning and preparing for upward mobility then I am certain that you are already aware of the need to be to work on time. To be able to complete a job efficiently one must have sufficient time to do that job well. Are you aware you were late this morning, Ms. Garth?"

"Uh, yes, I guess so. But it really doesn't matter that much. As long as I get my work done in a timely manner, that's all that really is important here," she replied.

"No not really," Tina answered. "You know there are some offices where no one punches a time clock. And you know what allows that system to be effective?"

"I'm not sure. What?" she asked.

"Honor, Ms. Garth. Trust and honor. When someone gives their word or promise that they will arrive at a predetermined time, then that is the time they are expected."

"I understand that. I was only two minutes late. I really could not have accomplished much if I had been at my desk working those two minutes. But this little meeting we are having is interrupting my work time. I'm sure you are aware of that, Ms. Taylor."

"Yes, and I am taking that into consideration, Susan. May I call you that?"

"If you wish."

"Susan, I would like your time with us to be mutually rewarding. I suspect one of the reasons your uncle wanted you to start your time with Hart in this department was because he wanted you to learn the basics of good management. And the ground floor lesson on that is honor. The first thing you need to demonstrate to me is that you have honor, Susan. If you don't have honor, you don't have anything."

"I have my honor. I don't understand why you seem to think I don't."

"By not getting here in a timely manner demonstrated it, Susan."

"What does it matter? I was ready to start working as soon as I put away my purse. That was until you interrupted me."

"I don't think you're getting my message here, Susan. Let me give you an example. Let's say that you agreed to pay, let's say just for a number, a thousand dollars for a coat that you wanted. The person selling you the coat agreed and you gave him an envelope of nine hundred and ninety dollars. He accepted the envelope from you trusting you that you put the amount of money in it you said you would. He gives you the coat. After you leave he counts the money and finds out you shorted him ten dollars. What do you think your actions did to your so called 'honor'?"

"It killed it. The man would think I didn't have any honor, or that I couldn't count."

"Absolutely correct. Now let's apply the same theory to your arriving at work on time. If you hired in, agreeing to arrive at your desk by eight o'clock, and you come in later than that, what would that do to your honor?"

"I see what you're saying Ms. Taylor. If my word is to be believable then I have to do exactly what I say I am going to do."

"Exactly! If you were a supervisor over other employees, which is what I think you will be someday, then you have to follow through on whatever you say you're going to do. Much like I have to do also. I would be remiss if I allowed my employees to come into work whenever they decided to arrive rather than at the scheduled time."

"Yes, I see what you mean. I really didn't think a minute or two would matter, but when you look at it as a matter of honor then it becomes imperative that one does follow through on their promises. I understand, Ms. Taylor. I'll try not to be late again. I appreciate you're explaining it in this way. Honor is important, and it is important to me personally now."

"I'm glad that you are in agreement with me in this. It really is the basis on which we build all of our training for supervision and management skills. You do realize, of course, that I will have to document our little discussion, and a copy will have to go into your file. If there aren't anymore incidents of this nature in the next year, then I'll mark the documentation before your annual evaluation so that it will not be reflected there," Tina told her.

"I understand. There won't be anymore, I promise. On my honor!" she said.

"I'm glad to hear you say that. You can go back to your desk now. I will have Ms. Pines contact you in a little while. I am sending you along with her to observe what she will be doing in relation to departmental instructional needs. It will be a great opportunity for you to learn constructive management in action. She'll come to your desk to get you when she has her paperwork ready. You will be visiting all of the departments in this building, so plan on being gone for quite a while. It will probably take most of the day. I hope you'll learn a great deal from this opportunity. Thank you for your time, Susan."

Tina stood up as their meeting ended. Susan stood as well and reached across Tina's desk, her right hand extended. Tina and Susan shook hands. It impressed Tina that Susan was acting so professional in doing so. She hoped it was just a natural thing, not a copied behavior that she had learned just because she had seen her uncle do the same. She was hopeful that it was Susan's sincere desire to be professional. She figured time would tell.

"Thank you again," Susan said just before she turned and left Tina's office.

After Susan closed the door Tina turned to her computer and typed up a summary of the meeting with Susan. Then she called in Marsha, her secretary, to time stamp it and put it in Susan's file with a tag on it. There would be a review of her attendance concerns before her next evaluation, also showing if there weren't any further problems in that area, this documentation was not to be considered in Susan's next evaluation, but it would remain in her file.

Marsha added Susan's name to her growing list of files to re-check before evaluation time. Then Tina headed back to her desk.

It was only minutes after she sat down when the com-line buzzed and Tina punched the button allowing the two women to talk without leaving their desks. "Yes Marsha?" she said.

"Miss Pines is here to begin her staff information update. Do you want to see her before she gets Ms. Garth from her desk?"

"Yes! Please send her in," Tina told her.

The door to her office opened and in walked Meredith Pine.

"Thank you for stopping in before gathering Ms. Garth. Please have a seat. We'll only take a minute, but there is something I want to discuss with you."

"Gladly! Is there something new I should know, Ms. Taylor?"

"Please, we're friends. You can call me Tina. The only time you need to call me Ms. Taylor is when we're in a meeting with other lower employees present. Sit! Be comfortable!" she said as she motioned to the two chairs in front of Tina's desk. As Ms. Pines chose a chair Tina moved around her desk and sat down beside her.

"The young woman that I am sending with you is the niece of our employer. She has very strong opinions, but is not well versed in management skills or knowledge. This is to be a learning opportunity for her. But I just want to warn you, she will probably be looking for things to critique in a negative way. I had to bring her into my office this morning because she was late for work. I discussed the importance of honor with her. I'm hopeful that she has grasped the concept. But just don't trust her too far. I'm sure she would like to find fault with how we do things so she could go back to her uncle and complain, just to make herself look good. I get the impression that appearance means a great deal to this young woman.

Don't give her any opportunity to catch you doing anything inappropriate, if you know what I mean."

"Ah, one of those, huh? Okay! I won't turn my back on her. And I'll watch how I say things when she's around. It sounds as though she might be one to twist things around to use to her own advantage. That's a shame! Wouldn't it be nice if she was an open slate, willing to learn things in an honest and sincere way? Perhaps you've caught her in time so she can be turned around. Thanks for the warning. I'll be watchful!"

"If you run into any problems just use whatever phone is at hand and give me a call. I'll be glad to help you any way I can. You do realize that the task ahead could be misconstrued to be employee harassment if handled badly?"

"Yes, of course. But it really is employee improvement, if anyone would research just what we're doing here. This program actually gives employees a second chance to clean up their act and improve. It's a shame that not everyone recognizes that."

"This isn't your first time doing this, and I really appreciate your ability here, Meredith. I know you'll do a wonderful job. You always do. Just watch how you say things in front of Susan Garth. We don't want her to misunderstand our management techniques. Let me know when you've completed your tour. I want to know when to expect Ms. Garth back at her desk. Hopefully my lesson on honor has sunk in."

"I hope it has," replied Meredith.

Tina gave her a big hug and walked with her to the door. "Good luck," she told her as she opened it.

Tina watched as Meredith walked over to Susan's desk and spoke with her. As she saw the two women getting to know each other she stepped back into her office and closed the door. She didn't want Susan to get the idea that she was watching over her.

Returning to her desk she pulled out some paperwork she needed to finish before the end of the day. It was a report that had to be on Mr. Michael Thorp's desk today and she wanted it to be thorough and complete, and without error. Since he was one of the two owners of Hart Personnel Development Corporation she wanted the report in his possession before the required time limit. She tilted her head down and brought her mind in line with where she had left off the last time she had worked on it. As she lowered her eyes to the paperwork before her, the words seem to swim. The page wavered and she thought she could glimpse something else entirely. There was a scene of a roadway, and a very old car traveling upon it, approaching her. It was as if she was watching an old movie. The action was there and she sat mesmerized as her head seemed to spin.

Tina shook her head as if to clear the cobwebs. She blinked and the scene was gone. What was going on? What just happened? Was the job becoming too stressful for her that she was hallucinating? She raised her eyes to look at the room around her. Everything seemed normal to her. Perhaps she just needed a cup of coffee. She stood to walk to the coffee corner, pulling her favorite cup from her desk drawer.

On her way to fill her cup with caffeine she thought about what had just happened. Where could that scene have come from? Was it from a dream she had and for some reason it just popped into her head? It made no sense at all, she thought. She couldn't remember such a dream.

Pouring her cup full from the fresh pot that sat on the warmer, she looked forward to the lift it would give her. She was feeling a little tired this morning. A boost of energy was just what she needed. She liked her coffee fresh, hot and black, and not too strong.

Taking a sip of the hot brew, she turned to return to her project. As she passed Marsha's desk Marsha looked up.

"Everything okay?" Marsha asked.

"Just needed some caffeine. Maybe now I can concentrate better," she said, smiling.

Sliding back into her comfortable chair behind her desk she took another sip of coffee, sat the cup down and proceeded to forget all about it. Her mind was totally on her report. An hour later it was complete. She sat back and crossed her legs, reviewing her progress page by page, looking for typing errors and mistakes. She found none. After she scanned the final page Tina lifted her pen from her desk and signed the bottom of the page. Then she reached for the com-line and asked Marsha to come in to her office.

Tina gave the finished report to her. "Don't forget to time stamp it and hand carry it to Mr. Michael Thorpe's office right away. It's due this afternoon and I'd like it to be on his desk before that time."

"Sure! No problem. I'll do it right away. Do you want me to make a copy for our files?"

"Yes, I think so. And it'll be on my hard drive in case we need it. Thanks, Marsha."

Her secretary was one of the most efficient in the entire building. Tina knew this paperwork would be on the appropriate desk within minutes. And she was glad. She didn't like waiting till the last minute to get required paperwork done. Somehow this report had just seemed to get pushed aside until almost too late.

Later Tina noticed the almost full cup of cold coffee sitting on her desk and grabbed it, and headed for the coffee corner to dump it out. As she stood at the small sink in the office's small kitchen she mumbled to herself.

"Pretty dumb! Needed some caffeine, and forgot to drink it. What a dummy I am," she said softly to herself.

"Is the job getting to you that you have to talk to yourself? Or is it you just want to control both sides of the conversation?" came the voice behind her. Thinking it was one of the male secretaries she said without turning around, "It's best to prepare for the worst. So if you get to be both sides of the conversation you're guaranteed to win the argument."

She turned to smile at the man behind her after rinsing out her cup, only to find it wasn't the face she was expecting. Before her stood one of her employers.

Michael grinned, aware she wasn't expecting it to be him.

"Oh!" she gasped. "Sorry! I just thought it was one of the guys from the secretarial pool. I didn't realize I was letting out secrets to someone important." She could feel the heat rising across her cheeks.

"Don't worry, I won't let it be know that our Supervisor over Personnel talks to herself. I just thought I would grab a cup of coffee. By the way, thanks for the report. From first glance it looks good to me." He stepped closer since Tina was standing near the coffee maker. He reached around her to get the coffee pot and fill his cup. His arm brushed hers as he moved closer to the coffee maker. Immediately she moved back to give him room.

"I didn't mean to be in your way. Sorry!" She was very much aware of possible sexual overtones that could happen in the office and wanted no part of such things. Even if he was the most attractive of the two brothers owning the company!

Michael was the dream date for most of the single females in his employ. So Tina vowed she wasn't going to become involved in an office relationship. It could only end badly. Yet, as she looked up at him she knew he had the darkest eyes of anyone she had ever known. And the nicest shoulders! His longer that usual hair was dark and shiny, and she longed to run her fingers through it. Tina wondered what it would feel like to be held in those arms.

When Michael worked at his desk he shed his suit jacket, and sometimes even rolled up his sleeves as they were now, showing the large size of his forearms and wrists. He looked as though he lifted weights. She wondered if his chest showed such muscle tone as well. Where did that thought come from, she wondered. She hadn't ever had such thoughts about him before. Maybe it was just because they were standing so close. She moved further back away from him.

Michael felt the attraction too. He smiled and said, "I don't bite you know."

"Maybe not, but I might," she tossed out, trying to cover her confusion. "I hope that pot of coffee isn't old. It looks a little on the dark side. Would you like me to make a fresh pot?"

"No problem. I'm used to drinking it strong. Sometimes I forget and leave a pot on the warmer for hours."

"You shouldn't drink it," she said before even thinking. "Just dump it and make some fresh. The thicker it gets, the harder it is on your stomach."

"This isn't anything compared to what I usually have at home." Michael turned to face her and moved closer to her. He towered over her since he was at least six foot three. Compared to her five foot five height she almost had to lean her head back just to get eye contact with him. Standing so close, she decided, could be dangerous to her health. Again she moved back and found herself against the wall.

"Or maybe we should just go down to the coffee shop on the first floor and continue this discussion. Then we could have fresh coffee as well as something with it. Care to join me?" he asked, standing very still. He knew his forward movement could be misinterpreted as sexual harassment and he didn't

really mean for it to be taken that way. He just wanted to get
to know this woman on a one-to-one basis. Her work was more
than excellent and she had the most interesting green eyes. He
wondered how she would feel in his arms, dancing slowly and
closely to some romantic music.

"No, I really couldn't. I'm sure you have much more
important things to do, Mr. Thorpe." she told him.

"Michael!" he said. "It's Michael! And we need to discuss
your report before your deadline runs out. I insist, Ms. Taylor.
Let's walk over to my office."

With that edict she couldn't refuse. She turned to leave the
coffee corner and walked with her empty cup toward Michael's
office. Michael paused in front of his secretary's desk informing
her that he would be in a meeting with Ms. Taylor and that he
did not want to be disturbed. Then he continued through the
open door into his private domain, turning after he entered to
invite her in.

As Tina stepped toward him he took a sip from his cup,
closed the door and proceeded toward his desk. He placed
his cup on a coaster she noticed there and he lifted her report
from the desk.

"Please sit down. Tina, isn't it? May I call you Tina?" He
waved his hand toward the conversational corner across the
room.

"Yes, it is Tina. Christina, actually! And yes, you may call
me Tina," she said, hoping he wasn't detecting her nervousness.

He motioned her into one of the two chairs that were
near the corner windows in his huge office, with a glass table
between. This was an area used with important visitors, not
employees, she noticed.

Tina sat in one of the comfortable chairs and watched as
Michael slid into the other one. He moved like a cat, smoothly
and quietly, as though he was stalking prey.

"I'd like to get to know the majority of our staff as quickly as possible. Since I've come in from our Houston office, I feel as though I have a million names to memorize. But since I'm going to be working out of this office for the next few years I want to get know the faces and the names of those that make the business effective."

"Sounds very understandable, Mr. Thorpe," she said.

"Please, call me Michael. Since you're in charge of all staff I'm sure we'll be working closely in the future. Just call me Michael, and I'll call you Tina, if that's okay with you?"

"Of course, Mr. Uh.. Michael. I'd be glad to be of any help to you that I can." She felt as though her smile wasn't quite pasted on correctly. She wasn't sure just how to take him. Was he flirting with her or was he serious? She wasn't sure.

Michael crossed his legs and leaned back in his chair. He had a lock of hair that had fallen across his forehead and she felt as though she should brush it back for him. Suddenly she was very much aware of this man across from her. Her instincts weren't exactly maternal.

"Would you verbally explain the purpose of this report so I don't have to read it in it's entirety? That would simplify it a lot." He looked at Tina, waiting for a short synopsis. She could make his job must easier, or more difficult, whichever she wished to do.

"In short, the review is being done as we speak. My team is currently visiting all departments in this building, speaking with each department head, and ascertaining what disciplinary needs have appeared in the last six months. As soon as I receive that information I can see what type of in-service retraining is necessary and I'll be setting up workshops, inviting specific employees that have had problems in that area. Then I allow each department head to invite two other employees to attend as well. The list of names will generate invitations, to only those needing the program along with the chosen employees selected by their immediate supervisor. Then the invitations will be sent through our in-house mail. All invited employees will be informed attendance is mandatory. Attending gives them the opportunity to improve their skills. The training workshops are held on paid status during the workday and the employee that seems to have a problem is given the opportunity to learn how to improve their work skills without feeling singled out."

"I see! Sounds as though it would be a very efficient way to correct behavior problems while offering improvement training at the same time."

"And it seems to lift morale as well. The two extra employees that are chosen by each department head allows that management individual the ability to assist the employees that he or she knows could use such training to strengthen their ability." Tina sat quietly, her hands folded in her lap. She could feel his eyes on her, as though he was evaluating her. It made her feel very uncomfortable.

Michael hadn't moved a muscle since they had sat down. He appeared almost too still. Tina kept her back straight and her posture professional. She couldn't remember ever feeling so self-conscious before.

"I see" he remarked. "Keep it simple, but necessary. I like it Tina. It's direct and to the point. It hits the current need and hopefully corrects it. Have you any records so as to show the effectiveness and improvement rate of those concerned employees?"

"Yes! My secretary keeps a running record for each year so we can actually see if we have helped any troubled employee. If we see it hasn't then we try a counseling session for the individual with their supervisor, with a notice that lack of improvement will be recorded in their files and will be considered in the following evaluation."

"I'd like to see the report for the current year Tina. You can have a copy sent over to me this afternoon. Do you enjoy your work here? Is there anything that you would change if given that opportunity?" he asked.

Tina was surprised to be asked such a question. Quickly she scanned her memory for any areas of concern she had had in the past. "Actually, I find the work rewarding and challenging. I'm sure as time goes by I'll find there are other needs that will need to be met, but right now, I think we're dealing effectively with our employees." She discovered she was pressing her thumbs together and consciously made herself stop it. She left her fingers interlaced on her lap.

"Excellent! Well, I guess I haven't anything to add to that, at the moment." Michael stood, and Tina did likewise. He reached out to take her hand in his as he turned toward the door. He pulled her after him and stopped two steps before the closed exit.

Pulling her closer to him he released her hand and placed his hand in the middle of her back. She saw his head come down toward hers and felt his lips as they laid softly against her own. She was afraid of something like this. Perhaps he was testing her. Then she heard a soft moan coming from between his lips and his kiss became something totally different. Immediately she pulled back, releasing their lips and his eyes opened. Those dark eyes were even darker now, and she could feel heat radiating from his body. They stood, with their chest's bearly touching, looking into each other's eyes. Moments ticked by and neither of them moved.

"You feel it too, don't you?" he asked. "What have you done, bewitched me Christina?"

Gasping her surprise, her mouth dropped opened. Immediately his eyes went to her mouth and he was kissing her again. And since her lips were open she felt his tongue brush against her bottom lip, and then her front teeth, and then gently begin a dance with her tongue. His arms tightened around her pulling her up tightly against him.

Without even being aware of it she had somehow moved her arms around his neck and was pulling him closer. "Oh,.." she moaned. She felt his hands slide down her back pressing her against him. It felt so good. She didn't want it to stop. Stop! Then she was saying it, "Stop!"

Suddenly he released her. They were both shaken. They stood for a moment in silence just peering into each other's eyes. She felt his hands slide from her back along her arms to her hands, and he held them in his large hands, between them.

"Christina!" he whispered. Then he was apologizing. "Christina, forgive me. I don't know what caused me to do that. I'm sorry. No I'm not sorry, I love the way you kissed me back." He began to lower his head to kiss her again and she stepped back away from him.

"Michael, I don't know what is going on here but this isn't right. You're my boss. No one kisses the boss," she stammered. She could feel the heat rising across her cheeks. She had embarrassed herself twice in one hour in front of her employer.

He started to laugh. "No one? Does that mean no one is allowed? How terrible! No Christina, this is one time it is allowed. I'm sorry to take you by surprise like this. But I wanted to taste your lips. Please forgive me. I didn't mean to do anything improper." His eyes sparkled as though he was laughing inside. "I love the feel of your lips. Let me kiss you once more."

"No Michael! You shouldn't be doing this," she managed to say just before his lips claimed hers again. He kissed his way across her bottom lip, as gentle as a raindrop. Then she felt his tongue as he licked her lips from one side to the other.

"So good. You taste so good." He continued his assault until she opened her mouth to speak, to try and stop him. Immediately his tongue found hers and began a dance that could only lead to trouble.

She tried to pull back but he held her tightly. He leaned into her as his arms tightened around her. His left hand slid down her back to just above her hips. He was pressing her tightly against himself as if he wanted to climb inside of her. Oh no you don't, she thought to herself. Tina placed both of her hands flat against his chest and pushed. He got the message and released her. "Michael! Stop it!"

"Yes, Christina! You're right. We must stop. I don't know what got into me. But you have the most kissable lips. I can't remember anyone making me feel like this." He released her and she stepped away from him. "I'm sorry Christina! Forgive me?"

"Only if you promise that this won't ever happen again," she replied, trying to put an angry tone in her voice.

"I think I'm going to regret this, but you have my word." He physically took a step backward away from her. She could see his eyes were very dark and his chest was rising with every breath. He stretched out his hand to her, enfolding her hand in his. "Forgiven?" he asked.

"Forgiven!" she replied. She pulled her hand from his and reached for the doorknob. She opened the door and took a step toward her path to freedom. She paused and looked up into his face. His eyes were on hers and she could feel his heat radiating again. She stepped quickly through the doorway and pulled the door closed behind her.

Chapter 2

That afternoon, after she had her lunch, Tina received a memo stating there would be an upper staff meeting the following morning at nine o'clock. As she paced back and forth across her office carpet she contemplated facing Michael in that meeting. He had promised no more kissing, but did he mean it? How could she look him in the eye? It just seemed much too embarrassing.

After several passes across the room and back she decided that no matter what happen she would just have to deal with whatever happens when it happened. There wasn't any use in worrying about it ahead of time. Okay, she thought. Then with that out of the way I can get back to doing my job.

Settling behind her desk again she pulled out some paperwork that she wanted finished before she went home for the day. As she worked, her mind became more engrossed with the needs before her and when she finally looked up, Marsha stood just inside the office door telling her good night and that she would see her in the morning. Looking at the clock Tina realized it was five o'clock all ready.

After saying goodnight and wishing her a nice evening she returned to the material before her. She decided to change her formatting and update a course outline for one of the previous workshops so that in the event the same subject was used again it could be more easily followed. She figured by changing the format the training information would flow better and be more easily understood. Happy with that small change she continued on, reviewing and changing as instinct guided her.

The next time she glanced up she noticed the clock showed almost seven in the evening. She decided it was time to call it a day and head on home. She returned the training material to it's folder, slipping it into the main drawer of her desk. She would come in early the next morning and try to finish this project before the staff meeting.

Even though her office door was a solid core door, the wall of her office facing the interior of the building was made of glass blocks, allowing light to penetrate. Anyone walking through the offices would be able to detect the lights were on in Tina's office as they walked through the hallway or adjacent office.

Michael walked out of his office at six forty-five. He decided he would stop by his favorite 'watering hole' on the way home, and have a bite to eat while he was there. Cooking at home for one just wasn't much fun. He really didn't consider himself a very good cook. Oh, he could pop a TV dinner in the microwave as well as anyone, or open a can of something, but other than putting together a sandwich, fresh food just didn't happen at his house.

Strolling along the hallway he noticed some office lights on. He watched, expecting to see the custodian making his rounds, or even security, but didn't see anyone. He altered his path to see if anyone was in the personnel office. There shouldn't be anyone there at this hour, he thought to himself.

Following the glow of light, he opened the door to the private office of the Personnel Supervisor's office. He stood in the doorway, surprised to see Tina gathering her purse and locking up her desk, obviously preparing to leave for the day.

"I'm surprised to see you're still here," he said.

"Oh!" she cried out. She hadn't heard the door open. "You startled me!"

"Sorry! You have something you just had to get done?" he asked.

"Yes, actually. I was reworking one of the workshops. I felt it ought to have an overhaul, and I guess the time just got away from me. I'm heading out now. You're working late too, I see." She thought she ought to toss the ball back in his court since his comment seemed to be censoring her lateness in leaving.

"You know how it goes. The boss doesn't quit when the rest of the employees quit for the day. If there is something that needs doing, that's the best time to do it. Besides, it's easier to work when the phone quits ringing and the place is quiet."

"Yeah, I have to agree with that. Just when I really get into something a call comes in and interrupts my train of thought. Even when I get off the phone it takes a little while for me to get my head back into what I was working on."

As Tina locked her desk she stepped away from it and headed toward the door. By the time she reached it Michael was standing directly in her path. She stopped and looked up into his face. "On your way home?" she asked.

"I thought I would grab a bite to eat first. Why don't you join me? It's more interesting when there is someone to talk with over dinner. We shouldn't be long, and I'm sure you have to eat dinner too. Why not enjoy a little company?"

"Thanks, but I think I'll just go on home. I'd like to slip out of my shoes and be comfy." She told him.

"I'll let you kick off your shoes during dinner. I won't even tell anyone," he replied quickly.

"I think I'll pass. But thanks anyway," she told him fearful that he might break his promise to her if she spent time with him.

"Suit yourself," he said. He stepped back to allow her through the doorway, and Tina reached up turning off the lights as she passed through the exit. Michael followed behind her, closing her office door behind him.

They started toward the main hallway and turned toward the bank of elevators.

"You know, my favorite hangout has the best Chicken Fried Steak. And it comes with home made gravy, not that pork gravy that most restaurants serve. It's just like homemade.

"Do you eat that stuff on a regular basis? I'm surprised you don't weigh a ton, if you do. That fried stuff alone will pack on the pounds. And homemade gravy as well? You know, my mom used to make the best biscuits and gravy."

Tina's feet stopped moving and Michael stopped beside of her. Looking down at her he said, "What?"

"Look what you did? You brought back a memory and you made me hungry for biscuits and gravy. What's wrong with you? A woman doesn't need to be eating that fattening food. That's for the very young, or the very old who don't care anymore if they get fat."

"I just figure if I put on a couple of pounds then there's just that much more of me to love," he told her. "Up to a point, that is."

"It's too bad that place of yours doesn't have biscuits and gravy. I'd be tempted to check it out."

"If they have the gravy for over the Chicken Fried Steak, I'll bet they have biscuits somewhere in that big kitchen of theirs. Come with me and we'll find out."

"I couldn't, really. I just need to get home."

"You're chicken. You're afraid to have a quiet little dinner in the same place as I would be. Tell me that isn't true?" he chided her.

They talked about it in the elevator all the way down to the first floor. By the time the doors opened and they stepped out into the foyer he had tempted her enough that her stomach was craving biscuits and gravy. "Okay," she said, giving in. But I'm not staying long. Just let me get my car and I'll follow you there, so I can leave for home from there?"

"We can walk from here. The place is only about a block. Come on," he said grabbing her hand and giving a tug.

Tina pulled her hand out of his and followed his lead toward the front sidewalk. They turned left and he stepped between her body and the curb. Tina noticed immediately. She enjoyed the chivalry of the act. She smiled at him to thank him.

"What's the smile for?" he asked.

"It's nice when a man is a gentleman,' she told him.

Ah, he thought. I'll be sure to remember that. I can be gallant.

They walked quietly into the next block and suddenly he grabbed her elbow to turn her into one of the bars that were scattered throughout the area. "Here we are!"

The hostess put them in a booth that was a little out of the way so they didn't have so much noise around them. She figured they were in for dinner more than the bar and dancing. She pulled the table out so it would be easier to slide in behind it. Tina slid in easily, then Michael sat down beside her. After the hostess handed them their menus and wished them an enjoyable meal she stepped away, just as Michael caught Tina's eye.

In the quiet of the moment she trembled. What was she doing here with him? This is the man all of the women in the office were dying to kiss. Everyone except her, that was.

Tina was afraid he might sense her fear. She tried to smile at him, but she knew it didn't come out well.

"It's okay. I gave my promise. I won't bite, or kiss you. But I knew it was a mistake to make that promise." His eyes never left hers as he said that.

Tina was ready to slide right out the other end of the booth. He knew what had crossed her mind, even though she had hoped he didn't.

Sudden the spell was broken and he looked down at the menu in front of him. "Look on the third page. That's where they hide the dinners. I tell you, they must have someone's mother back there in that kitchen because everything I've tried so far tastes like it came from a kitchen in the Midwest."

"When the waitress came to take their order she assured Tina that they did have the ability to create her biscuits and gravy and that it was one of her favorite things. With a recommendation like that how could she not try it? So Tina ordered a plate of two biscuits covered with homemade gravy, along with a small dinner salad. Michael ordered the Chicken Fried Steak with mashed potatoes and gravy, and veggies. When their meals arrived she was amazed at how much food was on their plates.

"As long as we only do this once and a while I'm sure we could get away with it," he told her. Besides, the walk back to the parking structure should get rid of a little of this."

Tina looked up and grinned. He didn't really believe that, did he, she thought to herself.

Some time later, over cups of rich hot coffee Tina and Michael were sated and more relaxed.

"So what did you think of the food, Tina?" he asked.

"It was wonderful, just as you said. But I wouldn't want to eat this heavy or rich very often. Light salads with some protein is just fine for me."

Tina turned to her purse to pull out some money to pay for her meal.

"No, no! Let me treat this time. I'm the one that coerced you into coming. It's the least I could do."

"No, that wouldn't be right. We're going 'Dutch'. I insist!" she informed him.

"You're a tough one Tina Taylor. And you're a lot like another Taylor I know. You're just as evasive! No one can grab hold of you."

"That's a good thing. If you were able to grab hold, you would probably regret it," she answered, smiling.

"Oh I don't know about that. I think you might be a nice handful."

"For some, a handful can be too much at times. If you don't think so, just ask some the guys in the office. They stay clear of me. They're scared to death of me."

"That's because they don't have the eyes to appreciate what they are actually seeing. You know, not everyone has the ability to see what is real."

"I'll take that as a compliment, thank you. Now, I really should be going." She grabbed her purse and began to slide toward him, hoping the body language would encourage him to also slide out of the booth. But he sat very still. His eyes stayed on hers as she moved. When she came within touching distance of his leg she stopped.

"I like a woman that likes to touch," he told her with a smile on his face. He was acting as though she was going to cuddle up to him.

"I don't think that's what is happening here, Mr. Thorpe. Would you please slide out of the booth? I do really need to get out of here."

Her eyes came up to meet his and his expression looked serious. He laid his left arm over the back of the booth as though he was going to pull her into a hug soon.

Without even blinking she hardened her expression and said, "Don't even think about it. Now move!"

Michael's face broke into a big grin. He realized he couldn't bluff her. "Okay, mom. Geesh! You're too tough!" he answered, sliding out of the booth.

As soon as he was standing he reached down to offer his hand to help her up. It caused her to pause. She looked surprised, he thought. I guess she isn't used to having a man treat her like the woman she is. I think I'll have to remember that being gallant is just what she needs.

Tina put her left hand in his right one, holding on as she stood. Why does he have to be so nice, she pondered. He seems so over bearing until he does something like that. If he'd just lighten up the rest of the time, maybe he wouldn't be half bad.

"Thank you," she said softly as soon as she was on her feet.

"That's what I'm here for. Always glad to help a lady," he stated softly, as he leaned close to her ear.

They had paid the waitress already, and had left their tip on the table, so they didn't have to stop on their way out of the bar. Tina walked directly toward the exit and reached for the handle on the door when Michael's hand got there first.

"Allow me," he said.

"Thanks!" was her curt reply. He may be the boss, but he is not going to intimidate me, she thought to herself. She felt smug and confident until the next thought came through her mind. That is, until he puts his arms around me again.

Her shoulder rubbed his as she tried to step around him to exit through the doorway. Immediately she caught her breath and paused. Her body warmed and she stopped all movement.

Looking up into his eyes she saw they were sparkling and his lips began to turn up in the beginning of a grin.

That did it! Instantly her anger came up and she walked out to the sidewalk. She paused just for a moment as he exited the bar, then her feet began moving in the direction of the office. She wasn't going to play games with this over-sized teenager whose hormones seem to be in overdrive.

As Michael stepped quickly and caught up with her he moved to her left side to put her away from the curb. As he did so her steps seemed to slow a little. He liked watching her and he noticed her eyes came up to his, in silent thanks for doing what he did. She may be a spit-fire, but she was all lady inside.

Chapter 3

The walk back toward the office helped her temper cool a little. It actually felt good to be moving. And the soft breeze felt good on her hot skin. Nothing was said during their 'hike' back to their vehicles. Instead of going into the office building itself, Michael took hold of her elbow and led her into the pedestrian path that led into the parking structure. As soon as they stepped into the building they turned to their left, going only a few feet to stop in front of the elevator.

"Evening, Mr. Thorpe," came the greeting from the security guard behind the desk, hidden out of sight from the driveway.

"Good evening," Michael replied automatically.

"Do you want me to send for your car, Sir?" the guard asked.

"Yes, thank you. I'll return in a moment. I'm just going to take Ms. Taylor to her vehicle."

"Yes Sir. It'll be here whenever you're ready Sir," came the reply.

Tina had pressed the button for the third floor and noticed the light go out, telling her the elevator was just arriving at this floor. The doors opened and she stepped inside. "You don't have to walk me to my car. I'm a big girl now," she told him.

"Never let a lady walk unescorted to her car after dark," he tossed back at her. You never know what masher might be lying in wait."

"That would be one very sorry masher," she answered.

"Then I'm glad I'm not a masher."

"Sounds like a lesson well learned." She glanced up at him and grinned.

"Yes, it seems to spring up whenever a lady seems 'vexed' with me. I have to remain ready to defend myself just in case she might feel she needs to put me in my place."

"I can't imagine you not being able to handle such a wimpy thing as a little woman, Mr. Thorpe."

"Michael, please. I'm just Michael. Anyway, thank you for joining me for dinner. I thought you would enjoy it. And it was very nice to have company across the table. Perhaps we can do it again, some time."

"Maybe! Thanks for the suggestion. The biscuits and gravy really were great. But I'll have to wait a long while before I dare have them again."

The elevator was moving upward now. As soon as the doors opened she moved forward, stepping quickly toward her car. Michael walked sedately beside her, trying to match his steps with hers.

"That's mine over there. The silver one," she said. She began to pull her keys out of her handbag. Pressing one of the buttons they could hear the soft "beep, beep" of the locking system releasing. She stepped up to the driver side of her small Mercedes. Before she could reach for the handle to open the door his hand was there. He opened her car door quickly. Before she could toss her purse on the opposite seat he grabbed her elbow and turned her toward him.

"Thank you Tina, for having dinner with me. I enjoyed having you with me."

"Thank you. Guess I'll see you at the meeting in the morning."

"Yes! I'll be there. Good night. Drive safely!" He reached for her hand to help her in, which she took. She straightened her skirt, since it had risen up as she slid onto the seat. She really did prefer cloth covered seats rather than leather, only it did cause her to have to straighten her skirt every time she got in.

As soon as her skirt slid up she grabbed for it. Glancing up to see if Michael noticed her legs showing too much she caught his smile before he could wipe it from his face.

"You could have left it that way. I didn't mind."

"Don't be crude," she told him. "You know it can't be helped when you have cloth seats. You're supposed to be a gentleman and not notice."

"How could I not notice such beautiful legs? Besides, you ought to have leather seats. Then you wouldn't have that problem."

"I actually prefer cloth. It's more comfortable on a hot day. No skin sticking to the seat when I wear shorts."

"Perhaps you have a point there. If you had leather, I wouldn't have gotten such a terrific view."

Tina flashed her eyes at him, and he immediately got the message. He knew that if he was closer to her he might have gotten slapped. He watched as she put the key into the ignition and started the engine. Then he made sure her skirt was out of the way of the door, before gently closing it for her. She reached for the power window and opened it.

"See you in the morning. And thanks again," she tossed at him.

Michael stepped back as the car began to move out of the stall. Suddenly it stopped. "Oh, since they're bring your car down to the first floor, do you want to ride down with me? I can drop you off by the exit."

"Sure, why not. I didn't really want to work off the love handles I was trying to create at dinner, by walking." He laughed a soft laugh. It sounded almost sexy to Tina.

She hit the button that unlocked the doors as he walked around her car. She thought to herself, even his laugh is appealing. Bet all the women love to hear it.

The door opened and he slid in. "Are you a safe driver, Tina?"

"Of course. Why do you ask?'

"Then I won't need my seatbelt just to go down a couple of floors, will I?"

"You never know. We might meet a cop on our way and it would just be my luck he would give me a ticket for your not wearing your seatbelt. You better put it on."

"Such a stickler for the rules, you are. Okay, you convinced me. But if we met an officer on the way down to the first floor, he'd probably only ask you out on a date, not give you a ticket."

"Pretty words! Uh huh!"

She waited for him to buckle up, then continued backing out of her assigned stall. Then the silver car was heading for the exit. She braked gently as they approached the security area where his navy blue Jag sat waiting for him.

"Good night, Tina," he said as he stepped out. "Thanks for the lift." He closed the door gently and waved as she began heading for the exit.

In her mirror she saw him get into the already open door of his car. The security man had left it running for him and she noticed his headlights came on immediately. Then she was leaving the structure, headed for home. Reaching for the radio she turned up some soft music that would help her relax and forget that she had just had dinner with her boss. Her very handsome boss. Her very arrogant boss.

Tina was finally starting to relax. She noticed there wasn't much traffic at this time of night, and was grateful for that. Home was only a few miles away, but she always enjoyed the drive. It was her time to unwind. Listening to the soft music she noticed as she made her next turn that there were only a couple of cars behind her. As she accelerated onto the next street she observed the car behind her turning onto the same street. She tried always to stay alert as to what was going on around her. A little niggling feeling went down her spine. Something about the car behind her made her feel uneasy. She turned quickly into the complex where she had her townhouse. The car slowed and turned in as well.

Tina drove on through the complex making several turns, then pulled into her private parking spot adjacent to her home. The car was still behind her. She began to feel uneasy about getting out of her vehicle. But the car hadn't made the last turn with her, so apparently it was just another resident going home. She shut off the engine and climbed out, locking the car as she stepped away from it with her remote control in her key. She stepped quickly toward her front door, looking around her for anyone that might interfere with her safety. Just as she unlocked her front door she glanced up and saw a navy blue Jag stopped at the corner. In it was her employer. He had better not be stalking her. It had better just be that he wanted to see that she got home safely. She would speak to him about it at her first chance. She moved inside into the safety of her home.

Chapter 4

The following morning Tina was at work early. She sat behind her desk, her first cup of coffee of the day beside her, working on the last of the course outline that had not been completed the day before. As she finished it she leaned back in her chair with a sigh. She felt good about this project. She knew her efforts here would make the next workshop for this subject much more enjoyable.   She reached for her cup of coffee and realized it had gotten cold.

"Rats!" she said. "What a bad habit that is." She rose, cup in hand, and headed for the coffee corner. She rinsed out her cup in the small sink and turned to pour a fresh cup. As she grabbed the pot to pour a fresh cup she mumbled, "Maybe I'll get to drink this one."

"Still talking to yourself?" came the voice behind her. She turned quickly to see who it was that had caught her talking to herself.

"Oh!" she cried out as the hot brew sloshed over the rim onto her hand. Quickly she sat the cup on the counter and stepped to the sink where she could run cool water over her hand to stop the stinging.

"I'm sorry, Tina. I didn't mean to startle you and cause this to happen." There was true sorrow in the sound of his voice.

Tina looked up into the face of Michael Thorpe, who was standing perhaps, she thought, a little too close for comfort.

"Here, let me help," he said softly. She didn't seem to be doing anything. She appeared dazed. He turned on the cold water tap and held her hand under the running water. "Does this hurt?" he asked as he touched the area between her thumb and index finger where the coffee had splashed.

"Only a little. I'll be all right. Here, let me do that," she told him. She had been startled and for a moment couldn't move.

Michael stepped over to the paper towel holder and pulled out a couple of towels and began wrapping and patting her hand dry. The entire time Tina just stood there in shock. "Tina," he spoke her name softly. "Tina! Are you sure you're all right?" He was standing very close holding her hand wrapped in paper towels, peering down into her face. She looked a little pale to him.

"What? Uh, what did you say?" she asked not quite sure what was happening. She looked up at Michael and she felt like she was just waking up from a dream, and she wasn't quite awake yet. As his eyes seemed to draw her line of vision up to his, he seemed to waver. Light waves rippled across his face. She blinked slowly.

Michael was afraid she might faint. She wasn't looking too good. He was surprised that just burning her hand would make her faint, but, he decided, there's no telling how some women's systems worked. He grabbed both of her upper arms and just as he did her eyes closed and she slumped toward the floor. He quickly released one hand and wrapped his arms around her back and the other then went under her knees as she sunk further toward the floor, and he lifted her into his arms. Looking around he noticed no one had come into the office yet so he walked quickly toward her office and laid her on the couch there.

"Tina? Tina?" he said to her as he gently shook her. Then he gently slapped her cheek, hoping to revive her. As he watched, her eyes slowly opened and she began to blink.

"What happened?" she asked. "Why am I lying down?"

"Because some jerk surprised you in the coffee corner and caused you to spill hot coffee all over your hand. I think it was such a surprise that your mind just quit functioning and you fainted," he told her.

"That can't be right. I never faint," she said.

"Well you're the one on the couch, not me. I think you did. Maybe you've been working too hard and were just too tired. Maybe what you need is a day off. I'm taking you home, Tina. I don't believe in making my staff work so hard that they faint."

"Quit saying that, I don't faint. I can't understand this!"

"And what time did you get here this morning, anyway?" he asked.

"About six or so. What does it matter? I'm not charging you overtime?"

"I'm not worried about your pay Tina. Just your health."

"I need to get my head straight. We have a meeting in a little while and I need to feel better than I do right now."

"No we don't, I'm canceling that meeting so I can take you home. We'll reschedule it for in two days. Now do you feel well enough to walk or shall I carry you?"

Tina looked at him in shock. "You can't cancel. The boss scheduled this meeting and it's important that I be there. I,.." she just stopped talking and looked at him. It was as if her mind was trying to walk through deep mud.

Michael stepped away and wrote a note from the notepad on her desk. He cancelled the meeting for two days and said he was taking Ms. Taylor to a special meeting that had come up suddenly. Then he went to his office and taped the note to his secretary's phone, telling her to reschedule it for him.

Returning to Tina's office he grabbed the phone and called security to have his car at the elevator doors immediately. Then he went to where Tina was laying and gathered her into his strong arms. Gently he carried her to his private elevator, hoping it would arrive quickly so they would not be seen. When the doors were opened he stepped quickly inside. One finger pressed the button that would take them to the garage and in only moments he was stepping out and walking rapidly toward his car.

The security man saw them coming and rushed ahead to open the passenger door for him. "Mr. Thorpe? Is there anything I can do? Do you want me to call an ambulance?"

"No thank you Tom. She just fainted. I'm going to take her home. Don't mention this to anyone. I'd rather not embarrass her, understand?"

"Yes Sir, I mean no Sir. I won't mention it to anyone. I hope she'll be okay, Sir."

"Yes, I'm sure she will be fine. She's just been working too hard. Thank you for being so helpful."

"That's okay Mr. Thorpe. I'm glad to help." He stood there watching as the owner of the building left the parking structure with one of his employees unconscious on his front seat.

Michael drove quickly toward the same townhouse that he had followed her to the evening before. Thank God he had, he thought, so he knew where she lived. Thankfully he had remembered to grab her purse as he left her office so he would have her keys.

He parked in the same spot he had seen her park in the previous evening and shut off the engine. He dug in her purse until he found her keys and went to the front door to unlock it and see if there was an alarm that needed to be shut off as well.

He unlocked the door, stepped inside and looked for an alarm. There wasn't one. He would suggest to her that it might be wise to install one. Then he returned to the car and opened the passenger side door and lifted her from the seat. Hoping no one would notice them, he quickly walked into her home with Tina nestled close against his chest. As he crossed the living room and stopped in front of her couch he thought how nicely she seemed to fit in his arms. She felt good there, as though she was a perfect fit.

Gently he laid her down, placing a small pillow under her head. Then he tried to wake her again. Man! This woman really was tired. Perhaps he needed to look into how often she came in to work early and left late. Maybe she needed an assistant. She shouldn't be so exhausted.

Michael gently slapped her face, while calling her name. He noticed her eyes were slowly opening.

"Tina! Wake up! You're home now so you can rest. If you don't wake up, I'm going to call the paramedics after all. You're scaring me here." He thought about what he had done. Perhaps there was something else wrong. Maybe he should call for paramedics. As he contemplated doing just that her eyes opened and he could see that her eyes were clear now. She was awake!

"What do you mean, I'm home now? What am I doing here? The meeting…" she stammered.

"No meeting today. The boss has canceled it. It's rescheduled for day after tomorrow. How do you feel now?" he asked.

"Like I'm been run through the ringer. What happened?"

"Actually, I surprised you in the coffee corner and when you turned around too quickly to see who was behind you,

you spilled your hot coffee all over your hand. And then you fainted. You acted rather 'out of it' there, so I decided I'd bring you home so you could rest. I suspect you've been working too hard. Tell me, how often do you get to the office so early?"

"Oh now and then. I like to get in before the rush so I can get things done while it's quiet. I'm sure you know how that is."

"Yes, but just now and then for something special. Not everyday! And I know for a fact that you worked late last night. How often do you do that?"

"Just when I have something to finish up quickly and wasn't able to do it. Why are you so worried? I don't understand why you brought me home."

"You weren't in any shape to stay at the office. If anyone had seen you in that condition I'm sure the paramedics would have been called, and your reputation as strong and tough would have flown right out the window. Yeah, I know about your rep!" he told her.

Tina tried to sit up. Her head felt like it was spinning. She swung her feet off the couch but then had to reach up to hold her head on. She leaned back against the back of the couch. Michael immediately sat down beside her and put his arm around her to help hold her steady.

"Are you sure you want to sit up? You look a little shaky here. And a little pale."

"I'm all right," she told him, not sure that it was true. "I never have this problem. This doesn't make sense."

"Well, good sense or not I decided to get you out of there before anyone saw you like this. I hope that was all right. I figured you just needed some rest."

"Maybe you're right. I have been putting in quite a few hours lately. It's just that there is so much to do and the day just seems to fly by, no matter how organized I try to be."

"Sounds to me like perhaps I ought to consider getting you an assistant." He liked the feel of her under his arm and he pulled her closer against him. Her head just seemed to naturally fit into his shoulder. Without even thinking he laid his chin on top of her head. She smelled so good, like strawberries.

"Ummm," she said, half asleep again. She was snuggling into his chest as though she was going to go back to sleep. Maybe it was for the best. She did seem tired.

Wrapping his other arm around her he decided he liked the feel of her in his arms. Quite a lot, actually. So he held her as she slept.

Suddenly he found himself kissing the top of her head. He seemed to be drawn to her. He felt very protective of her. He wasn't leaving her alone like this. He would put her on her bed, remove her shoes, and let her rest.

Lifting her up from the couch as though she was a small child, he easily carried her up the stairs and found her bedroom. He laid her across the bed and pulled off her shoes. Feeling her skin she felt a little cool to him, so he grabbed the extra blanket she had lying across the foot of her bed and spread it over her.

She moved in her sleep, rolling on to her side, slipping her hand under her cheek and drawing her other hand to rest on that wrist. Standing beside the bed looking down at her Michael felt a strong instinct to want to protect this woman. She looked just like a little girl to him, lying there like that.

He was surprised to have such feelings. He had known many women and had enjoyed most of them, but not one of them drew him to her like this one did. Michael shook his head. He wasn't sure why he felt so protective of this one woman but since he did he was honor bound to follow through until he knew why.

Michael wasn't sure how long he stood there watching her sleep. He was certain that was all she needed. But he liked watching her. He looked around the room and saw a wooden rocker sitting next to a table pilled high with books and a tall lamp next to it. There was a plaid blanket strung through the opening near the top of the back of the rocker, apparently to cushion the person's back, or be thrown over a lap if needed. He dropped into the rocker and just watched this woman sleep.

Later, as he became more aware, he realized he was rocking the chair back and forth. It felt soothing to him. He laid his head back, and slowly his eyes closed and he slept.

Two hours later he thought he heard something and his eyes popped open. As he looked across the room he saw Tina was awake and looking at him.

"Hi Sweetheart!" he said. It came out before he even thought about it. "How are you feeling?"

"Better! But what are you doing here? And why am I in my own bed? Michael? I don't understand what's going on."

"We went through this earlier, but I guess you don't remember. I startled you when you were pouring a cup of coffee for yourself in the coffee corner. You turned around so quickly you spilled your coffee all over your hand, burning it. You acted a little funny as you stood at the sink to rinse your hand with cool water, so I took over for you and did it myself. Then you fainted."

"But that doesn't make sense. Why would I faint just from that?" she asked.

"I suspect it was from more than that. I think you were excessively tired and when this happened it was just too much for you. Your mind just shut down and decided it needed rest. So, before anyone came into the office I carried you down to my car and brought you home so you could rest. Do you remember our talking about it this morning as you sat on your couch? I told you then that I was considering getting you an assistant. Do you remember any of that?"

"No, I guess not. I've been feeling rather tired lately. I've been trying to update some of the course outlines for our various workshops, along with keeping things going as usual. I have been putting in some extra time to try and get it all done." She raised her hand to her temple and rubbed. She had a bit of a headache.

Suddenly her head came up and she looked worried. "What about the meeting?" she asked. "We're late," she said, looking down at her watch. It was already after ten in the morning and the meeting was to have started at nine.

"The boss cancelled it. It will be rescheduled to the day after tomorrow."

"Oh, that was nice of him. That will give me time to get things together."

"You're welcome, and thank you for the kind words," he said. He realized she was thinking that his brother had cancelled the meeting, not himself. "Tina, I cancelled the meeting. I left a message for my secretary that you and I had to go to a special meeting that just suddenly came up. That explained why the meeting was cancelled and why neither one of us is in the office."

"You? You cancelled the meeting?"

"That's right!"

"But you can't cancel it. You didn't schedule it."

"Oh, but I did," he told her calmly.

"But, how?"

"What do you mean? I'm your boss too! Oh, maybe you just don't think of me that way. Is that it?" he asked.

Tina thought for a moment. "I guess so. I guess I was thinking that you just worked there."

"I do! But I am also sixty five percent owner of the business." He wasn't bragging, just calmly stating facts.

"Oh! I guess you can cancel the meeting then," she admitted.

"You got that right! Now, how are you feeling? Better? Would you like some lunch?"

"Better! Yes!" She put her hand on the mattress and pushed to sit up. She swung her feet over the side and just sat there on the edge of the bed for a moment. She was rubbing her temples with both hands as Michael left the rocking chair and moved over to the edge of the bed to sit beside her. He put one hand behind her and the other over her left shoulder. He didn't want her pitching onto the floor and hurting herself.

"Are you sure you want to be up? I can go check out what is in your frig and see what I can put together for lunch. I think you ought to have some food in you to give you some stamina."

"I'll be fine. I'll go with you. But I'm not sure we'll find much in there."

Tina slid forward until her feet touched the floor and she put her weight on to her feet. So far she felt okay, so she stood and Michael stood right along with her, still holding on to her in case his strength was needed.

"See, I told you I was okay. Let's go." She led him downstairs and through her living room then on through her small dining area into the small kitchen. "Why don't you look in the bottom drawer in the frig to see if there is some lettuce and maybe some tomatoes in there? And if you come across any jicama, pull it out too."

Michael went to the refrigerator and pulled open the door, leaned down to open the bottom drawer and found lettuce, tomatoes and the jicama. "Hey I found all three, how's that for lucky?" Bringing his items to the counter he laid them there, waiting for further instructions.

Tina had been pulling out large salad bowls and plates to set them on, from her cupboard. She sat one bowl on each small plate and asked him to put them on the kitchen table for her. Then she reached for a large knife and began preparing a salad. "Did you by chance see a red onion in there too?" she asked.

"I'm not sure. I'll check." He walked back over to the frig and found what she wanted and brought it to her. He laid it on the counter near the other veggies while standing next her so he could watch her hands working. She had lovely hands with long tapered fingers and she moved gracefully. He continued to watch as she quickly cut up the lettuce and tomato. Then she prepared the jicama and sliced the red onion, pulling the red rings apart and laying them on top of the salad.

"Would you pull a couple of tall glasses out of that cupboard door over there, pointing to the first door beyond her sink. And the napkins are under the counter on the first shelf. The flatware is in the last drawer next to the frig."

She turned to head to the refrigerator to pull out the package of boneless chicken thighs she had picked up at the store two days ago after work and hadn't gotten around to using. Pulling out her cutting board she grabbed her sharp knife and began to cut the raw chicken into bite size pieces. When that was done she pulled a skillet from the bottom drawer of her stove and put it over a fire to heat. After dumping in some cooking oil she tossed in the chicken, sprinkled some herbs on top and let them cook while she found her favorite turner. She sat it in the spoon holder next to the stove and waited as the chicken cooked. She knew it wouldn't be long before she would have to stir it. She glanced up to see if Michael had the table set for them to find him watching her.

"You do that like you're comfortable in the kitchen. I like a woman that can cook," he told her. "The only cooking that gets done at my place is micro waved to death. Maybe you'll teach me this recipe so I can do it myself. What do you say?"

"You already know the ingredients. Just cut them up and cook some boneless chicken with some herbs and toss it on top along with your favorite dressing. Nothing to it! But it is one of my favorite things," she told him, smiling. When their eyes met she turned shy and looked at the floor. She didn't know why she felt so shy around him now. She wasn't ever like that at work.

She turned the chicken over a couple of times in the next several minutes to make sure it was cooked through and nicely browned. Then she pulled out a plate from the cupboard, placed a paper towel on it and put the chicken on the paper towel to drain. After dabbing it with the edge of the paper towel to get as much oil off the meat as possible, she pulled the towel from the plate and grabbed a large spoon and stepped over to the table. She put half of the meat on top of Michael's salad and half on top of hers. She put the plate in the sink and turned toward the refrigerator one more time. "What type of salad dressing do you prefer?" she asked.

"Most anything you have will be fine," he told her.

She pulled out her favorite creamy Poppy Seed dressing and sat it on the table. Then she got a box of Ritz crackers from the cupboard, dumped them into a bowl and put it on the table as well. She turned toward Michael and said, "I guess it's time to eat. Hungry?" And she headed for her favorite chair at her own kitchen table.

Michael was there and pulled her chair out for her. "You don't have to be chivalrous for me" she told him. But she did enjoy it.

"Glad to be of service," he said with a smile. When he had sat down she remembered the iced tea in the frig.

"Oh, I forgot the iced tea," she said.

"Don't get up. I'll get it. In the frig?" he asked.

"Yes, in the white pitcher. Do you take lemon or is plain okay?"

"Plain is just fine for me," he replied.

Tina jumped up anyway, just to get the sugar bowl from the cupboard and the long iced tea spoons. Then she went back to her seat and sat down.

They both enjoyed the salad and the quiet lunch. They felt very comfortable in each other's presence. It was as though they were an old married couple.

"Tell me, why is this chicken so much more moist than the kind I get in a restaurant? It really is good."

"Because I prefer to use the thigh meat rather than the breast, like most restaurants do. I hate the white meat. It's just too dry for me."

"Now there's something I should remember. I've learned something new. This really is good Tina. You're a great cook."

She couldn't help but smile over his compliment. "Thanks!"

After lunch was over they stood side by side as she washed the dishes and he dried them. They worked well together, and seemed to enjoy it.

When everything was put away they wandered into her living room and sat down.

"How are you feeling now? I hope the cooking didn't tire you too much."

"Oh, I'm fine now. I don't know what got in to me this morning. I've been rather tired lately, but nothing I couldn't handle."

Michael looked into her face to see if she was telling him the truth. Her eyes looked weary, but her skin was creamy and lush. Now where did that come from, he wondered. She looked as though she could stand to take a little afternoon nap, he thought.

"You don't have to baby sit me you know. I'll be fine. If you want to go back to the office you can."

"Are you trying to get rid of me?"

"No, I just thought you would rather get back to work. Oh, I just remembered. My car is at work without me."

"Now that's an interesting way to put it. At work without you! Do you think your car might be working?" he laughed at the thought.

"Don't give me a bad time or the next time I'll put arsenic in the salad dressing," she said grinning at him. "And if it is working while I'm gone, I hope it gets everything done for me."

"Thanks! At least now I know I'm going to be invited back."

"Yeah, you can handle a dish towel very well, and you don't pick on the cook too badly. I can deal with that," she smiled back at him.

"Actually I would enjoy a day off. It doesn't happen often enough to suit me. Think you could stand the company for the rest of the day? Then, after the office empties out we can drive over and pick up your car."

"Okay, but what are we going to do all afternoon?" she asked.

"You're going to take a little nap. And maybe I will too. Then we can decide from there what else we want to do."

"You sound like my mother," she told him. "I haven't been told I need an afternoon nap in years."

"Well, get used to it because today you're going to have one. I want my employees well rested, Ms. Taylor." He smiled softening his harsh words.

"Yes Sir, Mr. Thorpe Sir," she told him saluting him as though they were in the Army.

"Why is it, all women aren't as easy to boss around as you are?" he queried.

"It's only because you helped me do the dishes, is all."

"Okay, I'll buy that. Do you want me to walk you to your bedroom for your nap or are you going to nap on the couch?"

She looked at him surprised he would suggest his accompanying her to her bedroom. Then she remembered he had already taken her there and sat in her rocker watching her sleep until he himself, fell asleep.

"Okay, you win. I'll go up and lie down and you can nap on the couch, or on the bed in the guest room. That would probably be more comfortable."

They walked up the stairs together and he took hold of her elbow before she could disappear into her bedroom. Turning her toward him he pulled her into his body and kissed her softly on the lips. "Sleep well, Tina." "If you wake up before me come wake me up. And if I wake up first, I'll come and get you."

Surprised and stunned by his tender kiss all she could say was, "uh huh!" Then she turned and headed toward her bed. She realized this entire time she had been barefoot and loved every minute of it.

She sat on the edge of her bed smiling. What a sweet man he is, she thought. Then her head hit the pillow and she was almost instantly asleep.

He slept for over an hour and woke, momentarily disoriented as to where he was. Then he remembered he was in Tina's guest room. He stretched to get the kinks out and rose from the bed. Walking down the hall he stopped just outside her bedroom. She was still asleep, stretched out with one arm over her head, her long eyelashes fanned out across her cheeks, looking so feminine. He watched as her chest rose with her gentle breaths. What a picture of feminine beauty she was, he thought.

Walking softly so as not to wake her he walked around her bed. He knew she might be terribly angry with him for doing this, but he wanted very much to lie down beside her. And that was exactly what he did.

The movement of the bed was minimal and he laid on his side, minus his shoes, just watching her sleep. There was something about this woman that made him just want to take her into his arms and not let go. He couldn't understand why.

With his head on the adjacent pillow he laid very still, just watching her. Somehow it felt right, and very comfortable. Then she moved in her sleep, turning over toward him. He was afraid if she felt him it would wake her. But it didn't. In fact she snuggled up to him as though she was used to having him with her, so he couldn't help but put his arm around her. She moved closer laying her head against his chest. Their thighs were resting against each other's. He was afraid to move.

He laid very still. She moaned in her sleep and she snuggled as though she wanted to get closer. So he pulled her tightly against him. He laid his hand on her back and felt as though his heart was going to burst with the joy of it.

Now he was afraid to close his eyes for fear he would drop off to sleep. So he just tried to relax and enjoy the moment. After a little while he noticed her breathing changed. She was beginning to wake up, but still he didn't move. He wanted to hold her as long as he could. He would deal with the anger when it came.

He listened. Her breathing had stopped. What was wrong with her? He looked down into her face to find her eyes were open. But she wasn't breathing! "Christina!" he said. "What is it?" He rolled back to be able to see her face better.

She took a breath. "What are you doing here?"

"I woke up a little while ago and wanted to check on you. You looked so peaceful sleeping I just decided to lie down here and watch you. But then you rolled over next to me and I was afraid I was going to wake you up, so I just laid still, until now. That's all! I wasn't trying to get fresh or anything. You just rolled over against me in your sleep."

"But you weren't suppose to be in here," she said sleepily.

"I know, but I couldn't resist temptation. You looked so peaceful there."

She raised her face to see him more easily. They peered into each other's eyes.

The temptation was too great. His head came down and his lips touched hers. Immediately electricity sparked and her chin came up, leaning into his kiss. He rolled over toward her, pinning her to the bed and the kiss deepened. His hands came to hold her head in place so he could devour her lips.

He laid butterfly kisses at each end of her mouth. Then he drew his tongue across her bottom lip and she took a breath. As her mouth opened he invaded it with his tongue. He gently touched her teeth, then the inside of her lips. He touched her tongue brushing it top and bottom. His kiss created such heat that their bodies had to follow suit.

His hand slid down her shoulder holding her upper arm in place, as if he was afraid she might move away and he didn't want her to do that. His lips spread their warmth across her cheekbone and her eyelids. She heard herself moan softly.

He laid soft kisses down her chin and along her throat. She heard him say her name as his lips lay against her throat. "Christina! My sweet Christina!"

She was melting in his embrace. She began to kiss him on his throat and she licked him. He moaned for her.

Then he realized what he was doing and paused. It was long enough for them both to pull back. "Oh Christina, you drive me crazy. Your skin is so soft, and your kisses make me want more of you."

"Michael, how did we get into this? You feel so good to me. It seems as though we have known each other before today. How can that be? But your kisses, your touch seems so familiar to me. I feel safe in your arms. Why is that?" she asked.

"I don't know Sweetheart, but I don't want to let go of you yet. It's as though I just got you into my arms and I don't want to lose you. I don't understand it either."

She stopped kissing his neck and pulled back, so they both rolled over onto their sides. "I don't understand it, but we shouldn't be doing this. You're my boss, for heavens sake."

"That doesn't mean anything. You're a desirable woman, and I am very attracted to you.

I don't know why, I only know I want to keep you with me. I've never known a woman that made me feel this way before. That has to mean something."

"Oh Mike. You feel so right to me. Hold me a little longer."

It was just what he wanted too. He pulled her close, her head was on his shoulder now. His hand laid on her head, and his other one was low on her back, keeping her tight against him. She scooted closer so their stomachs were against each others. She moaned for him.

"I love when you do that Sweetheart. You make me feel so good. I think I'd like to make you do that often," he told her sincerely from his heart.

"Uhmmm," she told him, closing her eyes, her arm around his chest. And they stayed that way for the next hour.

Finally they decided it was time to get up. It was around three o'clock in the afternoon, and they felt they needed to stretch and move around a little.

They slid off the bed and each went to their respective bathrooms to splash water on their faces to help them wake up. They met again in the living room. When she saw him she stopped dead in her tracks. He walked right up to her, pulling her into his arms. He figured if she didn't want to be there she would let him know, but she came willingly. He lifted her chin and kissed her. I don't understand it, but I don't want to let you out of my arms my Sweet. Do you mind?"

"Uh uh," was her only answer. She reached up to place her hands on both sides of his face to draw him down to her. She kissed him, and he picked her up, holding her in his arms with her feet a foot off of the floor as he kissed her.

Michael enjoyed holding her. He literally carried her over to the couch and sat down, placing her on his lap. He kissed her again. "I don't think I can stop."

"Please don't, Mike. I like it too," she told him. They stayed on the couch, with her on his lap until time to go fetch her car.

"It's as though I can't quit touching you Christina, my Love. I think you are my love, Sweetheart. What would you say to that?"

"I don't know, Mike. But I feel the same. I just want to keep touching you. What's wrong with us?"

"Wrong? I don't think it's wrong. I think if this keeps up, I'm going to claim you for myself. And no other man better be touching you. I guess you can tell, I'm a very possessive man. What is mine, is mine only."

Tina didn't understand it. Maybe it was lust. Who knew? All she was certain of was having him touch her just felt right to her. And apparently to him as well!

Chapter 5

They sat together on the couch, just enjoying each other's company. They talked about work, and food, and cooking, and then about each other. He told her about his childhood, his favorite color, favorite food, and the like. Then it was her turn to do the same. They had similar taste in food, simple American fare. They found they were only two years apart in age, he being thirty-six and she was thirty four.

Tina usually wore her shoulder length hair pulled up either into a French twist or held in place with a clip that had teeth that would reach into her hair to hold it in place. Michael asked, "Why don't you wear your hair down sometimes?"

"I do when the weather is cool. Otherwise it just gets too sticky and uncomfortable on my neck. And I hate that," she told him.

It was May in California, and it really hadn't gotten awfully hot yet. Leaning closer Michael reached around her head and released her hair clip. Immediately her brunette tresses fell to her shoulders. He couldn't resist temptation so he ran his fingers through her hair to comb it. He grabbed a fistful and pull gently, forcing her to move toward him. He continued to pull until his lips touched hers, then his hands opened and he held her head in place as he ravaged her lips.

"I like it down. It's beautiful down. Will you wear it down for me tomorrow?" he asked.

"Tomorrow? I guess so," she stammered. She hadn't gotten around to thinking about tomorrow yet. Everything was happening so fast between them that she wondered how long these feelings could last. She had heard somewhere that if it started out hot, love died quickly. She didn't know if that was true, but she was almost afraid to find out, since their passion had definitely been hot.

"Tell me what color you think you will wear tomorrow, Christina?"

"I don't know. Whatever grabs my eye tonight. I usually lay out my outfit the night before so I can get ready quickly in the morning."

"I'll wear light gray with a soft blue tomorrow. If you have something that would match that, why not wear it. We'll look like a 'pair'."

"Are you sure you want to do that Michael? I think we ought to keep our relationship low profile, at least for a while. We wouldn't want anyone to think you were, well, you know."

"Go ahead Sweetheart. You can say it. There can't be any secrets between us now."

"Well, someone might think you were favoring me in other areas if we suddenly started looking like a couple. Especially if you were serious about considering getting me an assistant."

"Not a chance. Besides, the boss should be able to do as he pleases. Our relationship is no one else's business. And if I choose to add another staff position at my own expense I think I should be able to do just that. No Christina, I won't dance to someone else's tune. Unless it's yours."

The sun was going down and the shadows were lengthening. It was the time of the day that most of the employees had already started their trek home. "I guess we could head over to pick up your car now Sweetheart. Are you feeling up to it?"

"Yes, I'm fine now. Those two naps made a lot of difference for me. How about you? I suspect you rather enjoyed that short nap yourself."

"Yes, it was nice. But the best part of the day was holding you in my arms. But I think I'm going to need more of that soon. How about right after we pick up your car? I'll follow you to make sure you're all right, just like I did last night. Only I'll come in this time, if you'll let me."

"Of course I'll let you. Okay, let's go get my car. I'd like to settle in for the evening soon anyway. And by the way, I wanted to talk to you about last night. You know you scared me half to death?"

"Hum, was that an invitation?"

"Yes, to come to visit, not to stay all night. Don't get the wrong idea here."

"Okay! You're too tough. Let's go!"

"Do you have anything to say about scaring me last night on the way home?"

"Not really. I'm sorry if I scared you. I just wanted to keep you safe."

They drove back to the parking structure at the office to pick up her vehicle. He drove slowly up to the third floor.

"You know, it feels funny driving in here. I don't usually get that opportunity. Ted, the attendant usually takes my car just inside the gate. Weird feeling, driving around in circles in here."

"See what joy you're missing out on?" she asked him, laughing.

It took only minutes to get her back to her complex. She put her car in her usual stall, while he parked in one of the visitor stalls a few steps away. Then they went inside. They curled up and watched a movie, ordering a pizza to be delivered. By ten o'clock she was sending him out the door. They stood in the doorway as he kissed her goodbye.

"Drive safely," she told him.

"I will," he said. "I have a reason for doing so now. And you get some rest. I'll see you in the morning at the office. Good night!" He gave her lips a soft kiss before slowly walking toward his vehicle. She stayed by the door until he drove out of sight, as she waved. She felt as though she had a very dear friend in her life now, and she liked the feeling.

Chapter 6

The following morning she was up at her usual time of five thirty. She was out the door by six thirty and sitting at her desk by six forty five. She felt good that she had been able to complete that course outline, but there were still several more to also be updated. She stepped to her files and selected one that she figured might be needed in the near future, pulling it out and laying it on her desk.

Then, before she sat down she pulled her coffee cup from it's place in her desk drawer and walked over to the coffee corner. She poured a cup, wondering who had come in early and made this pot. It really didn't matter that much as long as the coffee was palatable. Many of the management personnel had a habit of getting in early. She carried her cup back to her desk and sat down. An hour later she could hear voices and sounds of the office coming to life. Then her secretary, Marsha stuck her head in.

"Morning! How did your meeting go yesterday? I understand you went to something special with one of the bosses."

"What? Oh, yes, it went fine. It took longer that I had anticipated. Sorry I was out all day."

"Is he as harsh as he looks? He looks as though he could be pretty tough if he wanted to be. Tough, but soooo handsome," she said with a dreamy look in her eyes. "He really is a hunk isn't he?"

"Handsome? I guess so. He's seems to be a very caring person. What did I miss yesterday, Marsha? Any messages?"

The morning went as usual and passed quickly. She managed to get all the way through this next course outline update by four in the afternoon. Just as she was putting it back into the file the com-line on her phone rang.

"Tina Taylor," she said automatically.

"Good afternoon Sweetheart. Are you awfully busy right now?" He hadn't even said his name, but she knew that voice. It felt like kisses were coming through the phone.

"Only partially busy. I was able to complete another course update today. Feels good to complete something."

"I'm glad. So you feel pretty good today? How did you sleep?"

"Oh, fine. I'm feeling back to normal again, thanks. How about yourself?"

"Couldn't sleep. Kept thinking about this certain employee."

"You're having an employee problem? Is there anything I can do?" she asked, uncertain if he was joking or serious, so she decided she had better do her job and offer to help.

"Well, you see, this certain woman has…., perhaps you ought to come to my office so we can discuss it. Can you come now?" he asked, sounding serious.

"Yes, of course. I'll be right there," she told him. As soon as she hung up the phone she was walking toward the door. Pausing at Marsha's desk she told her that she had been summoned to Michael Thorpe's office for a conference, and that if she needed her that she could call her there.

Marsha thanked her for the information and asked, "Would it be all right if I left a few minutes early today so I could stop at my pharmacy before it closed at five?"

"Sure, I don't have a problem with that. You can write in your time in the morning and I'll initial it. You go ahead. You aren't sick or anything are you?"

"I'm fine. It's my daughter. Her prescription ran out and I need to get a refill," came her reply. Marsha was raising her twelve year old daughter, Stacy, by herself. She had gone through a divorce several years back, so she had discovered being a single mom was a harrowing job sometimes when there was only one parent to handle all the problems.

"See you in the morning, Marsha," Tina told her. "I'm glad it wasn't anything serious." She strode away quickly toward the far side of the building where the two executive offices were located. They were actually large suites. Stepping into Michael's secretary's office she told the young woman that she had a meeting with Michael, and asked if he was ready for her?

"Just a minute I'll check," she said, turning to her com-line and telling Mr. Thorpe that Ms. Taylor was here for their meeting. Then she said, "I didn't have that on my schedule. Did I miss something?" she asked.

Michael quickly informed her that it was a spur of the moment thing and he was sorry but that he had forgotten to tell her to jot it down on his calendar. Then he said, "Please send her in."

The young woman told Tina to go right in, that Mr. Thorpe was expecting her. And she did just that. She stepped into the room and as she was closing the door Michael had risen from behind his desk and came toward her. She stepped forward, expecting to be seated with him in the conversation area near the window, or in the two chairs in front of his desk, but instead he walked right up to her and pulled her into his arms. He lifted her chin with one hand and said, "How I've missed you. Come here woman."

His kiss was all encompassing. All thought left her mind. The only thing she could think of was how good his lips felt on her and how his tongue was sliding across her bottom lip. She gasped and he took advantage of her opening her mouth. His tongue invaded and touched her, searching as though it was looking for something. Something very sweet and special! Then it tangled with the tip of her tongue and suddenly their bodies began to heat with a burning fire. His hand came up to hold the back of her head just where he wanted it. Tina began to feel weak in the knees.

She started to pull back to stop this feeling, but he wouldn't let her. One of his hands slid down her back to just above her hips, rubbing and exciting her as he pulled her closer to him.

Finally Tina put both of her hands on his chest and pushed. Suddenly he got the message and released her. But as soon as he did, his lips returned for one more light kiss across her bottom lip. His large hand found hers and he pulled her with him onto the couch in the corner.

"So did you miss me?" he asked.

"I think you know the answer to that already," she answered. "I thought you wanted my help with a employee problem?"

"I do. You're the employee and this is my problem." They had sat down already, but he leaned in close, laying his lips on hers. "Oh!" she said when his lips left hers. "I thought you were serious."

"I am serious. I couldn't sleep last night for thinking about you. I think you've bewitched me." His hands came up to capture her upper arms and he was pulling her to his chest again.

"Michael, what if your secretary came in? I'm not so sure we should be doing this here." She was beginning to be concerned about professional appearances.

He released her and leaned back against the couch. "What am I going to do with you? She knows not to come in when I'm in conference. She would page me on the con-line first."

"Michael, I feel very uncomfortable doing this in the office. Perhaps we ought to keep our relationship out of the office. When we're here, I think we should continue as though nothing is going on between us."

"If you think so, Sweetheart. But I just had to hold you and kiss your lips. I've wanted to do that all day. What a day this has been. It's been one thing right after another without a moment to myself. I hadn't noticed how little time I had for myself before."

"Maybe you haven't wanted time for yourself?"

"That's probably true. But now I want time to touch you, and be with you. I'm going to have to find a project that we'll have to work on together so I can at least see you each day. I've missed your touch." He reached for her again, taking her upper arm and pulling her close. He wrapped his arm around her, pushing her head to his chest as he laid gentle kisses across her forehead. Didn't you miss me?" he asked.

"You know I did. I love your kisses, and the feel of your arms around me. You know, I can't remember any man's kisses that make me lose control like yours do," she admitted. She lifted her hand to his face and laid her fingers along his cheek. "Do you know that most of the women in the office would love to know how it feels to be held in your arms?"

"The only one these arms want to hold is you, my Sweet." He lifted her chin with his hand and laid little kisses at both sides of her mouth. She moaned and was lost in his sweet kiss.

"That's the sound I love to have you make. It's a sound that I don't want any other man to hear. Just for me, Sweetheart, only me." His hand slid down her arm, then to her back as he crushed her to him.

"Michael! I love what you do to me, but I'm nervous about doing this in the office. When I walk out of here all anyone has to do is look at me and they'll be able to figure out what we've been doing in here. They will see it in my face, and my bruised lips."

"Am I bruising your lips, Darling? I don't want to hurt you, but after I kiss you they look so beautifully swollen. And your lipstick is gone. Am I wearing it?"

She laughed as she sat back up straight. She searched his face for any trace of her lipstick on his mouth. Nothing there! "No, Darling, it's all gone."

He smiled quietly at her.

"What is it?" she asked.

"I think that's the first time you've called me that, and I like the sound of it, coming across your lips. Your soft, kissable lips." He was leaning forward again, taking not only her lips but her will as well.

"Are we having a conference or not, here?"

"Of course! We're conferencing on how to best keep you close to me while I try to wear out your lips so you won't be tempted to share them with anyone else. You don't do you? Let anyone else kiss you? Is there a man in your life Christina, other than me?"

"No!" she answered him honestly. "I've been too busy to even think about it."

"Then it's definite! I'm getting you an assistant. Is there a small area that can be enclosed to make a small office for her near yours? I want you to make up a job description for me and we'll begin accepting applications immediately for the position. As soon as you give me the list of job duties I'll see if I need to add anything to it, then I'll have flyers made up to send to all offices in case anyone in-house is interested. And then personnel, that's you Love, can include the position to the standard hiring list. I want to have this position filled within a month. My Lady needs a respite from all of this." He smiled down into her face expecting her to be excited about all of this. Yet her eyes were large with wonder, not sparkling as he would have expected.

Are you serious?" she asked.

"Absolutely! It appears your workload is in need of some assistance. There's no reason that you should have to be at your desk long before anyone else in this building is and staying late almost every night. Not even I do that."

It was common knowledge in personnel circles that if the job couldn't be done within a forty hour workweek without constant overtime needed, then the position was too much for one person. An occasional late night might be required, but not on a regular basis.

"Okay Michael. I have to agree with you there. I'll draw up a job description with a list of duties. Then I'll forward it to you for your approval."

"I'd love to add to that, that the current position holder needs time to spend with her boss." He grinned at her like a kid who had just discovered lollipops.

Tina couldn't help but smile. He was like a little boy who had found that special friend. And she knew that he had become special to her as well. What the future held in store for them she wasn't sure, but she was hopeful. But she still wasn't certain whether it was ethical for her to be dating her boss.

Yet she hadn't been out on a planned date with him yet. Not officially. Yes, he had kissed her that first time they had met in his office that day. And yes he had kissed her socks off the day he took her home when she was so ill. But as far as actual dating, that hadn't happened yet.

She stood, figuring their conference was over and he stood as well. He closed the distance between them and laid his hand on her upper arm. She saw his head dipping down toward hers just before their lips touched. It was as though they couldn't get enough of each other. Whatever was going to become of them in the future she was afraid to consider, because what they had right now was blazing hot. They couldn't keep their hands off of each other. At least, he couldn't. Out of sheer fear of professionalism she was able to maintain some poise, at least at work.

She began to step away and his hand tightened on her arm. Then his other arm came around her and she felt herself being drawn up against his broad chest. She liked the feel of it, under her hands. He was a very viral male and he exuded sex appeal like mad. It was getting more and more difficult to be around him and try to keep a clear mind at work.

He just hugged her this time. His hand came up to the back of her head and he held her against his chest. Her forehead rested over his heart and she could hear the beat of it. Her hands slipped around his waist and they just held each other in silence. It was a precious moment.

When she lifted her head he blessed her with a light kiss on the forehead, and stepped away from her. He walked toward his desk as though he knew he had work to do and should get to it. Then he stopped and looked at her.

"Christina!" he said. Then he was returning to her, dragging her into his arms and kissing her as though he was drowning without her. "Christina!" His breath was coming in gasps and her heart sped up just hearing him.

"What is it Darling?" she asked.

"I feel as though I can't bear to let you go away from me. I don't know how, but you have truly bewitched me."

"It isn't me, it's your own heart. I just happened to be here when your heart made the choice. I'm the lucky one here." She grinned up at him and she realized that was just what she suspected happened. His loneliness made him see her as something special, was all. And when he got over that lonely feeling and his mind was interested in his work once again, he would walk away from her. She felt that in her heart. This wasn't going to last. She knew now that she needed to guard her heart, for once she gave it away, there would be no getting it back.

Suddenly she had to get away from his kisses and his touch. It was as though her heart was already breaking, just at the thought.

"Thank you for wearing your blue and gray for me, Christina. It looks lovely on you," he told her.

"I wasn't sure if I should, actually."

"Well, I'm glad you did. Thanks!"

"I'll get that job description and duties together right way and send it over," she told him and stepped back from his arms. She started for the door. She wanted to get out of his office before the tears started. It had felt so right yesterday, but today, in the daylight she saw the truth. How could he want her? She was just his employee! A captive lover who just happened to be in the right place at the right time.

Tina's head went down along with her shoulders as she walked toward the door.

Michael felt something wasn't right. She felt so good in his arms and then it was if someone had opened the refrigerator door and let out all the cold. He watched as her body language was telling the story. She was only two steps from his door, when it hit him.

She's hurting. What did I do to hurt her? He didn't know but he had to fix it. She was walking away as though she was almost in pain. He covered the distance in a moment, grabbing her arm and turning her to face him. He peered into her face to try to see it. Finally he said it. "What's wrong Sweetheart? What have I done? Somehow I've hurt you. Please tell me and I'll fix it. I can't let you go like this."

She couldn't look him in the eye. Tina tilted her head down, placing her head against his chest. She liked the feeling that being loved by him gave her. She didn't want to give it up, but she had no choice.

"It's nothing. I just realized that this can't work between us. It just wasn't meant to be real."

"What do you mean, Honey. It is real. As real as it can be! Don't you see what you mean to me? How can you say that? Sweetheart, tell me. Let me make it right. Something has gone through your mind just now that is pulling you away from me. I don't want that, Christina. You're everything in the world to me right now."

"I know, Michael. I guess I just have to realize that what we feel right now may not be around later. Nothing is forever. I was just dreaming, I guess."

"Then dream with me Christina. Be my angel, my love. Let me love you while I can."

"Yes, you're right. Yes, Michael. Love me while you can."

He lived her chin and laid a butterfly kiss on her lips. "It's true you know. I've fallen in love with you Christina. Don't ever forget that."

She decided to enjoy it while she could so she made her face smile as she looked up at him. "Yes my Love, you're right. I love you too," she said to him, knowing after a while he would no longer want her love. She laid a kiss on her finger tip and placed it on his mouth. Then she turned and walked out of his office, her shoulders up straight. She may be dreading the change that she knew was coming in the future, but she was going to proudly enjoy the time he could give her. And the assistant she would have. She knew that when the change came she would have to leave this place. She would not be able to work in the same place with him then. She wouldn't be able to stand seeing him day after day.

She knew he though he was in love with her now, and maybe he was. But later he wouldn't be. If he had really heard all that he had just told her he would know that everything was in the 'now'. And she wanted the 'forever'.

Chapter 7

Tina walked back to her office and paused at Marsha' desk. "Would you come in to my office please?" she asked. The she continued on to her desk.

When Marsha came in she had her steno pad in her hand, along with a pencil. "What can I do for you Tina?"

"We need to figure out a couple of things rather quickly here. I want your input on this Marsh. I want to create a small office somewhere close to mine. We can put up temporary walls to enclose it, along with a door. But it must be something that can be done rather quickly. What section of the office would you suggest we use?"

"Wow! Sounds exciting. What will the office be used for?"

"I'm considering creating an assistant position. By the way, if this goes through, you might think about applying for this job. You know almost as much as I do about what it takes to do my job. Now lets see, is there a space that is all ready partially open that we should consider?" she asked.

"Well, we have the copy corner just the other side of your office that could be moved over along the far wall. It would mean a few more steps to get to it and back to everyone's desks, but if the priority is the new office space rather than having a centrally positioned copy corner, I would suggest that area. We could move a couple of desks over a few feet. The desks could actually be paired up, face to face for those who are sitting at them, rather than have everyone facing the same direction. That could gain us several feet. We could move my desk closer to your door, or even on the other side of it, creating even more room."

"How much room do you think that would allow for the office space itself?"

"Oh, I would guess probably fifteen feet by ten or twelve. That might work."

"Do you think we might turn some of the desks to create even more width? It would be much nicer if the new office could be at least twenty feet across. Granted, it wouldn't be that deep, but at least it would give a sense of some space."

"Yeah, I think that's possible. And you could have one wall with mirrors on it, perhaps on the front of closet doors behind which you could put a few files. Without visible files in the room, and the mirrors there, you should get the illusion of space."

"Marsha, you're terrific. See! You might just be a perfect fit for this new job. But don't whisper a word of it until I let you know it's a 'go'.

"Okay, I think I want you to call maintenance and find out if they have the material for putting together an office that size, including phone lines, computer connections and more lights. And I'm sure we'll need electrical outlets as well. Tell them I want a price by quitting time tomorrow on this, and how quickly it can be done. And tell them Mr. Thorpe has requested it. That ought to light a fire under them. As soon as they have it together have them fax up some paperwork on it. And remind them it's tomorrow by the end of the day. That's their deadline. Tell them, if it's necessary to cancel out some other project they have going to get this done on time, tell them that's okay too. Tell them that this is urgent! Thanks Marsha. I really appreciate your help here."

"No problem. That's the kind of thing that keeps my job interesting. I'll get right on it. As soon as I have some information I'll let you know."

After Marsha went back to her desk Tina sat down at her own desk. She sat and pondered all that seemed to be happening in her life right now. Something good had seemed to happen to her, yet there was a big gray area right in the middle of it. Yes, Michael had said he was in love with her, but something told her it was a passing fancy. She just hoped she was wrong. She really was falling in love with him. But she was afraid to trust it just yet.

Tina leaned her elbows on the top of her desk and sat her chin in her palm. She wondered how other women handled their concerns about their futures. And as she pondered her head began to drop further down.

Tina closed her eyes and pictured the possibility of marriage to Michael. It was a fact he was a very strong personality. But then again, she could be also. He was willing to consider her thoughts and feelings, which was good. She would definitely be willing to consider his as well. And if marriage happened, there could possibly be children in the future. Would that mean she would have to quit working? There was so much to think about. But the feeling was still very strong that he was really only considering the present and how he felt now. After he got to know her better perhaps he would begin to see her faults. And there were many of them, she thought. Perhaps then he would decide it wasn't worth it to him to maintain the relationship. She didn't want something temporary. She wanted unconditional love to be generated by both of them so there would be some built in give-and-take. She hoped there would be room for mistakes and forgiveness. And that each of them would be willing to forgive the other when mistakes happened, because they happen just naturally. She sat quietly just thinking about it.

Suddenly her desk seemed to dissolve into nothingness and she saw the same dirt road she had seen a couple of days ago. It was like a dream. She was standing at the edge of the road and she could hear an antique car approaching. There was a man driving it, dressed in the attire of the early nineteen hundreds. A man that appeared to be about her own age.

She wondered why she was having this same dream again. What was her mind trying to tell her? Suddenly she felt as though she was falling. She grabbed her desk to keep from going down. She felt her fingers sliding across the mat that covered her desk. She grabbed for the edge of the desk, just for something to hold on to, yet her fingers felt as though they were greased. No matter what she tried to grasp with either hand her fingers seemed to just slide over it, unable to hold on. She truly felt as though she was falling as though through a trap door into,…into what? "Noooo!" she heard herself call out. Then she felt the wind knocked out of her as she hit something hard. She blinked her eyes, then reached out to touch something to steady herself. She still had her eyes closed. She opened her eyes and saw she was sitting on the ground. The ground! How could she be sitting on the ground? She was in an office building on the tenth floor. This couldn't be happening. She must be dreaming. Yes, that was it. She had closed her eyes and fallen asleep. All she had to do was wake herself up and she would be back at her desk. This was preposterous. This couldn't be happening. This was the twenty first century.

All the time she could still hear the old antique car getting ever closer. She looked around. It appeared she was out in the middle of no where. She couldn't see any buildings of any kind.

Just trees and a dried up river bed beyond the road. The road itself wasn't even paved.

This just didn't make any sense. She leaned forward and pressed both hands into her temples. Her head was aching and she felt lightheaded, as though she had been drinking. Only she hadn't. She closed her eyes and held her head in her hands. She could hear the car getting close now but the sun light was so bright it made her head hurt even worse each time she tried to open her eyes. What was happening?

Sudden the automobile was upon her. She tried to remember if she was on the road or beside it. Well, she decided, if the fool saw her on the road he should have enough sense to at least not run her down. She just couldn't open her eyes yet. The pain was too great.

She could hear the engine running close by. It sounded as though it was no longer moving. Then she felt someone touch her.

"Miss, are you all right," came the deep voice. "Miss! Miss?"

"All she could do was hold her head. It hurt to even think about speaking, so she didn't.

"Miss, how did you get clear out here all by yourself? What happened? Did you fall off of a buggy, or out of a car? Miss? Can you talk? Miss, how can I help you?"

Even just listening to the sound of his voice made her head hurt. She reached up to let him know she needed his help. She felt a strong hand take hold of hers. Then she saw what little light that was getting into her vision fade into blackness. And the pain dropped away.

Jefferson Michael Marlboro was a man on his way up in the world. He owned his own business and had plans for purchasing more before the year was out. He had two small hotels and one barber shop, as well as a restaurant next to one of his hotels. If things panned out he was going to go into the business of selling gasoline for all of the new automobiles that the general public was dreaming of purchasing. Along with that there was the possibility of garages to service those automobiles.

Yes there were many possibilities in his future for making money. And he planned on getting in on the ground floor on several of them. He might even consider becoming a automobile dealer himself, selling vehicles to the public.

He'd been dreaming of the many possibilities as he came around the curve and spotted the woman sitting on the ground. It was a good thing he wasn't so involved with his dreaming that he missed seeing her. Whatever could a lovely woman be doing out here, ten miles from any town? It didn't make any sense. And when he discovered she was unable to speak it made it all that much more sad. Who would leave a woman out here like that? That's almost the same as murder. No true gentleman could do such a thing. If he found how who abandoned her, they would have a lot to answer for, to him. He would certainly take the man to task. He was certain it had to have been a man. He couldn't imagine a woman leaving another woman alone like that. Most women were more compassionate than that. If he hadn't come along she could have been in serious trouble. What if she had lain out there for the night? He didn't want to imagine it.

Since she was unable to even open her eyes he had had to pick her up in his arms and put her into his vehicle. She just fainted as he picked her up. Her clothing appeared to be very thin and he was immediately concerned she may be chilled, so he took off his coat and wrapped it around her to keep her warm while they traveled. He put her in the back seat so he could lay her down to travel. He couldn't drive and hold her at the same time. And he certainly didn't want her falling out of her seat as he drove.

He tried to drive slowly so she wouldn't be bounced around so badly. He sincerely hoped she had only fainted and would be coming around soon. His place was a little over a mile this side of town, so he would take her there. His housekeeper would know what to do for her and if a doctor was needed.

It only took him about thirty minutes to get home. As he drove onto the long driveway leading up to his house he began to honk the claxon horn. And as he circled around the driveway in the front of the house the big front door opened and his housekeeper stepped out.

"Mrs. Braxton, come quickly. I found a lady on the Old Post Road. She was just sitting there on the ground as though she had fallen from a buggy or perhaps out of an automobile. She was holding her head as though it was hurting her. By the time I got to her she wasn't able to speak. And just as she reached out to me for help she fainted. She's in the back seat."

"Oh my land!" she said. Bring her in and we'll put her in one of the guest rooms. The one at the top of the stairs would be good. It's more feminine. Let me get the door for you," she said as she ran to open the wide entranceway door as he carried the woman up the front steps.

He passed quickly through the vestibule and on into the entrance hall. Then he hurried up the wide stairway leading to the second floor. Just as he approached the first bedroom door Mrs. Braxton passed him, opening the door for him. He carried her over to the tall bed that stood in the middle of the room. Gently he placed her on the soft bed. He hoped he hadn't hurt her further by jarring her as he hurried up the stairs.

Mrs. Braxton stepped quickly to the side of the bed. She looked the woman over carefully, watching for injuries on her head, neck and extremities. Then she checked her eyes. They appeared to be very dilated. Other than that she couldn't find anything wrong.

She had Mr. Marlboro step out of the room so she could undress the woman and slip a light gown on her, while she checked the woman's body for cuts, bruises, or possible internal injuries. When she had completed that she opened the door, letting her employer back into the room.

The young woman was covered with the sheet and one blanket from the bed. All that was visible of her was from her shoulders up. Mrs. Braxton had put the ladies arms on the outside of the blankets, with her arms crossed over chest.

"So what in the world do you think is wrong with her, Mrs. Braxton?" he asked.

"The only thing I found was that her eyes looked as though she was having a terrible headache because her pupils were really large. No bruises of any kind, and no other injuries that I could find," she told him.

"Well, I guess we should be grateful for that. You didn't discover any bump or any head injuries?"

"No, nothing on her head that I could find. If she hit her head there isn't any mark of it." She shook her head. It doesn't make a lot of sense to me. It's as though she just maybe had a bad headache and fell out of the buggy, or automobile. But the moment she fell out you would have thought someone would have missed her. Why wouldn't they go back and look for her?"

"I don't know, Mrs. Braxton. This seems most unusual to me. But we'll do our duty to her. She is welcome to stay as long as necessary so she can get well. Did you find any label or anything that might identify her in her clothes?"

"Nothing! It's a shame. You would think someone would be looking for her."

"Perhaps I ought to post a sign on a tree close to where I found her. Then if someone comes by looking for her the sign would direct them to us."

"An excellent idea. You should do just that," she said. And perhaps you could ask around if anyone knows of a missing young woman. There must be people around somewhere close that know of her. She couldn't be that far from home, I would think."

He stood at the foot of the bed looking at the woman. "She really is quite beautiful isn't she?" he asked.

"I suppose so. Each woman has their own beauty, in their own way. You know, even an ugly woman may look beautiful to the right man. But yes, I think she is quite pretty. I just don't understand how such a thing could have happened. You say she was awake and alert when you found her?"

"Yes! She was sitting up holding her head, with her eyes closed as though the sunlight bothered her, or she was in pain. Most likely she was in pain from the tumble she took. Then, as she must have heard my voice she reached up as if to take my hand so I could pull her up from the ground when she fainted. I had hoped she would have come around by now."

"You know, sometimes with a brain injury a person doesn't wake up because of pressure in their brain. And folks have been known to die from that. I guess all we can do now is hope and pray. I'll stay close to her, to watch over her. You go on with whatever you have to do, Mr. Marlboro. She'll be in good hands now. I promise. We just have to wait for her to wake up." With that she straightened the blankets and brushed the woman's hair away from her face with her hand. "The good Lord will guide her from here. You've done all that you could."

He stepped away from the bed, shaking his head from side to side. "It's just so sad to see such a thing happen to a lovely young woman. What a shame." He headed toward the door.

"Oh, would you ask Maisey to bring me my knitting? I may as well keep my hands busy while I sit here."

"Yes, gladly Mrs. Braxton. Thank you for all your care. I'm going to go into my den and make up that sign and then ride out to the place I found her and tack it onto a tree. Then I think I'll go into town and ask around if anyone knows anything. I'll be back after that."

"Yes Sir. I'll be right here. I'm sure she'll wake up eventually. If there's pressure in her head, lets just hope it lets up so she can wake up."

He left the room, headed for his den on the first floor. Marching into his home office he walked directly to his huge walnut desk to sit and write out a brief message about the woman. He took his pen and began to write. He printed the word FOUND in large blocked out letters so as to draw attention to his flyer. Below that he filled in the information as he knew it, finishing with his name and address so that anyone looking for this woman could locate him, thus locating her. Looking at his work he felt satisfied that this was sufficient. Getting to his feet he walked quickly to the kitchen where he knew he would find Maisey.

Striding into the large kitchen he could see his cook, Mrs. Booth and Maisey, sitting at the counter cutting up some vegetables.

"Maisey, please take Mrs. Braxton's knitting up to her. She's in the pink guest room at the top of the stairs. And do it quietly because she is sitting with a very ill young woman."

"Yes Sir," came her reply. "I'll go immediately." She jumped up and literally ran from the room in the direction of the servants quarters to do her errand.

Maisey entered the Pink Room with Mrs. Braxtons knitting held tightly in her hand. She rapped her knuckles on the door as she opened it. Peering around the heavy door she could see the housekeeper sitting in a rocking chair beyond the big bed.

Mrs. Braxton waved her into the room and signaled for her to quietly walk around the bed to her. Maisey handed her the knitting and stepped over toward the end of the big bed.

"Who is she?" she asked.

"We don't know yet. Hopefully she'll wake up soon and tell us. Otherwise all we can do is watch over her. If you know any good prayers perhaps you could use them in her behalf. You go on back downstairs and help cook as much as you can, since, as you can see, I'm going to be busy here. If we need anything here I'll let you know. Thank you Maisey," she said in a soft voice.

Maisey stood for a moment just looking at the lady. What a pretty one she was, Maisey thought. What a sad thing to have happen to her. Then she turned and walked quietly out of the room.

Mrs. Braxton rocked back and forth as her hands worked over the yarn that slowly unwound from the skein on her lap. Occasionally she would look over at the woman to see if there was any change in her condition, but spying none her eyes returned to her hand movements. She was so adept at knitting now that she could do it without even seeing what her hands were doing. It seemed a natural thing for her. Again her eyes drifted over to the bed. Something unusual was happening, her mind was telling her. Laying her yarn and needles aside, she stood and walked to the side of the bed. She watched as she could see the eye movement behind the woman's eyelids. She watched as the woman's eyes seemed to be moving back and forth as if she was looking for something.

Mrs. Braxton remained very still as she observed the woman on the bed. She seemed to be re-living what had happened to her. She watched as the hands reached up as though the woman was trying to grasp something in front of her, her fingers bending, reaching for something to hold on to. Suddenly the woman's mouth opened and she spoke. She shouted "Nooo!" in a frantic cry, as though she was trying to keep from falling. Then her hands went into the air as if she was sailing downward through the air. Her head went back and her shoulders bounced off of the bed momentarily as though she had just landed on the ground. Her arms landed on the bed, spread wide just as if she had fallen. Then her hands came up to cover her eyes, then hold her head between them as if she was in pain.

Mrs. Braxton was amazed as she watched the scene play itself out before her. She saw the woman sit up, her eyes still closed and turn her head as though she was hearing some sound. Then one of her hands shot up into the air as though she was reaching for something. And just as quickly it fell to her side as she collapsed onto the pillow, as though she had fainted.

She waited a moment longer to see if the scene was played out completely, or if something might occur. As the minutes passed she was certain this young woman had just re-lived what had happened to her. Apparently she had fallen, crying out in her fear. She must have hurt her head in the process, since she was holding it in her hands.

Mrs. Braxton reached to pick up the woman's hands, laying them at her sides. Then she positioned her back down in the bed where she had been before. In her movement she had ended up with her head against the headboard. After getting the woman back onto the pillow properly, she again drew up the sheet and light blanket over her to keep out any chill. She felt for a pulse along the woman's throat and found it to be normal. Gently she again brushed the hair from the woman's face. As she did so, the woman moaned, turning her head to the side. Perhaps she was beginning to wake up.

Standing patiently beside the bed the housekeeper watched as the woman's hand came up to her head. It was a certainty now in the housekeeper's mind, there was pain there.

She moaned softly again and began to blink her eyes. She was waking up. Perhaps the re-living the scene was what awakened her.

Mrs. Braxton watched as the woman's eyes came open, looking around as if to find out where she was. Then the bright green eyes settled on her own.

"You're going to be fine, Dear. You've had a bit of an accident, but we're going to take good care of you. Don't you worry about a thing. There aren't any injuries anywhere, so you just rest and get better. Do you want something for your headache?"

The young woman blinked again as if trying to comprehend what was going on. She squeezed her eyes shut, wrinkling up her forehead as if to push away the pain there. "Where am I?" she asked.

"You're safe in the home of Mr. Marlboro, Miss," the housekeeper told her.

Tina looked around, trying to understand exactly where she might be. It appeared as though she was in an old house that apparently was the home of some fellow by the name of Marlboro. She couldn't help but wonder if he was any relation to the Marlboro Cigarette maker.

She would have to try again to find out exactly where she had ended up. "But exactly where are we?" she inquired of the older woman.

"Oh my!" replied the housekeeper. "I wonder if you have lost your memory? You're in the lovely home of Mr. Jefferson Marlboro just outside of Los Angeles, Miss. Does that help at all?"

Tina still wasn't getting enough of the picture. She looked at the long dress that encompassed the housekeeper. Most housekeepers don't wear such long dresses and haven't for many years. Even though she was all in gray with a white apron over it, she looked to Tina as though she was from a time long past.

"What year is it?" Tina asked.

"Why, silly girl, it's 1912 of course."

Tina could hardly believe her ears. "Nineteen twelve? But it can't be. I was just at my desk working, and it was 2004. It can't be 1912." Shock was evident in her face.

The housekeeper didn't believe what she thought she had heard the woman say. Whatever did she mean she was at her desk working and it was 2004. Why that was almost a century away. Such a thing wasn't possible. And besides, women didn't work.

"You just rest, Miss. I'm sure you're just confused right now. Mr. Marlboro will be back shortly and you and he can talk about all of this. Just close your eyes and rest while I get you something for your headache. I'll be right back," she told her, starting for the door.

Tina tried to relax and figure out what was going on. Only minutes ago she had been at her desk. How did she get here, and where exactly was here? She began to suspect that she may have dropped through a tear in time. This woman certainly wasn't dressed in modern garb.

Tina's head was throbbing so badly she didn't want to try and think anymore. Perhaps it would be best if she just rested for now. She was certain things would work themselves out in time.

Tina let her eyes close and she rolled over on her side. The light coming in the tall window was so bright that it made her head hurt worse, so she turned over in the other direction and faced toward the door. As her eyes drifted around the room she noticed the place was full of antique furniture. There was a tall secretary along one wall with an uncomfortable chair before it. The desk section was open so she could see the many cubbyholes along the back. The top of the secretary had glass doors so she could see what was on the upper shelves. It appeared to be full of books.

Near the fireplace she had noticed a horsehair couch. It must be a true collector's item. No one even made them anymore. Over the fireplace was a beautiful marble mantle which held a candle stick at each end. And in between was a picture of some lady, in the dress from the early 1900's or possibly earlier.

Tina decided she wasn't going to be able to figure all of this out at the moment, so she closed her eyes. It was only minutes until the housekeeper returned with a glass of water in one hand and a bottle of aspirin in the other.

The housekeeper sat the glass of water on the table next to the bed and pulled a spoon from her pocket. Then she put the spoon on the table as she opened the bottle, laying the lid on the table as well. Picking up the spoon she dumped a white powdery substance into the spoon and dumped it into the glass of water. Quickly she stirred the concoction and handed it toward Tina.

"Can you drink this on your own, or do you need my help in sitting up?" she inquired of Tina.

"I think I can sit up on my own, thanks." Tina did exactly that and accepted the glass from the woman. "What is this?" she asked.

"It's aspirin. Now be good and drink it down quickly so it can start working on that headache of yours."

"But aspirin comes in pill form. Why do you have it in powder?"

"Young lady, I don't know what you're talking about. Just drink it so you'll start feeling better."

Tina did so. She could feel her stomach burn a little in only moments. She had always been sensitive to aspirin. That was why she made a point of getting the buffered kind.

"Thank you," she said to the kind looking woman. I'm sorry to be a burden. Maybe if I just take a little nap I'll feel better."

"Yes, I agree with you there. Your body just needs rest after all of that excitement. Just rest and I'll come back later to check on you. Now, don't worry about a thing, Dear."

Tina closed here eyes and immediately dropped into a deep sleep. The trauma of the past hour or so was more than she wanted to think about with this headache.

Chapter 8

When Jefferson Marlboro returned he went to the kitchen to locate his housekeeper. Finding her there he assumed that it meant that their houseguest was awake.

"How is she?" he asked quickly.

"She's sleeping. But she woke up while you were gone. I was with her as she seemed to be re-living what happened. She seems confused."

"Confused in what way?"

"She asked where she was and I told her in your home. I used your name figuring if she lived around here she would know of you. But she didn't respond as if she recognized your name. Then she asked me what year it was. And when I told her, she was a little upset. I don't know. I suspect she may have lost her memory because of the fall. She said something about that it couldn't be 1912, that she was, let's see, ... what did she say exactly? Oh yes, she said she was just sitting at her desk and it was the year 2004."

"Two thousand and four? So she thinks she came from the future?"

"Well, if you took her words seriously, that seems to be the case. Of course we know that isn't possible. So I suspect it's just in her mind."

"What an unusual occurrence. I wonder why she might think such a thing."

"Who knows! Perhaps she was dreaming of what the future might bring when she fell. We'll never know. I guess anything is possible."

"Do you think I might be able to talk with her? Would you go up with me? If she's awake I think there are some answers we need to get from her."

"Yes, I agree. I figured you would want to do the asking of questions, so I didn't ask her who she was or anything."

Both Jefferson and his housekeeper headed for the stairs that led toward the bedroom where Tina rested. As they topped the stairs he stepped forward, knocking on the door twice, then slowly pushing it open. He directed her to enter before him, just in case their guest might have gotten up and was not presentable for visitors.

He waited in the hall just out of the sight of the bed until she invited him into the room. Stepping into the bedroom he could see his guest sleeping, her light brunette hair fanned out across the pillow in a very feminine way. He noticed her color seemed better.

He stepped to the end of the bed as Mrs. Braxton stood at the side of it. She reached over and laid her hand on the young woman's hand. Immediately the young woman's eyes came open. And the first person she saw was Jefferson. She quickly pulled the sheet up to cover herself and made a gasping noise, surprised to see a man in her bedroom.

"Who are you, and what are you doing in my bedroom?" she asked before he could say anything.

"I might ask you the same. This is my home and I am Jefferson Marlboro. I found you along the road as I was traveling home. Can you tell us your name?" He tried to ask gently, trying hard not to upset her. As yet, they weren't sure if her brain had been affected or not.

My name? My name is Tina Taylor. That is Christina Taylor. Where are we?"

"As I said earlier, you're a guest in my home."

"Okay! And where is here?"

"We, my staff and myself, live on the outskirts of Los Angeles. We are several miles from town actually."

"I see. And what year is it?" she asked, almost afraid to do so.

"It's the Year of our Lord, 1912. Does that make a difference to you?" He lifted his one eyebrow, trying to see how she might respond to such a question.

"But it can't be 1912. It just can't be!"

"And why not, young lady?" He could tell by her raised voice that she was truly concerned about it. He wanted to keep her as calm as possible. He didn't want her becoming unduly upset.

Tina looked at Mrs. Braxton, and then at Jefferson. They could both see in her face that she wasn't sure they were telling her the truth.

"Miss Taylor. Can you tell us why it might upset you that it is 1912?"

"Because I was just in 2004, that's why. How could I be in 1912? The only way that could happen was if I accidentally slipped through a hole in time. And I don't believe in such things."

Tina reached up and rubbed her temple. It felt as though her headache might just come back full blown. This just couldn't be happening. It wasn't possible.

"Neither do I. Can you tell us Miss Taylor where you lived in the year 2004?" He couldn't help but look at his housekeeper and smile.

"Of course! I lived in Los Angeles, California. I have a townhouse at the Midtown Estates. Do you know where that is, Mr. Marlboro?" She looked into his face to see if he was going to lie to her.

"No, I don't think I've heard of that place. You say it's within the Los Angeles city limit?"

"Of course it is. It's just north of Wilshire Blvd. About a mile or so. It's a gated community. That's why I bought it. I wanted the security of living behind gates. The city is getting much too dangerous and a woman alone doesn't need to take unnecessary chances." Her eyes seemed to sparkle as she gave them this information. "Although I do hold a black belt in Karate, you just never know who is going to jump out at you from the shadows." She made her statement as though it was suppose to impress them, but since neither of them knew what Karate was, it fell on deaf ears.

"And can you tell us what Karate is, Miss Taylor. It's a term I don't recognize."

"Oh! Figures! 1912, indeed! It's a form of self defense using hand and foot movements."

"I see, I think." Jefferson told her. And you mentioned you work? What type of work do you do?"

"I'm the Personnel Supervisor over all employees who work for the Hart Personnel Development Corporation in Los Angeles. Have you heard of them?"

"No, I'm afraid not. Miss Taylor, I really can't believe that you traveled through time to get to us. Is there anything that you might tell us that might convince us that you really are from the far distant future?" He wanted to chuckle but decided it might embarrass his guest.

'Well, I'm not sure. You say this is 1912. What month is it?"

"This is April. It's one of my favorite months. It means Spring is just around the corner," he told her.

"Uh huh! April what?" Quickly she was trying to remember the date that the Titanic sunk, killing 1500 people. That ought to shock him.

"This is April 14th, 1912. Does that date mean anything to you, Miss Taylor?" He was looking at her wondering what she might come up with to try to convince them she knew the future.

"I believe it was April 15th, 1912, not long before dawn, maybe two or three in the morning, that the ship known as the Titanic sunk with a loss of over 1500 lives in the North Atlantic. It was on it's maiden voyage across the Atlantic from Great Britain."

Jefferson's head came up. "What did you say? A loss of over 1500 lives? But that's not possible. That ship was built with a double skin so that if the outside one ruptured for any reason, the inner hull would keep it afloat. Mr. Guttenheim designed it that way for double protection. Why there are many wealthy and well-known people on that ship, Miss Taylor."

"Since you don't believe me, you just wait until tomorrow, or actually the day after tomorrow, and it will be in the news all around the world. A terrible loss of life! And millions of dollars went down with it, locked in the safe. I understand some of those wealthy patrons took valuable paintings with them to hang in their suites, and everything was lost. Just you wait and see." She nodded her head at him as if to say, so there.

That's unbelievable!" He just shook his head at her.

"And it gets more interesting than that. I can't remember the year, but I believe it was in the 1990's when they finally were able to go down to her and bring up the ships safe, plus china plates that survived hitting the bottom of the North Atlantic, and many other articles that laid there twelve thousand and fifty feet down. Can you imagine the pressure down there? Of course all of the divers had to be either in a special made sub or deep diving suit. The pictures I saw showed it was very dark and there was stuff growing all over the ship. They took pictures of the grand staircase and several places on board. Then they showed drawings as to what it looked like before it left port. If I remember correctly the ship broke up into two pieces when it hit the bottom, the two parts landing a ways away from each other. A couple of movies have been made about the story. I have a copy of the most recent one in my DVD collection. But it's so awful, the way that they kept the gates locked shut to keep the poor people that were traveling in the hold, down there, that it made me angry. Even when they knew the ship was going down they wouldn't let them out. They didn't want them filling up the too few lifeboats. They wanted to get the wealthy passengers off first. How some people can be so inhumane to their fellow man is beyond me." Tina frowned at them both. Just thinking about what happened to those poor people made her blood boil.

Jefferson looked at her face. She actually believed what she was telling them.

"Tell me, Christina, what is this 'sub' you mention?"

"Oh, sub is short for submersible or submarine. It's a ship that can go underwater and is pressurized so that it can withstand the great pressure deep in the ocean. You know, the deeper you go the greater the pressure, and our bodies weren't made to withstand that. It would simply smash us. And when men go down that deep they have to stop at different levels before coming back up to de-pressurize or they get something called the 'bends'. That means that their bodies would literally explode if they don't do it right. Like I said, our bodies weren't meant to handle that kind of pressure changes all by itself."

"And what is a movie, or a DVD?" he asked.

"Movies are moving pictures projected onto a screen. As you watch them it appears you are actually seeing life itself. A DVD is the latest technique in movies. They used to put movies on celluloid tape and as the frames of pictures flashed by, what you saw on the screen looked like the real thing. But that film, as they called the celluloid, was very flammable. Now that we have computers which can store memory, they put the memory of the movie on a disc and you simply have the movie on a disc. The discs are called DVD's. I'm not sure what the first 'D' stands for, but I think the 'V' is for video, and the last 'D' is for disc. And these DVD's are almost unbreakable. Maybe the first 'D' is for digital."

Preposterous! It's a shame, such a beautiful woman having such a mental state, he thought. "Well, perhaps we ought to discuss this later. I can see this upsets you."

"Certainly! We can discuss it in two days. That is, if I'm still here!" She gave him a look that scared most of her employees. It only made him shake his head.

"Yes, of course," he said, trying to placate her. "How are you feeling, Miss Taylor? Do you think you'll feel up to coming down for dinner?"

Tina was feeling better, except for the anxiousness that she felt because these people didn't seem to believe her. And also, because she didn't know when, or if, she might suddenly slip back through that hole in time to 2004. But personally she was more than ready to go home.

Mrs. Braxton spoke up. "I think Miss Taylor might want to freshen up a bit before dinner, Mr. Marlboro. If you would excuse us, I will help her get up, and if she feels up to it, I'll bring her down to dinner. Otherwise, I can just bring her a tray. I'm sure she must be famished."

"Yes," Tina said, I think it would feel good to get up. I feel as though I need to get my blood moving again." She looked up at Jefferson as if to say, hurry up and get out of here.

After the door closed behind him Mrs. Braxton pulled the blanket and sheet back and reached to help her to her feet.

"Are you sure you feel well enough to be on your feet, Miss Taylor?" She was a rather small woman, but she would do her best to help this poor young woman move around and wash up, if she chose to do so.

Feeling her feet touch the floor Tina rested her weight on her feet and paused, hoping the lightheadedness would go away. After a moment she stood up and took a step. The fuzzy feeling in her head was letting up and she was beginning to feel normal again.

"Where is the bathroom?" she asked the housekeeper.

"Right through that door. Are you sure you can do it on your own?"

"Yes, I think so. I just feel a little stiff. My head is feeling much better now." She walked slowly toward the door to which Mrs. Braxton had pointed. She kept her head high and just took her time getting there. She put her hand on the doorknob and turned it. Stepping into the bathroom she couldn't help but smile at the tiny white tiles laid like diamonds across the floor. She had seen that same pattern in many old apartment buildings that had once been large homes in L.A.

She was tickled with the pedestal sink that had come into style, gone out, and come back in again in the 1990's. She remembered hearing that styles came and went several times, and apparently this was one of them.

Looking at the old style clawfoot tub she could remember many time as a child she had taken a bath in just such a tub.

She used the toilet and then washed her hands. She decided to strip off her clothes and treat herself to a hot bath. She turned on the hot water tap and began to slip off the gown that apparently the housekeeper had put on her. She just wished she had some clean clothes to put on, but that just wasn't to be.

She heard a soft rap on the door. "Are you decent dear? May I come in for a moment?" It was Mrs. Braxton so Tina called to her to come in.

"I thought I heard the water running. While you are taking a bath, how about if I take your clothes and get them cleaned. You know, Mr. Marlboro's sister used to stay here before she got married. I think she was just about your size. She left some clothes here. I'll go look and see what I can find. If you can fit into some of her things, I'm sure she won't mind if you use them. I seriously doubt she will even miss them. I'll be right back. If it turns out you don't fit her things then I'll just brush this outfit off and air it out so you can slip back into it." She nodded toward the clothing over her arm.

"Thank you Mrs. Braxton. You've been so helpful. I really do appreciate everything you and Mr. Marlboro have done for me."

"Oh posh, it's nothing. I'm sure you would do the same if the shoe was on the other foot. Now you just enjoy that hot bath and I'll go look in the closet where Tilly left those clothes."

She turned to leave and Tina closed the door behind her. Soaking in a hot bath sounded wonderful.

Chapter 9

Dinner that evening was delicious and refreshing for Tina. She had not sat down to an actual dinner in someone's home in quite some time. Outside of having had dinner with Michael the other evening in that bar, she could not recall the last time she had enjoyed good food with some interesting company besides.

Mrs. Braxton had been able to locate some of Jefferson's sister's things and when Tina tried some of them on they fit her as though they were meant for her to wear. The dress she selected went to her ankles and had short sleeves and a princess line to it. The empire waist emphasized her breasts and draped beautifully. She felt as though she was a princess for a day, or at least a few hours.

As she entered the formal sitting room Jefferson stood to greet her. He stepped up quickly to her side and took her hand in his, lifting it to his lips. His kiss on the back of her hand made her wish he would turn it over and kiss her palm as well. Where did that come from, she wondered as she considered her last thought.

"Would you care for something to drink before dinner, Christina?" he asked.

"No, nothing for me thank you. I'm still getting over the last dredges of that horrid headache."

He walked her over to a huge horsehair couch and seated her. He sat with her, leaving a proper space of air between them. "I'm glad you're feeling better. I'm still not sure I believe from where you've come. But we can worry about that another time. Can you tell me more about why you think you have traveled through time?"

"Certainly you could see that my clothing wasn't from this era. If nothing else, the length of my skirt alone should show you that. I don't believe anyone wore things that short in the early nineteen hundreds. We have many manmade fabrics in my time that you don't have now."

"The length of your skirt idea does make it have a ring of truth to it. Tell me, how did you fall into the hole in time?"

"I haven't any idea. I was sitting at my desk when I seemed to have a vision of the roadway where you found me. I could hear your car coming. I was looking around just before I felt the impact with the ground. I think I hit rather hard."

"I suspect so. That may have been why you were unconscious."

"Or," she imposed, "it might have been caused by the distortion of passing through time," she told him. "Since we don't have any knowledge of such things, we'll never know."

"Tell me, why do you call my automobile a 'car'? What does that mean?"

"It's a term that has been adapted. Automobile is just too long. Good advertising companies would tell you that in a minute. Make it short and easy to remember they would say. That's what sells things to Mr. and Mrs. John Q. Public. I'm sure you have things commercialized now that are known to have catchy phrases attached to them. Perhaps a little jingle."

Mrs. Braxton appeared at the door, interrupting their train of thought, and announced that dinner was served. Jefferson rose and extended his hand to help her from the couch. She took it and stood. With her hand remaining in his, and his glass of wine in his other, he escorted her into his formal dinning room. He seated her at the far end of the table, and walked to the opposite end, sitting in his usual chair.

"I must tell you, Christina, if I may call you that, that I am grateful for your company. Dinner isn't as enjoyable alone."

"Yes, of course you may call me that. It is my given name. Although in my time everyone calls me Tina, or Miss Taylor."

He smiled and said, "Perhaps it would be more proper for me to call you Miss Taylor, since we haven't been properly introduced as yet." He sat smiling at her.

She was at a loss of words. The formality of his statement blew the wind right out of her sails. She didn't know what to say.

He lifted a small bell that sat on the table, and rang it. Almost immediately Mrs. Braxton appeared in the doorway.

"You rang, Mr. Marlboro?" she asked.

"Yes, Mrs. Braxton. We just realized that we have not been properly introduced, which seems to be causing a bit of a problem in our conversation. Would you come in and do us the honors?"

"Of course!" she replied. Stepping up toward the table she stood beside the chair in which Tina sat. Jefferson stood and walked over to them.

Mr. Jefferson Michael Marlboro, I would like very much for you to meet Miss Christina Taylor. Miss Taylor, this is the honorable Mr. Jefferson Michael Marlboro."

Jefferson took her hand in his and kissed it, as he had done previously, and stated, "It is a great honor to meet you officially, my Dear." Then he turned to his housekeeper. Thank you Mrs. Braxton. At least now we can safely use each others given names, rather than remain so formal."

Mrs. Braxton disappeared back into the kitchen to fetch their first course of meatball soup.

Tina lifted her spoon and tasted the beef flavored broth. It was delicious. Until that moment, she hadn't realized that she was really very hungry.

She had almost polished off the wonderful soup when Mrs. Braxton returned with the next course. She sat a small salad of fresh vegetables before each of them and placed a small boat of creamy homemade salad dressing by each of their plates. Removing their bowls, she left them alone again.

"My goodness. In my day, we no longer serve courses. This is such a treat," she told him.

"How would you serve dinner if I was a guest in your home this evening, Christina?"

"Well, first of all, I'm not much of a cook. It would be just you and I, without any servants. There would be a salad, followed by a plate with the entre and vegetable. Breads or rolls would be offered, then fruit or dessert, with coffee. But most of it would be brought to the table all at one time," she informed him.

"Practical, of course. And very efficient. I understand. It sounds as though in your day things are done in a hurry, just to get them overwith. Is that not true, Christina?"

"Yes, I'm afraid so. Expediency is important there. You see, there is so much to do, and it seems, so little time to do it that we hurry, hoping to have more time for leisure."

"And what do you do during your leisure, Christina?"

"Personally, I like to read, or take a drive, or swim, or even just take a nap. There is a small pool at my townhouse and I love to do laps. It's very good for the heart you know."

"Is that true?" he asked. "In what way? Do you mean it keeps you from being lonely?"

"Well, yes, perhaps. But I meant that it strengthens your heart. So it helps to keep a person healthy." Tina reached for her goblet of water and took a sip. "And drinking lots of this is a good thing too. Many people don't understand the need for hydration in my day. They will go hiking, or just walking in the hot sun and forget to take water or an energy drink with them. Then they end up with a headache, and could pass out if they really become badly dehydrated."

"How interesting. And how would someone on that day trip to nature carry water along with them?" he asked, "in a canteen? Somehow I can't picture lots of people carrying one."

"No, water is a big business in 2004. You can purchase many different size bottles of it to carry in your knapsack, or even on a clip on your belt. Women even carry them in their purse. Nowdays, or rather, in my time, it's not unusual to see people going most anywhere with a tall bottle of water in their hand."

"How unique! Sounds like a most profitable business. And what is this energy drink of which you speak?"

"Oh, they're flavored drinks that have either sugar in them, or electrolytes to hydrate your body."

"I see,...I think," he answered.

"What other ways are their to become financially wealthy in your time are there?"

"Many, actually. Why, if you knew what I know, you could make investments now, or as the business's begin to appear, and very quickly become quite rich. Of course, there's always the possibility of what happened in Silicone Valley. Many people who became millionaires over night lost everything in the same time span."

"What do you mean, Christina? How could someone become so wealthy over night and lose it overnight. In the stock market?"

"Well, yes, kind of. You see a young man created a microchip that could store memory. It was an electrode that was tiny, but able to retain a vast amount of information. The young man also invented a computer to house it, with the ability to type in information and several keys that would allow the operator to do many different functions. And the world-wide-web was invented."

"The what?"

"The web. Or as it is sometimes called, the internet. It's a series of computers with microchips that record information. People very quickly started putting all the information in books into them, plus their own ideas as well. When you go to the internet you can research any subject that you can imagine. Only you have to understand that some articles are written in such a way to expound on the author's opinion, not just pure fact."

"And anyone who had one of these, computers, is that what you called it, could gain access to this internet information?"

"Yes. People and companies began to create things called web sites where you could visit through your computer and gain information or opinions."

"That's unbelievable. And you say something went wrong with this 'internet'?"

"Well, not exactly. You see the ability of the microchip became so prevalent that it was no longer unique, and it's value 'crashed'. What was worth millions in company investments became almost worthless, since there was so much available. People that had moved into multi-million dollar homes suddenly could no longer pay for them. And they lost everything. When you discover a need for something, and you fill that need, you can make lots of money. But when you glut the market with too much of that needed thing, it floods the market and the price for that item plummets. And investors take a great loss."

"I see. That applies even today, I'm sure. One simply needs to keep the supply short so there is always a need for the product."

"Yes, exactly. That is effective product management to maintain financial security," she said.

"Understandable!"

They talked all through their meal, almost not aware of what they were eating. Finally when Mrs. Braxton brought their coffee they were sated and comfortable in each other's company.

"You know, Christina, usually when men and women get together for a dinner, it's the men that get to enjoy the interesting conversation. But this had been most enlightening and enjoyable. The company of such a lovely woman and the conversation of such interest has been marvelous. Most women haven't any idea what goes on in the business world and could care less."

"Ah yes! I'm still waiting for the announcement of our first lady President."

His head came up in shock and bewilderment. "What? Whatever made you say such a silly thing? It's not possible. The men of our country would never consider such a thing."

"You might be surprised, Jefferson. Anything is possible. They said man would never walk on the moon either!" she told him with a smile.

His face became serious and he simply sat and looked at her. His mouth dropped open and still no words came across his lips. Then he said, "You jest."

"Definitely not! Mr. Neil Armstrong not only walked, he jumped and bounced. It was 1969, I believe." She sat and watched his face from across the long table. She could see he was feeling very dubious.

After their second cup of coffee he suggested they move into the parlor and relax. She suggested why not walk outside onto the patio area where they could enjoy the evening sky. So he rose from his chair and walked to where she sat, extended his hand to her and she laid her hand in his and rose from her chair.

He tucked her hand into the crook of his arm and they strolled toward the French doors and out into the night.

The air was warm for April and the night was clear. He escorted her over to the two wooden Adirondack chairs and seated her in one.

The chairs were constructed so as to lean the user backward slightly, which was perfect for looking into the night sky.

"You know, these chairs are still popular in my day. But quite expensive. I guess it's the same old thing, supply and demand, and the high cost of shipping." She laughed.

Jefferson couldn't help but laugh with her. He enjoyed the lilting sound of her voice. And he felt drawn to the intelligence he found in her.

Tina leaned her head back against the back of the chair. Her stomach was full, and her head had stopped aching. She was feeling pretty good, for a woman without a century of her own.

"There!" she said. "There is Ursa Major. You know, The Big Dipper?"

"Yes, I understand it is the most recognized constellation. It really is interesting."

"I understand the dipper is part of what is known as the Great Bear. See, the bear's tail is the handle and the cup of the dipper is his flank. I think I read somewhere that in the handle the second star from the left is called Mizar and is made up of four different stars, only it takes a telescope to actually see all four," she told him.

"You are a delight, Christina. You seem so well versed in many areas. I can't help but wonder in what areas you aren't," he said as he grinned at her.

"Oh, it's just stuff I learned in school. Funny how you can remember things sometimes."

They sat quietly for a few minutes, just enjoying the night. Finally he stood and reached for her. She took his hand and stood also. They headed back into the house and on into the parlor. He put her in one of the Victorian looking high back chairs and walked over to a small box on one of the tables. Opening it he pulled out a cigar. He offered her one. She shook her head.

"Do women smoke in your time, Christina?"

"Yes, but mostly cigarettes. They make a small form of cigars that some women prefer. But I don't smoke. I prefer to keep my lungs free of tar," she told him.

"Tar?" he asked her.

"It's been proven without a doubt that smoking causes lung cancer which kills thousands every year. Even when someone else smokes in the same room, a person that isn't actually enjoying the cigar or cigarette is breathing in the smoke and can get cancer just as quickly as the one smoking. I'd really rather you not smoke around me."

"All right," he conceded. He put the cigar in his pocket, planning to enjoy it later.

They talked into the night about many things, until Mrs. Braxton appeared and informed them that she was going to bed and wanted to know if there was anything else they required.

"Thank you, no. Good night Mrs. Braxton."

"Good night Sir, Miss." She walked softly out of the room.

"I think I should be retiring as well," Tina told him. It's been a most unusual day for me. I haven't any idea when or if I will be returning to my time, but if I'm not here in the morning I want you to know I've enjoyed your company and your kindness to me. Allowing me into your home like this has been more than generous. I don't think most people in my time would have done such a thing." Tina stood and walked toward him. He was on his feet immediately.

"Let me walk you to your room, Christina? And we will say good night there."

As they climbed the stairs and approached her bedroom door she said, "It almost feels as though we've been on a dinner date. Thank you again, Jefferson. I'm glad you came along and found me."

"Since it feels like a date perhaps it was. And somehow I feel as if you found me," he said softly. He leaned forward and Tina knew he was going to kiss her. Somehow she didn't even mind. As his lips touched hers she closed her eyes and just enjoyed it. There wasn't any passion in it, but just a nice feeling of trust. When she felt him pull back she opened her eyes and blushed.

"Good night Jefferson." She turned and opened the door to her bedroom and stepped inside, closing it softly behind her.

Chapter 10

The following morning Tina woke just as the sun was rising over the horizon. She was more like herself again after a good night's rest. She felt as though she needed to stretch and move to get some kinks out. So even though she didn't have her running clothes with her, she decided to run anyway. She would just do it barefooted. She'd just have to watch where she laid her feet.

Tina searched through the clothes that Mrs Braxton had brought her that belonged to Jefferson's sister to see if there were any shorts or slacks there. Clear in the back of the closet she found a pair of slacks. They were full, not fitted a she would have preferred, but they would have to do. After a quick sponge bath she slipped into the blouse and slacks, and headed downstairs. She went quietly out the back door not sure as to where she might run without being seen.

Checking her watch she saw it was six thirty. Thank goodness she had it, as well as her cell phone that was in her pocket of her skirt when she fell through the hole in time. She had noticed Mrs. Braxton had placed it on the table by her bed. Tina was surprised that Mrs. Braxton hadn't asked her about it.

Tina stepped off of the steps and turned to press one foot than the other against the step second to the bottom to stretch her muscles. Then she stood and spread her feet to do some warm up exercises. Feeling warmed and ready, she glanced around to decide what direction she should go. Finally she just started. She wished she had her CD player with her. She enjoyed running to music. It seemed to give her more of a rhythm. She began to hum one of the tunes she knew was on her running CD and it seemed to stabilize her.

She followed a path that led into a group of trees. It was only minutes and she was at her rhythm and moving smoothly across the meadow. She followed the path, not knowing where it might take her. It led her out of the woods and across a beautiful meadow and on up a slight grade. As she crested the hillock she could see the ocean. What a wonderful sight. She wasn't aware she was that close to the water. Her townhouse in Los Angeles was fifteen miles from the beach.

The path ended up in the sand at the beach. A perfect spot, she thought to herself. She kept on running as she checked her time. She had only been running for twenty minutes. On she went following the edge of the water while running on the wet sand. She was smart enough to know that running in the dry sand used up more energy and slowed her speed.

She ran as she watched the tide moving in and the sun rising into the sky. Finally she knew she had to turn around. At least now she had someplace to run where she would be hidden from the eyes of the public. She was certain that the people of 1912 would not like to see a woman running. They would never understand.

Slowly she made a wide arc and circled around onto the dry sand and returned to the wet sand to continue back. She checked her time and saw it was seven fifteen. She had been running for forty-five minutes. Then she started back the way she had come.

The sun was getting warmer, and it felt as though it was going to be a warm day. She hummed to herself and tried to keep her rhythm smooth. Breaking through the woods with the house in sight she could smell a stinky old cigar. That must mean Jefferson was up and smoking. Ugh! How could anyone enjoy the awful taste that must go with that smell? She continued to hum as she crossed the lawn to the same steps from where she started. When she stopped she checked her time. She had been running an hour and a half. She usually averaged about twelve minutes a mile so she knew she had probably traveled about five miles. That was a good distance, she thought to herself. She again pressed first one foot than the other against the step to stretch her muscles. She did a few stand and stretch movements, and finally she spread her feet and touched the ground five times. A couple of twists for her waist line and she was finished for the morning. She climbed the steps and found Jefferson standing just outside the doorway, watching her.

"Good morning, Christina," he said.

"Morning Jefferson. What brings you out so early?"

"I am usually up early. It's a habit I guess. I like to take care of some of my paperwork while the house is cool and quiet. Did you sleep well?" he asked.

"Yes, thank you. I feel much more normal now. And since I've had my run, I'm ready for a shower."

"I'm afraid you won't be able to get one here. But you can take a nice hot bath instead. I've been thinking of putting in showers in the bathrooms, but just haven't gotten around to doing it yet," he told her.

"Well, once you have a shower you'll wonder why you ever enjoyed a bath. That is, unless you have sore muscles that need to soak."

"You may have a very good point there. None the less, I'm curious. Why are you running? That seems to be something only children do."

"Not where I come from. It's good for the heart and lungs. Keeps them healthy and your body strong. Not to mention, it feels good."

How far did you go?" he asked.

"I followed the path to the beach. Then I went down the beach a ways, then turned around and came back. I think it was about five miles all total."

"That's amazing. How can you go so far? I mean, that's quite a distance for such a small person."

"Not really. Size doesn't really enter into it. Once you get used to the rhythm and get to where you can breath easily as you run, you could actually go much further if you were so inclined. But five miles is what I'm used to doing twice a week. It gets the kinks out."

"Interesting!" was his only reply.

"Well, I'm going to get that bath and freshen up. I just wish I had my running shoes with me, and my regular running outfit. Oh well, those who fall through holes in time can't be choosers, I guess."

He was smiling as she brushed past him and headed for her bedroom.

Tina enjoyed soaking in the hot water. She washed her hair and wished for her bottle of conditioner. When she was through she wrapped her hair in a towel, slipped into the robe that Mrs. Braxton had brought her, and went looking for a comb and brush. She walked over to the chest of drawers in her bedroom and began opening drawers. In one of the small drawers in the top area she found a silver brush and comb set, along with a hand mirror. Mrs. Braxton thought of everything. I love this woman, she thought to herself. She makes me think of my mother.

She unwrapped her hair and walked over to the French doors along the front wall of her bedroom. Pulling open one of the doors she noticed there was a balcony there overlooking the front driveway. And as she stepped outside she saw there were two chairs and a table sitting in the sun. Standing along the railing she began to brush out her hair. The warmth of the sun felt good on her head and shoulders. Slowly, but surely, she dried and styled her hair. Then she went back inside and pulled one of Jefferson's sister's outfits from the closet and got dressed. She wished for her deodorant and perfume.

She looked through the small drawers again and found some powder that smelled like Jasmine. She decided to put some on. She finished dressing and opened her bedroom door. She was definitely ready for some coffee.

As she stepped out into the hallway she saw Jefferson walking toward her.

He stepped up to her side and smiled. "You smell wonderful, Christine. Is that Jasmine?"

"Yes. I hope it's all right I used it. I found it in one of the drawers."

"Of course. Whatever Mrs. Braxton put in the room for you is yours to use as you please. Avail yourself. You look radiant after your run. I can see your running really does make a difference in your health. But naturally the bath helped too."

"Yes. But I miss my own amenities. I can't help but wonder how long I am going to be here. I'm wondering if I should try to see if there was something that I did to trigger my moving through time. Then I could trigger it again so I could return to my own time."

"But wouldn't you miss me, if you went back? We've become friends I think."

"Yes, that's true, but my place is there. I don't really think that I could affect history in any way here, and hopefully I wasn't going to do anything important there, but I just want to go home."

"You are welcome here for as long as you like, Christina. My home is your home. So you mustn't worry about anything. It would be nice to have you stay. I enjoy our talks. Is there someone there who would miss you?"

"Actually, yes. I was just beginning a new relationship with someone. It was just beginning to get serious when this happened. Now I don't know what will happen. Or if I will ever get back there. He's a very busy man, so if I don't get back soon he will probably move on and forget me."

"If he loves you he won't move on or forget you, Christina. Not if it's real. Has he told you so?" Jefferson asked.

"Yes. He asked me to let him love me while he can. I think back now and wonder how he meant that. And I can't help but wonder if he didn't have some forewarning something was going to happen to me because look where I am now? But that isn't possible, that someone would have subconscious knowledge of such a thing. But I would have said it wasn't possible that I could pass through a hole in time either."

"We just don't know, but I want to help you in whatever way I can. Would you let me help in this? I'm not sure what good I can do except to give you whatever you need as long you are here, but I want to try."

"I understand Jeff, and I appreciate it." She smiled as his eye brows went up as she called him Jeff rather than Jefferson. "May I call you that? Jefferson seems like such a long name. Of course, if you really prefer it, I will call you that."

Jefferson's face broke into a smile as he peered down into her face. No one had ever called him anything but Jefferson. To be called Jeff was quite a change, once he thought about it, and he liked it. And he liked the little woman that was suggesting calling him that. "I think I like it," he told her. "So I guess I have a new nickname. This is really something new to me. Thank you Christina for putting new life in my name."

"Oh silly, it's just a nickname. It fits you, and it's easier and much more friendly. You can call me Tina if you wish. Most people do, or did, in my time."

"No, no!" he answered quickly. "Christina is so feminine and beautiful, just like the person within. I couldn't call you anything but that. I love your name, Christina." As soon as the words were said his face started turning pink. He was feeling embarrassed.

"You may call me either name, only just don't call me late for dinner," she said, laughing.

"Ha Ha!" he laughed loudly. "That's good Christina. You really are a delightful creature. And such good company! Let's go down for breakfast and we can continue our conversation. And maybe even try to work out some solution to your problem." He took her elbow and proceeded to the staircase.

They sat in the formal dining room as Mrs. Braxton brought in their breakfast. She had several cups of coffee along with eggs and toast. Both Jeff and Mrs. Braxton tried to coax her into eating more, but she really didn't want more than that. But she thoroughly enjoyed the coffee. It was better than lattes and many other fancy drinks. Just a plain cup of black coffee made fresh and just right.

Sitting over her third cup of coffee she tried to remember what had happened just before she fell through the hole in time. "You know," she told him, "it seems to me that something caused this to happen to me. I don't know yet what it was, but

I would like to try to figure it out so I can try to return to my own time. I really don't think I'm suppose to be here."

"I don't blame you, Christina. Did you get any warning before hand that something unusual was going on? Anything at all?"

"No, I don't think so, I…wait a minute. Yes! A day or so before this happened, while I was sitting at my desk, I was thinking about getting back to some paperwork that I needed to get taken care of, when I seemed to go into a trance, or something. Maybe it was foreknowledge of what was coming, I don't know. But all of a sudden I wasn't looking at the papers on my desk I was seeing the road where you found me, and I could hear your car coming. Then it was just gone. I was looking at the paperwork again. And then one other time I was looking at my boss when he seemed to disappear in shimmering light. I don't know if that has anything to do with my going through time or not. I fainted right after that session, and I fainted when you found me. So I don't know if the two are connected or not. The only reason that that time comes to mind is because I never faint. That was totally out of character for me. I'm stronger than that. So whether the movement through time was causing the fainting because of the change of my blood pressure, or what, I don't really know."

"Well, your theory might be true. I should think that such a thing as moving through time would create some changes in your system. That would explain why you were fainting. I guess we should be grateful that was all that happened to you. Do you realize it could have killed you? I'd say you're lucky to be alive. Since we don't know how it happened, we can't begin to really understand it. In reality, I didn't think such a thing was even possible." Jeff rubbed the bridge of his nose as though he was feeling pressure there just trying to understand all of this.

"Yes, I think you're right. The time travel did seem to cause pressure on my system. Yet somehow I don't think it was suppose to have happened. I think it was just a 'fluke'."

"Here's another idea. Perhaps there really was a hole, or a tear in time. I think we ought to go back to where you found me. The cause might be answered there. Maybe the hole opened up as I sat at my desk and I just happened to be in the wrong place at the wrong time and fell through. And maybe this end of the hole is still there. If it is, maybe I find it and fall back through again and get back home."

"That sounds plausible. Let's do it."

"Can we go now? If there is a possibility of that hole closing up again, I think I ought to find it quickly, before that happens. Because when it closes, it may not open up again. Or it may open up in another place and I wouldn't know where to go to find it."

Jeff looked at her in astonishment. What a fantastic thought. You know, your thought processing excites me. You seem to rationalize things in a very structured way. You know, you just may have something there." Jeff stood, taking one last sip of his coffee and setting his cup back down in it's saucer. "Let's go, Christina. I'll get my automobile and meet you out in front in a minute or so. Grab a sweater or wrap of some sort. The air may be cool."

Tina stood up quickly and stepped away from the table. She almost ran as she went to her room to locate something to keep her arms and shoulders warm, since his car was a convertible, and she would have the breeze hitting her as they drove. After grabbing a sweater she found on a hanger in the closet she raced back downstairs and out the front door.

Just as she reached the edge of the porch she heard Jeff's car putt putt putting around the corner of the house. What a difference from the purr of a huge fuel injected engine, she thought. Wouldn't Jeff be surprised to see the cars of her day, and feel their power.

She stepped off the porch and down the steps. Jeff parked his car right in front of where she stood. Jumping out he reached for her hand and led her around to the passenger side. He helped her in and proceeded back to the driver's seat. In moments they were 'putting' down the driveway.

Tina couldn't help but wonder how difficult this vehicle might be to actually drive. Although her current car had an automatic transmission, she had driven a stick shift transmission before, and suspected she could operate this vehicle if she tried. She thought to herself, perhaps she might get the chance to try before she went home. But getting home was her primary consideration. She just hoped they might find the tear in time this morning. She was a little concerned that Jeff might not remember the exact spot where he found her.

Neither of them spoke as they traveled. Jeff seemed to be trying to drive as fast as his car would allow, which seemed to Tina only about thirty mile per hour. But then again, she rationalized, the road wasn't paved and who knows what might happen if they hit a pothole at that speed especially with only the mere basics in suspension. She leaned back against her seat and tried to remain calm.

Jeff was driving as fast as his automobile would go. He watched carefully for any holes in the road. He didn't want to hit one suddenly and maybe lose control. He just wished the place they were looking for was closer.

His mind thought about this lovely woman that sat beside him. Her wit and intelligence excited him to the point that he didn't really want to lose her. He suspected he would not find such an enjoyable companion in any of the women of his own time. Thinking back to the few he had encountered he realized they were more interested in clothing and what went on in a home then what went on in life around them. Not a one of them had any business sense or structured thought. How could he seriously think of letting her go? And there was always the chance that she might die trying to go through time again. Since it wasn't something that anyone really knew anything about, how could she be certain that it was safe?

The sun was bright and Jeff was grateful it was behind them. He didn't relish having to drive into the bright morning sun and not being able to see very well. That would have increased the possibility of not spotting a pothole until it might be too late.

Tina pulled the sweater closer around her neck. The air was a little cool. She had slipped her arms into the sleeves before leaving the house, but her throat felt the chill in the air.

Jeff already had the automobile in third gear, which was the highest, to get the most speed. He knew there wasn't a need to make any turns before they reached their destination, and there were only a few curves between here and there, so he would probably be leaving it in third for most of the rest of their trip. He looked over at Christina. She was not only an interesting individual, she was a beautiful woman as well. Any man would be proud to have her on his arm. She must have felt his eyes on her because she turned her head and smiled at him. Reaching over to him she laid her hand on his forearm. He realized she only meant to encourage and reassure him, but the warmth of her skin on his lit a fire that he had not felt with a woman in the past. This woman was not only special, she was a friend.

They traveled on, her hand resting on his arm. Apparently she felt drawn to touch him, and he appreciated that. It seemed to be an acceptance that they were in this together. They sailed around the first curve and continued on. Jeff knew he needed to keep both hands on the steering wheel, or he would have reached over to hold her hand. He was grateful for her touch.

Another curve loomed before them he decided it might be wise to slow the vehicle a little, since this curve seemed to be a bit tighter than the last. Lifting the pressure of his foot from the throttle they could hear the slowing of the engine. But as they cruised through the curve he accelerated again, and the centrifugal force propelled them onward.

Minutes ticked by and Tina thought about the possibility of locating the hole in time. The only way she could think of finding it was to walk methodically back and forth in a pattern that would cover the entire area. Perhaps Jeff could do the same starting at the opposite edge of the area. They could work their way toward the middle. The only concern she had was that he might fall into it and be transported to her time, and that by his passage through time the hole might close up again, thus trapping her in this time.

Tina released her hand from Jefferson's arm. She grasped her hands together as though she worried at the same time as she tried to methodically scrutinize all of the possibilities in covering the area to locate the hole.

Jeff looked over at Tina. He sensed she was thinking deeply and was a little worried. Her hands rubbed against each other as though she was washing her hands. Yet her gaze was ahead of them, up the road. She had to be excited about the possibility of going home. He began to wonder if it might be possible or desirable that he go with her. He just hoped she wouldn't be disappointed if they were unable to locate the hole.

He knew they were approaching the spot where he had found her. As he glanced over at Tina her instincts must have been telling her the same thing because she was now leaning forward in her seat, as if straining to get there.

Jeff began to slow the vehicle and he downshifted to second gear. Now Tina had both hands on the dash as if holding on for dear life.

Jeff slowed more as they approached the location they were seeking. He pulled his automobile off the edge of the roadway just in case another vehicle came past. He hoped that would not be the case while they searched.

He pulled up the parking brake and shut off the engine. He leaped out and rushed to the passenger side as Tina was already starting to climb down from her seat. Jeff reached up and grasped her around her waist and lifted her down so as to not catch her skirt on anything.

They walked to the edge of the roadway and she automatically looked both ways before crossing. Jeff looked surprised by her actions but didn't say anything.

They crossed the road and just stood there for a moment.

"Where was I was sitting when you found me?" she asked.

"Over here." He led her several steps further and stopped. "I think this is it," he told her.

"Are you sure?" She didn't want to start their search with the wrong information.

"Yes, I think so. I posted the sign right there," he said, pointing to the nearest tree. "Yes, I think this is it. Now what do we do?" They both noticed the 'bill of notice' was absent.

"Well, I was thinking we could each start back at the edge of this open section and walk a path from, say the line of trees over there," pointing to several trees over toward the creek, "to the far side of this area, being the roadway. It would be just like mowing the lawn. You would start over there at that end of the section while I start at this side and we work our way toward the middle. That way it would seem we should cover the area totally and thoroughly. What do you think?"

"I'm not sure. What is mowing the lawn?" he asked.

Tina started laughing. She laughed harder and harder and couldn't stop. It began to sound like hysterical laughter, even to her ears.

Jeff stepped closer to her and grabbed both of her arms and shook her. "Tina! Get hold of yourself. This isn't the time to get hysterical. Just be calm. Now what was it you were saying about mowing the lawn?"

"Oh, I'm sorry. I think the pressure is getting to me. In my time we have lawn mowers and they have an engine, just like your car. There is a blade that goes around and cuts the grass as we push the mower across the lawn, following the edge of what we just mowed. That way no section of grass is missed and when you're done the lawn looks even and totally mowed to the same height."

"I see, . . . I think," he said.

"Here, let me show you. If I start over here, as far over as I can get, along these trees, then I walk in a straight line toward the road, when I get to the road I have checked a path along this perimeter. Then I turn around and start back following along next to where I originally walked. When I get as far over toward the creek as I can go I simply turn around and cut another swath. See what I mean?" she asked.

"Yes, I think so. And how will we know when we've found the hole?"

"We'll have to watch each other. As soon as one of us feels something different, or begins to disappear, then I think we've found it," she told him.

"Let me demonstrate." She walked toward the creek that ran parallel with the road. She chose the furthest most path possible to her right as she faced the road. "From here I would have to keep an eye on where I'm walking, as well as on you, walking on the other side, so the minute you disappear, I will know it and stop and say something."

"Okay, I got it," he told her. "If either one of us feels something weird we should say something also, just to be safe. You said you had a bit of a premonition before you actually fell into the hole, perhaps one of us might sense something just before we fall in."

"Yes that's a good idea. We'll have to watch closely and probably walk slowly so as not to miss anything. Okay, you go over to that end of this open area, and I'll start here," she said.

Jeff stepped up to her and grasped her upper arms in both of his hands. "Christina, just be very careful, okay?"

She nodded her head, unable to speak. She could hear her heart pounding in her chest. "And you do the same, Jeff. I just hope you don't slip into it before I can get to you."

"Don't worry! I'll let you know if I find it. Okay let's get at it." He turned to walk away and turned back. Leaning forward he placed his lips on hers and left a quick gentle kiss. "Good luck!" he said.

"Thanks!" she whispered. She hoped she would be the one to find it.

Tina returned to her starting point and waited for Jeff to get to his starting point. As soon as he did they looked at each other and both nodded. They each glanced down at the path they followed but tried to look at each other more. Tina thought, he could step totally into it and just disappear right at the moment she looked down, and she could miss it, and he might be gone. She prayed that would not be the case.

Tina was moving four, five, steps, look down. Then she stepped again watching Jeff. After three or four more steps she looked down again to be certain she was on the same path. Four steps, look down. Four steps, look down. She began to feel perspiration coming out on her forehead and trickling down her back. She shed her sweater and not knowing where to put it simply dropped it where she stood. Then she continued on. Watching Jeff she saw he was also taking about four or five steps while he watched her before he looked down at his path.

Now she had made a full path across the area. She stepped to her left one step and turned to start back toward the creek. Looking up she watched Jeff. He too had just reached his turn around point. They both stepped out, watchful of each other.

They each had made several swaths across the area and were rapidly closing in on the center of the area. She had not noticed any reaction from Jeff, nor had any part of his body disappeared yet. And such a nice body it was too. Now where did that crazy thought come from, she wondered. This wasn't any time to be thinking of bodies. This was the time to be trying to find the hole so she could go home, away from that handsome body over there. She reprimanded herself for such thoughts. Tina, count your steps, she told herself. Again, watching Jeff she counted off five steps, then glanced down. As his eyes came back up she could see him counting steps as well, while his eyes remained on her.

Ten minutes later they found themselves passing each other on their last swath across the area. Then they each turned at the end of their path and began approaching each other on the same path. As they came within inches of each other they both stopped. Jeff reached for her and pulled her up against his chest.

He could feel her disappointment. He just hugged her to him, holding her silently and he felt her shoulders begin to shake. Her face was against his chest, right over his heart and he could hear her gasping for breath as she cried. His hands began to rub her back to try to sooth her disappointment. He knew she figured they would probably find the hole and that she was going to go home this morning. But now they knew otherwise.

One of his hands reached up to hold her head to him. He felt it was just like comforting a child that had fallen down and hurt himself. Only worse! He cuddled her to him and he said to her, "We tried Sweetheart. I guess it just isn't here anymore. Don't cry. I'm glad you're going to be staying here with me."

Tina took a deep breath and pulled back from his arms. "I was so sure it was here. I was just so sure. Are you positive this is the right spot?"

"Yes, I think so. Did you want to switch sides and we check it again?"

She looked up with hope in her eyes. Then she realized that between the two of them they had covered this area thoroughly. If it was there one of them would have found it.

"Maybe it could have shifted a little. Let's walk around all of the tree areas. We can use the same techniques so we don't miss any area."

"Okay!" he told her. "We can take the same area as before. You check the area around where you walked, and I'll check over there around mine."

Tina's face lit up with hope. She turned quickly and almost ran over to where she originally started and began to walk around each and every tree, making circling paths as she went. Then she remembered they needed to watch each other. "Don't forget we need to watch each other," she shouted to Jeff. He too had forgotten and he lifted his eyes to her and smiled.

Walking in circles and watching where she was going proved more difficult that walking in a straight line and trying to watch Jeff at the same time. She discovered she had to walk much slower to be able to do it.

"I guess this will take us longer Jeff," she shouted to him. It's harder to keep my eyes on you and walk in circles," she laughed. He could tell by her voice she was hopeful again.

"You're right about that. I'm having to move a lot slower to do this."

A half hour or so later they decided they had pretty much covered each of their areas, without finding anything. Tina walked over to where she had dropped the sweater and sat down on the ground. She drew her knees up and laid her head on her knees. She heaved a deep sign and just sat there in grief.

Chapter 11

It was a very quiet ride all the way back to Jeff's house. Tina just sat with her hands in her lap and looked straight ahead.

Jeff could feel her sorrow. He just wished there was something he could do about it. But he didn't know if there was anything that could be done. It felt as though someone had closed a door that couldn't be opened again.

Finally as they were pulling into his driveway Tina asked, "What if that wasn't the spot? Are you absolutely sure that was where you found me, Jeff?"

"I think so. Well,…" and he paused.

"Well what? Maybe it wasn't?" she asked, already moving in her seat to face him.

He stopped the car and looked at her. "I thought it was. Maybe it was that other open spot, just beyond where we went today. Now I'm not so sure." His face showed his pain. He wanted to help her find her way back home, but he wanted her to remain here with him also. There was a wrinkle between his eyebrows that told Tina that he was feeling stressed about this and now wasn't so sure that the spot they had checked was the correct one.

"We have to go back! We have to check that other section. Jeff, please! Turn around and take me back there. For both of our peace of mind, we have to check the other area."

"I have an appointment in a half hour Christina. It's an important one and I have to be there. Perhaps we could go back after the meeting, or in the morning. I promise I'll take you back to look."

She couldn't interfere with this man's life more than she already had, at this time. He had a meeting and that was all there was to it. The hole was either going to be there or it wasn't. "Okay, Jeff. We'll go after your meeting, or tomorrow morning at the latest. I'll wait," she told him.

Tina was beginning to fear she was going to be stuck in 1912. And it didn't exactly excite her. She'd rather be home in her own time.

Jeff started the car moving again and drove up to the front of his house to drop her off. He shut the engine off and escorted her to the front door, putting her inside before turning to leave.

"I'll be back later. My meeting is in the city so I have to go now to get there in time. Try not to worry, Tina. I know that's easier said than done, but try anyway. I'll be back as soon as I can."

"I'll try, Jeff. Drive safely." She gave him a little hug and went on into the house. She wandered up to her bedroom and sat down in the rocking chair. Three hours later, when Jeff came looking for her that was just where he found her. Her eyes were closed from her stress and exhaustion and she was napping.

Jeff rapped loudly on her bedroom door. "Christina! Are you in there? Christina!"

Startled awake she jumped up and went to the door. Upon her opening it Jeff stepped into her room. "Christina!

It happened! Just as you said! The Titanic sunk. With a loss of life numbering over 1500. It's unbelievable! I believe you Christina! I believe you."

Tina returned to the rocking chair and sat down. She didn't care about the Titanic. It was just history as far as she was concerned. She just wanted to correct her history and get back to where she belonged.

Jeff came over and sat down in the adjacent straight back chair across from Tina. "It's just almost too much to believe, you know?"

"I don't know why you're all so excited. I told you all about it last night. I don't lie!"

"I'm sorry, Christina. I didn't mean to infer you did. I guess I'm just flabbergasted with the possibility of it, and that you were right. This time travel thing is upsetting."

"So now you know a little of how I feel. I'm not trying to be mean Jeff, but I need to get back to my own time. My life is there."

"I understand. At least, I'm trying to understand. It's getting late, but if you want to go back out there we can go. It will be getting dark before very long though. It might be better if we wait until morning. We should do this in the good light, I think. But if you want to go now, I'll take you."

"That's all right, Jeff. We can wait until the morning. I just want to rest and take it easy right now. How was your meeting?"

"It was rather brief because of all the news about the Titanic. That was all anyone wanted to talk about. Christina, you look exhausted. Why don't you take a nap and I'll come and get you for dinner at six o'clock?" With that he stood and started for the door. I'm sorry we weren't able to find the hole this morning, but we'll keep looking. And if you want to keep on looking the day after that, we'll do that too."

"Thanks, Jeff. I think I will take a nap. I'll see you at six o'clock. And Jeff,.."

"Yes?" he answered.

"Thank you for all you're doing for me. I want you to know how very much I appreciate it. You've been a good friend to me."

"I'm sure it isn't anything you wouldn't do for me. See you later, Christina." He walked out of the door and closed it softly behind him.

The following morning Tina was awake before the sun came up. She bathed and dressed quickly, and walked outside to watch the sunrise.

The sky was clear and crisply beautiful. Not at all like most sunrises in 2004. There wasn't any smog, so there wasn't any pink, or orange tint in the sky. Breathing deeply she couldn't help but smile, in the coolness of the morning. At least there was something good in the year 1912.

She walked across the grass wondering if there was anything she might be missing that was pertinent to her slipping through that hole in time. She stopped and just thought.

She remembered she was sitting at her desk, looking at some paper work when it began to shimmer. Shimmering! That's it! What she was looking at began to shimmer just before it started, as if she was just entering the hole. It was like a warning. So maybe, as they pace off the other section of ground later this morning, they should be watching for the shimmering, and step away before either one of them slipped through the hole. That's it! That has to be it, she thought to herself.

She was so excited that she felt like a little girl again and she danced around and twirled, lifting her arms to the sky in gratitude for the memory.

Jeff was having trouble sleeping. Several times through the night he woke up thinking about Christina and her plight. What if they searched the second area and didn't find the hole? What would that do to Christina? It was obvious she didn't really want to remain in 1912. She was anxious to return to the time that was familiar to her. To where she felt comfortable.

Jeff had laid awake as the sun came up. Finally he just couldn't stay in bed any longer. He got up and wandered over to the window. His eye caught some movement down on the grass below. He watched as Christina walked quietly across the lawn, then paused for a few minutes. Then, as he watched her head came up and he thought he saw her smile. Suddenly she was twirling and dancing around, with her arms outstretched as though something wonderful had just happened. He wondered what it could have been. His curiosity got the best of him and he grabbed his robe and slippers and raced down the hall to the stairs. He went down the stairs as quickly as possible and exited the house onto the porch. He walked across the huge porch to where he could see the lawn that was below his bedroom window and there she was. She was standing still with her arms wrapped around her and she was smiling.

He stepped off the porch quickly. He felt he had to get to her and find out what it was that made her so joyous. It was as if he felt he had to share in that joy as well.

As he strode across the wet grass Tina's eyes came up and she saw Jeff coming toward her. She began to run toward him and as she approached him she opened her arms wide and grabbed him in a great big hug. She was pulling on him to move in circles with her and he couldn't help but rejoice with her. So with their arms around each other they jumped and dance around the lawn as she sang, "We did it! We did it!"

Finally he pulled her tightly to him and her feet stopped moving. They stood, chest to chest, and peering into each other's eyes as Jeff's lips came closer and closer to hers. She felt his tender touch and he was kissing her. The joy just seemed to pour from her into him, even though, as yet, he didn't understand why.

Then she pulled back and smiled. He looked down into her face and asked, "What did we do, Christina?"

"Oh, Jeff, we did it. We figured it out." Her face was radiant with excitement, and her eyes sparkled.

"And what is that? Tell me quickly Christina before you burst," he told her.

She stopped her movement and wrapped her arms around his waist. She did it automatically, without conscious thought. Jeff suspected that if he asked her if she had done it later she would not remember she was sharing her excitement with her arms wrapped securely around him.

"I was just trying to remember everything that happened just before I slipped through the hole in time. I suddenly remembered that as I was looking at the paperwork in front of me that it began to shimmer. That has to be the warning that the edge of the hole was near. Jeff, when we see the shimmering as we check the other area this morning, we'll know we've found it."

Jeff began to grin at her. "You may have found what we needed to know to find the hole, Christina. You have such an organized mind. You truly are a delight!"

"Can we go right now? I can't wait. Get dressed, Jeff. We have to go right now."

"No, Christina! You need to have some sustenance in you before we do this thing. And I need to take a bath and get dressed." Holding his arm around her he turned her to face the house and began walking in that direction. He ushered her through the front door and took her by her shoulders and gently shoved her toward the dinning room. "You go have some breakfast and I'll join you in a few minutes. I'm going to get ready for our expedition and be down shortly for breakfast. Now go, and just relax, if you can. I'll be with you shortly," he told her.

Taking two steps at a time Jeff hurried up the stairs to get ready.

Tina walked to the kitchen and sat down at the brightly sunlit table by the large window. Mrs. Braxton was so surprised to see anyone but the hired help sitting there she didn't know what to say.

"We're going back out to the site again this morning," Tina told her. Mrs. Braxton was aware that Tina thought she had traveled through time, but she hadn't shared it with anyone else for fear they might think Christina was crazy. She was such a nice young woman that she couldn't hurt her reputation like that. So she kept her thoughts to herself.

"Is there any coffee made, Mrs. Braxton?"

"Of course. There's very few times there isn't coffee ready and waiting in this kitchen," Mrs. Braxton told her. "Are you ready for one?"

"Oh yes, absolutely. I'm so ready for this morning I can hardly wait." Tina was smiling from ear to ear.

Mrs. Braxton poured her a cup and brought it over to the table. "Thank you, Mrs. Braxton. You make the best coffee I think I've ever tasted. And in 2004 that's really saying something, because there are coffee shops almost on every corner there. Coffee is a big thing there, right now. They whip it with hot milk, and put extra caffeine in it. They put whipped cream on top of it and candy sprinkles. They even add chocolate, or other flavors in it. It's becoming more of a dessert."

Mrs. Braxton didn't know what to say to that so she just smiled. Goodness gracious, she thought to herself, what is this world coming to that people wanted their coffee to have other flavors? "What can I fix you for breakfast this morning?" she asked Christina.

"Just coffee is fine for me, thanks. I'm so excited! We're going back out to the spot again this morning to look for the hole. I can hardly wait. I think we may just find it this time. I've remembered that when I slipped into it when I came here, everything began to shimmer, so I think if we can find a spot where our vision begins to shimmer, we will have found the hole."

Mrs. Braxton realized that this information, if it were true, could be very dangerous in the wrong hands. So she vowed silently to herself not to repeat it to anyone. Besides, Christina and Jefferson would probably be back later this morning, the same as always.

"You realize if you're going on a trip that you need to have a good breakfast in you? I'm going to fix you some scrambled eggs and bacon. And maybe even some of my homemade sour dough toast. Now you just sit there and relax while I get it ready."

"I spoke with Jeff already and he should be down soon as well. I know he'll want breakfast before we go."

"I'll just fix enough bacon for him as well so when he shows his face I'll just have to whip up some eggs. A good breakfast will stand you in good stead you just see if it doesn't."

Right after Mrs. Braxton sat a plate full of food in front of Tina, Jeff came through the door. "Why aren't you in the dining room Christina?" he asked. "I was beginning to think perhaps you had left without me," he said with a smile.

"Not a chance! Someone told me I needed breakfast, so here I am. I know how to follow orders," she grinned up at him. "Besides, this tastes great."

"It's different eating in the kitchen. But sitting here in the sunshine is nice. I like it. Maybe we ought to have breakfast here more often," he told them both. He sat in one of the hard wooden chairs and smiled. He was discovering that the kitchen felt warm and comfortable. It was much nicer that the stiff and formal dining room.

They polished off their breakfast in short order and Tina was on her feet, ready to go.

"Where's your sweater?" he asked her. "This early in the morning the shady area where we're going can get rather chilly, young lady."

"Okay, I'm getting it. I'll meet you out in front," she told him. Then she turned toward Mrs. Braxton and rushed over to her and gave her a big hug. "You're the greatest," she told her. "And you definitely have the best coffee in town! Thanks!"

Tina rushed upstairs to fetch her sweater. Before she left her bedroom she looked around. She figured this may just be the last time she saw this room. It had only been hers for a couple of days, but she had considered it home. Then she was racing down the front stairs to the front door.

As she was closing the front door behind her, she heard the putt putt sound of Jeff's car coming around the house. She quickly stepped down the steps to the ground to wait for him.

Jeff stopped his automobile right in front of Christina and shut it off. After climbing out he escorted her to her side of the car and put her in. Then he went back to the driver's seat and started the engine again. It was only moments and they were moving down the driveway.

They turned left onto the road and began their trek back to where they both suspected waited the hole in time. Jeff knew that the ride would feel as though it was taking forever if he didn't get her to think about something else. He asked her what else she could tell him about the future.

Tina leaned back and thought about how to answer that question. Jeff had been successful in getting her mind off of their goal, at least temporarily.

"Well, there's been great headway made in flight, as you must have suspected after my comment about man walking on the moon. Planes went from gas to diesel engines, then to turbo engines and jets. And huge propulsion rockets that took man into outer space."

"Uh huh!" he answered her. "And what else has happened that would make history?" he asked.

"Well, scientists discovered that the only area where Redwood trees would grow were in a section of California where a fog belt usually is, that runs from Point Sur north into Oregon. They found that area was the only place they will grow, so when there were a lot of fires a few years back there was a chance that some of the remaining redwood trees could have burned. Thank goodness the firemen were able to stop the wild fire before it reached them. It seems that the fire season is growing and the possibility of greater and greater losses every year are astronomical."

"Hummm," he answered. He just wanted to keep her talking, and thinking about something other that finding the hole in time.

"World War One started in August in 1914, when German forces invaded Belgium and Luxembourg. They overran it in only days and took over Brussels. It took the combined efforts of several countries to finally end it on Nov. 11, 1918.

World War Two started in Sept. 1939 and ended in Sept. 1945.

Let's see. The first electric refrigerator that people could have in their own home happened in 1913 and cost $900.00."

"I'm impressed," he told her.

"I excelled in history. I seemed to be able to remember things and dates well."

"Apparently! What else can you tell me?"

"Well, this is a Ford automobile. I seem to recall that Ford went into business in 1903 and was the first car manufacturer to use a moving assembly line in 1913. And they are one of the largest automobile makers in 2004."

"That sounds like a good place to make an investment. That is, if one has anything to invest. A lot has happened between my time and yours Christina. No wonder you want to go back. It sounds as if there are a lot of opportunities available there."

"I suppose so. It depends on what you're interested in, I guess. Personally, the horrible smog problems and the regulation of absolutely everything is amazing. And big brother is definitely watching."

"Who is big brother? And what is he watching?"

"Maybe I said it badly, but I can remember before there were cameras everywhere watching what you do. All major highways seem to be monitored by cameras now so that the Highway Patrol can watch whatever is going on. If there is a major accident, or if they're chasing someone who had stolen a car, they can watch the chase on camera now. I suspected the camera thing started because someone had the big idea that busy intersections ought to have cameras that can cite you for running a red light. You can get a fine and have it recorded on your driving record for stopping your car six inches into an intersection. And that fine will raise your insurance costs. You get very many of them and it can cause your insurance company to "drop" you, and then you really have to pay a lot more just to get the minimum required insurance before you can even put your car on the road. So you see, there's a lot more regulation in 2004 than in 1912. Enjoy your freedom, and your clean air while you can."

"Clean air? Of course the air is clean. Why wouldn't it be?"

"Can you guess what your neighbor would say if she hung out her white sheets to dry on the line and you come along and put your trash in your burning barrel and light it? The ash, not to mention the smell, will get all over her laundry and she'll have to wash it all over again. And you've just made your neighbor very upset with you. Now multiply that to factories all over the country putting out smoke and ash, and who knows what else. Some of that stuff could even be toxic. Next, you have millions of cars on the road and they are all putting exhaust into the air. And then come airplanes doing the same thing. Pretty soon you have polluted air and pink and orange sunrises and sunsets. It's called smog, and it affects how well some people can breath."

"Christina, it sounds as though you might be better off staying here with me. At least you'll have clean air."

"Probably so, but there's more to life than just having clean air."

"Yes, well, perhaps so. But your 2004 is sounding less and less like a place I would want to visit or live in."

"To each his own, I guess," she told him. "Myself, I was very happy there. I just try to stay as healthy as I can, and live my quiet little life the way I like it."

"And you're really happy with your life?"

"Yes, I would say so. I have a nice home, even though it isn't anywhere near as large as yours. I have my freedom to come and go as I wish. I like my job and I make a decent wage. Yes, I would have to say I like my life."

"Well, it sounds like you have good reason to want to go back to it then."

"Why are we pulling over?"

"Because we're here. You've forgotten our morning project already?"

"We're here? Let me out! I want to start searching the other area. I just know we're going to find it this time."

Jeff shut off the engine and rushed around to help her out. By the time he got to her she was halfway to the ground. He grabbed her by the waist to help her the rest of the way. Then he held her for a moment. "Remember, we're searching for something we may, or may not find. I don't want you to be too disappointed in the event we don't locate it."

"I understand! But I have a feeling we will find it this time. Just wait and see, Jeff!"

"Okay! Which side do you want?"

"I'll take the section to our left. You take the one to our right. Remember, we're going to do just as we did yesterday, only we're also watching for a possible shimmering."

"Right! Let's do it!" he remarked, not feeling as enthusiastic as she. They each marched off to their far corners and stood watching the other.

"And Jeff," she called out to him, "don't step through it without me right there. It might close after someone goes through and then I'd be caught here."

"Understood! Not a problem! Are you ready?"

"I think so. I'm so nervous I'm shaking."

"Don't be. We're going to work together on this. I'll watch you, and you watch me!"

"You're right! Okay, let's begin!" she said, looking over at him and smiling.

They began stepping out, counting to four or five steps and glancing down just as they had done the previous day. Tina noticed she was using her peripheral vision more this time. Perhaps that was a good thing, she thought.

Watching, stepping, then looking closely at everything close to watch for ripples or shimmering. Jeff realized they were moving much more slowly that they had the day before. Perhaps that was good. They both seemed to arrive at the end of their first swath at about the same time.

They both paused before starting their second swath.

"Are you all right?" he called to her.

"Yes! Are you?"

"I'm fine!"

They stepped out again, slowly but surely working their way across that swath. By the time she was ready to turn around and start back across the area again Tina had to shed her sweater. She felt like she was burning up.

She glanced toward Jeff and saw he was waiting on her. She nodded her head and they both began again.

She could feel the perspiration running down her back. Step four, step five, glance down. Eyes up again on Jeff, step one, step, "Jeff!" she shouted. "Stop! Back up quickly!"

Tina raced across her section into Jeff's. He had just shimmered and almost disappeared.

Jeff stepped backward. The shimmering stopped.

As Tina approached he said, "Did you see it Christina? All of a sudden everything in front of me was shimmering as if it was out of focus." He was both amazed and excited. They had found it."

Tina moved forward as though to step into the very spot. He grabbed her just as quickly and pulled her back against him.

"Are you certain, Christina? Is this really what you want to do?" he asked her, watching her face closely. He hated to let her go, but he couldn't say that to her. This was her life and her decision.

"Yes, Jeff. I want to go home. I'll never forget you. Never! Thank you for being my best friend ever." She turned from him as his fingers slid from her waist and she began to shimmer.

"Christina!" he called after her, but in that moment, she was gone.

Chapter 12

Tina sat at her desk, blinking her eyes and trying to remain calm. She was back where she had begun her adventure. At her desk. But she felt dizzy and she had a bit of a headache. But she was definitely back! Hooray!

Now she had to discover how much time had passed since she left. Did she come back to the exact time that she had left, or was it really two days later? She figured she could check her computer and check the date. That ought to tell her what she needed to know.

She turned to the computer that sat on the adjacent table and drug the cursor down to the time where it would show her the date. Amazing! She came back only minutes from the time she left. So no one would even suspect that she had slipped through time and traveled back almost a hundred years.

Tina scanned her calendar and discovered the staff meeting was still on for the following morning. Michael had done that for her. And he had spent that day, yesterday in fact, with her. She needed to get her head straight as to the day. She felt as though she had been gone a long time and the goings on at her office didn't quite make sense to her.

Tina looked at the paperwork lying across her desk. Oh yes, the course outline for one of her workshops was strewn in front of her. She hadn't started on the update on it yet. She needed a moment to give herself closure on her adventure. She leaned back in her chair and closed her eyes. She could picture Jeff in her 'minds eye'. He was standing right where she left him, next to the opening in time. She couldn't help but wonder if it closed behind her as she passed through it. She hoped so, so no one would accidentally fall into it.

She recalled Jeff grasping her waist just before she stepped into the hole in time. She almost got the feeling that he didn't want her to go. But how could that be? He knew she belonged here, in her own time. He was so nice. She would never forget him.

Opening her eyes she began to gather the papers into some semblance of order. Then she began to go through them, with her computer showing the same workshop outline on the screen so she could restructure it and then print out the new and better outline.

Quite some time later she finished her task and looked at the clock. It was already seven in the evening. She felt tired and rather bleary eyed. She assumed Marsha must have stuck her head in to say good night to her, but she couldn't recall it happening. Oh well, if she says I was acting funny tomorrow when I see her, I'll just tell her I was so engrossed it didn't even register that she was saying good night.

Tina gathered up her old material and stapled it together. Then she printed out the new course outline to go into the file. She wrote "old" on top of the old one and the new one showed the current date so when anyone looked at it later they will know the outlined changed. She dropped the file back into it's place in the cabinet and began to lock things up getting ready to go home.

Suddenly she heard a knock on her door. Looking up she saw Michael standing in her doorway. "Hey!" she said to him.

"Hey, yourself. You're getting to be just like me, staying late at the office. What are you working on?"

"Just finished another course outline for one of our workshops," she told him. She hoped he wasn't going to ask her to go to dinner with him. She just wanted to go home and sleep.

"Want to catch something to eat with me?" he asked.

"Not tonight, Michael. I'm pooped! Can I have a rain check?"

"Sure! Maybe one of the other gals will want to have dinner with the boss," he tossed out at her.

Tina wasn't aware any of her staff was still in the building. Perhaps he meant someone from another office. And why would he be asking someone else to go to dinner with him if she and he were going together? She was so tired that she didn't even want to try to figure it out.

"Well, aren't you going to say something? I figured you wouldn't appreciate my asking another woman to go to dinner after yesterday. Or was I mistaken? I was only joking with you about asking another gal to dinner, just to see if I could get a rise out of you. Apparently I can't!"

"Who am I to tell you who you can have dinner with? I'm just one of your department heads. You can enjoy yourself with anyone you please, Michael."

Michael's head came up and his face got serious. He stepped rapidly over to where she stood and felt her forehead with the back of his hand. "Are you feeling okay Sweetheart? Now that I am looking at you, you do look tired."

"Yeah, I am. I guess it's been a rather long day."

"How about if I come over and keep you company for a couple of hours. Maybe give you a back rub?"

"Thanks, but not tonight. I think I'm just going to take a hot bath and call it quits for today."

"If you think that would be best. I'm going to grab some chow and go home myself. I'll give you a call later to check on you. Are you sure you feel up to driving home, Tina?"

"Sure! Not a problem. I'll talk with you later. Thanks for the invite to dinner though."

"Anytime. Don't forget, we have a meeting in the morning at nine."

"Right! I'll be there. Thanks again for rescheduling it like you did. I consider that pretty darn nice of you."

"Just for you Sweetheart. Talk to you later," he said as he turned to walk out the door. Then he stopped and stepped back over by her. Taking her arm in his hand he pulled her into his arms and lifted her chin with his hand so he could kiss her. Be careful going home Sweetheart."

Then he turned and was gone.

Tina locked her desk and shut off the lights. It might have been nice if he had thought to walk her to the elevator so they could ride down to the parking level together. But, she figured, he had other things on his mind. And as the elevator doors were opening she saw him drive away in his Jag. Must be nice to have someone bring you your vehicle, she thought. Boy am I ever grumpy tonight. I guess I must really be tired. But not everyone has lived two days in only one. She walked over to the parking structure elevator and went in, punching the third floor button. When she stepped out of that elevator she hurried to her car and unlocked it, sliding in quickly. She felt uncomfortable for some unknown reason. She quickly pressed the automatic lock for all the doors and started the engine. In only minutes she was driving out of the structure and on her way home.

Tina tried to remain calm, thinking about all that had gone on the past forty-eight hours of her life. The more she thought about it the less it seemed to be real. Did she dream it? How could she dream up such a nice guy as Jefferson?

She figured it didn't really matter now, because if it was true, it was all behind her. It was time to move on with her life in the here and now.

When she got home she shed her shoes and decided to shower and put on her pj's to be comfortable. She wasn't going out, nor was she expecting any visitors, so why not be comfy? She showered quickly and washed her hair. Then she slipped into her favorite pajamas, the ones with the light blue lace on the front. She found her slippers hiding under her bed and put them on. She didn't see any need for her robe since she was going to be alone.

Going to the kitchen she didn't really feel like eating much, so she pulled out a bowl and decided on some cereal. She boiled some water to make herself a cup of hot chocolate to go with her cereal.

Taking her feast into the living room she curled up in front of the TV and began to munch while she watched the news.

She polished off the cereal rapidly and sipped at her very hot chocolate. Her first sip reminded her of the incident with Michael in the coffee corner. He was a nice enough guy, but it appeared he didn't always think ahead. Like today! It was obvious she was about to leave the office too, so why didn't he wait for her so they could go to the parking structure together, unless subconsciously he didn't want her company. And he had remembered to come back to kiss her goodbye. He had already turned to go to the door before he remembered. Then she wondered if she was thinking too much about all of this and reading too much into his actions.

I'm beginning to think my mind is working overtime here. Maybe all of this is better just left to chance. I ought to live my life and let what happens, happen. That's what I'm going to do. I don't need all this stress worrying about what is real or if Michael really cares or not. I really don't think he will continue to want me now that he had made his conquest anyway.

Tina sat her cup on the coffee table on one of her coasters she had put there just for such times that she wanted to eat in front of the TV. She leaned back on the couch, sliding down so her head could rest on the back and she watched the news. She felt bored with the news, thinking how interested Jeff had been in all of the many items of newsworthiness she had shared with him. Slowly but surely her eyelids began to feel awfully heavy and before she thought about going to bed she fell asleep. Three hours later she woke up and shut off the television and made certain the front door was locked, then went up to bed.

The next morning found Tina at her desk again at six o'clock. She pulled out another lesson outline to update and was just getting into it when she decided she needed a cup of coffee. Grabbing her cup from her desk she headed for the coffee corner. Very possibly, being the first person in she may have to make the first pot. She rounded the corner and could see the coffee maker when she realized someone was currently making a pot of coffee. She walked up and said "Good morning. I hope you make a good pot of coffee because I'm more than ready."

The gentleman turned around and she saw it was Michael. "Good morning Sweetheart. I see you're doing it again."

"Doing what again?"

"Working harder than you need to be. Why don't you hold off on those course outlines until I can get you some help? That would be a good project for the new person."

"Possibly but the new person wouldn't have the experience to know the needs and the best way to put them forth in the classroom."

"Oh, I see," he replied. "So that means you're going to do them anyway?"

"Probably! When and if you get me some help I'll be teaching her, or him, how my boss likes things handled so that person can then put together a course outline that would be acceptable to management, rather than an embarrassment or even a legal concern."

"Ah! Well put! I guess I have to agree with you there. Always protect the boss! Good plan." He smiled at her as he stepped closer to take her in his arms. She lifted her face up to his and he kissed her. What started as what seemed to be a gentle little good morning kiss turned into something quite different. His arms tightened around her and she was pulled up against him. She couldn't help but snuggle closer since it felt so good, and she moaned softly.

Lifting his lips from hers he said, "That's what I like to hear. The sound of satisfaction. I love it when you do that." Then he was kissing her again.

Beginning to feel a little uncomfortable about kissing the boss where anyone could see them she pulled back, breaking off the kiss.

"Don't tell me you're afraid of someone seeing us?" he asked.

"Yes, actually, I am."

"Then lets go into my office and continue this. I think I need a lot more of this even more than I need coffee." He took her hand and was going to lead her toward his office when she pulled back.

"No Michael. I have work to do and you probably do too. That's why we're both in early. So I think we ought to go do it."

"Okay Sweetheart. You go on back to your office and as soon as the coffee is ready I'll bring your cup to you. And, if I get lucky, I just might get at least one more kiss for delivering the coffee." He grinned just like a little boy trying to manipulate his mother. And it worked.

"Okay, I'll buy that." She grinned up at him and turned to walk back to her office. Before she could get two steps away he had her arm in his hand and he was pulling her back to him for one more kiss.

"I may as well get all I can, while I can get away with it!" he told her, grinning.

Tina couldn't help but think, yeah, it's too hot not to cool down. It won't last.

She slid back into her chair at her desk and started arranging pages of outline. Then she turned on her computer to bring up this current outline so she could start updating it. She became so engrossed she didn't hear Michael when he tapped his foot against her door instead of knocking, since he had two cups of coffee in his hands. He managed to get her door open and stepped in.

Looking at Tina working at her computer he couldn't help but be proud of her. She was not only a trusted employee, but a beautiful woman and a great kisser as well. He wasn't sure how far their relationship would go, but he was anxious to find out. He hadn't told her how much he had thought about her the evening before, and how he almost drove over to her townhouse, just to be with her. The only thing that kept him from doing it was that tired look in her eyes. He figured she would stay up later than she should just because he was there with her, and he decided that wouldn't be fair. So he stayed home and had a bowl of cereal. He figured she would never have a bowl of cereal for dinner. No, not his Tina! She probably had a very balanced meal and relaxed watching the news.

"Coffee's ready, Sweetheart!" he said as he brought her coffee to her desk. After sitting the cup down he stepped behind her chair and leaned over her, kissing her on her neck.

As soon as they touched she leaned to give him access to more of her throat and he took advantage of the offer.

Michael sat down his own coffee and turned her chair so she faced him. And he laid gentle kisses across her throat and down to her collarbone. Then he had her hand and was lifting her from her chair, pulling her into his arms as he stood up. Looking into her face he wanted to see if she was more rested this morning. He could see she looked better, less tired. Then he smiled into her eyes, causing her to smile back as her eyes lit up. What a wonderful gift that was for so early in the morning. He kissed her softly.

"I thought about you last night. I almost came over, but I figured you were resting."

"Oh? Why didn't you come over anyway? We could have rested together on the couch."

"Now you tell me! If I had known that last night..." he couldn't stop smiling at her. He scooped her up and sat in her chair, placing her on his lap.

"This is where you belong, Woman! Right here! Right where I can touch you and kiss your lips, and anything else I want." His lips were on her cheek and he laid butterfly kisses across her cheekbone, across her eyelids, and down her other cheek. You make me want to take you home and keep you. And never share!"

"Hmmm,.." she told him.

"Yes, I agree. You do taste good." He pulled her tightly against him and nestled his face into her throat. "I can't get enough of you," he mumbled to her.

"Michael! We shouldn't be doing this here. Michael,..." he pulled back from her throat and took her lips to stop her words. The kiss deepened and she forgot about her argument of making out in the office.

When the kiss finally ended Tina stood up and pulled him from her chair. She handed him his cup and led him to the door. "Didn't we come in early to get some work done?" she asked.

"But this work is so much more fun, Sweetheart." He didn't want to leave her, but knew he should.

"Go do what you have to do" she told him.

"Okay! I have to kiss you one more time," he said leaning down to catch her lips with his.

"You silly nut. You know that wasn't what I meant. Now go to work. And thank you for the cup of coffee. You're a wonderful man for bringing it to me."

"You're having dinner with me tonight. We're leaving early, or at least on time and we're going to have a meal together. I like eating with you. I like doing everything with you. Tina?"

"We'll see what happens, okay?"

"Marry me? We should be coming to work together, and going home together. You know we're perfect together. Be with me always?"

"Go to work, Michael. You know you don't mean it. Your hormones are just working overtime. Go away! Go back to work."

She had managed to get him as far as the door where she let him kiss her one more time and then she pushed him out and closed the door. She could tell he was standing just outside the door contemplating coming back in. She waited to see if he would. Then she heard footsteps that told her he was headed back to his office.

"He is just like a teenager who has found what he thinks is love, but actually it's only lust. She was sure that was all it was. That is all it is, her mind told her heart. It isn't real, only he doesn't understand that yet. One of these days he'll meet another woman, maybe at his 'watering hole' bar. And maybe then he'll realize what our relationship really was.

Slowly she walked back to her desk. She knew she needed to get busy on that next handful of paperwork. Because she was spending so much time on those course outlines she was slipping behind on her regular work. She wondered if he really was going to get her some help.

The morning passed quickly and Tina asked Marsha if she would like to go out to lunch with her. She said, "Sure! We haven't done it in a while."

They decided on the time and the place. They both liked the little Italian bistro in the courtyard below their office and they began considering their delicious chopped salad and bread sticks. So with that decided they both went back to work.

Tina didn't get to have lunch with Marsha very often. It seemed as though there was always something that needed doing so that they both couldn't get away at the same time. Finally they were going to get to do it. Tina was looking forward to it. She considered Marsha a friend. And she was actually hoping that she would apply for the new position, if it opened up. Tina felt certain that Marsha could handle it.

They had decided to beat the lunch rush and go at eleven. That was the time the bistro opened up. And that was what happened. At one minute till eleven Tina was standing next to Marsha's desk with a big grin on her face.

Marsha glanced up. Is it that time already? She grinned too. They both felt like two kids that were getting away with something. "Let's go!" she said as she quickly grabbed her purse. They locked arms and strolled out into the hallway, arm in arm.

Just as the two women approached the elevators Michael stepped out into the hall. Glancing down the hallway he spotted the two of them, arm in arm. He couldn't help but grin. He knew that Tina rarely even went out for lunch. She seemed to have a one track mind when she started something. She worked early, often through lunch, and late into the evening. She worked too hard and too long, he thought. He knew Tina and Marsha worked well together. He wished them a nice lunch. The only problem was he wished it was himself she was locked arm in arm with and having lunch with.

Over their chopped salads Tina asked Marsha if she was going to apply for the new position.

"Absolutely! I think we'd make a great team. The only problem will be training someone to take over my desk as secretary." Marsha's brown eyes sparkled as they discussed the possibility of her promotion. She had been with the firm for eight years now, and it was definitely time for her to move up. She understood what happened in their department and how to keep things running most effectively. She had made connections and ties with other offices that could help get items needed, or actions taken quickly.

Their lunch flew by and slowly but surely they locked arms and strolled back to the elevator. Just as the elevator doors opened on their floor and they, still with locked arms stepped forward to exit, Michael appeared.

"Caught you! I can't believe you actually do take a lunch break once and a while," he grinned at them. You two are the busiest. How was lunch?"

"Great! The bistro has the best salad." Marsha wasn't afraid to talk to the boss. She had done so several times, so she wasn't the usual shy woman around him. So she grinned back at him.

Turning to Tina he said, "Do you have a minute? Can you come into my office after you drop off your purse?"

"Sure! Be right there," she told him. He lifted his hand as she stepped by him, brushing her arm with his palm. Immediately her eyes went up to his, and he smiled at her.

After she passed him his hand came up quickly and touched her back. She could feel it sliding down her spine. She couldn't help but slow her movements to enjoy the contact. She looked back over her shoulder at him to see his eyes sparkling and a slight smile turning up his lips at the corners. He was trying to be professional while he was being romantic, and failing the professional part horribly. If anyone had been watching they would have seen what was in his eyes

Tina and Marsha went to their perspective desks and put their purses away. As Marsha checked for messages Tina grabbed her notebook and started in the direction of Michael's office. As she approached his secretary's desk she told Tina to go right in, that he was waiting for her. Tina thanked the young woman and stepped toward Michael's door. She couldn't help but wonder why he hadn't tried to date her. Because he saw her all the time, and she was definitely single and available, she wondered if he had already. She wondered if there was a way to ask him.

Tina turned the knob and stepped into the private domain of her employer. As soon as the door closed he stepped up behind her and encircled her with his arms. He had been hiding behind the door.

Tina let out a little yelp that she hoped his secretary didn't hear. Then he was turning her around to face him. She couldn't help it, it just came out, probably because he had surprised her. "Do you do this to your secretary very often?" she asked.

"Never!" came his reply very quickly. "She's not my type!" He pondered where that had come from, and suddenly realized that she really did care for him, because she was showing some jealousy. And he liked it. Not that he wanted her jealous, but just knowing that she truly cared about him, and apparently didn't want to share him any more than he wanted to share her made his heart sing. He was so happy about it he pulled her against him, kissing her deeply and rubbing her back. He felt her relax and give in to him. He knew she had gotten the answer from him that she had hoped to hear. He loved being able to figure her out like this.

Five minutes later when they came up for air he could see she was speechless. And as he listened he realized she was breathing very shallowly. He liked the feeling he could do that to her.

Finally they pulled apart and he took her hand in his, pulling her over to the couch by the window. "I'm jealous I didn't get to go to lunch with you, Sweetheart."

As he seated her he positioned himself close enough so that their thighs were touching. He wanted to continue to enjoy the power he had over her. He could sense her continued breathlessness and wanted to make her desire him, as he desired her.

"What was it you wanted to discuss with me, Michael?" she asked.

"Many things, my Sweet. But I have to talk about the new position with you. I received your list of duties and responsibilities. It's different enough from yours that I think it will work. I'm going to send out a flyer, in house, to allow anyone who is qualified to apply. Is Marsha planning on applying?"

"Yes, we discussed it today over lunch. I think she would be perfect for the job."

"Maybe we should do away with the applications then and just promote her. That would save me a lot of time and expense, since she would be ideal for the position."

"Would that create any legal problems for the company? Would it be setting a precedent that would allow a legal concern for later promotions?" she asked.

"Not if we word the promotion to cover that area. Have you figured out how you would rearrange the office to be able to create another private office in there?"

"Yes! And I've had Marsha talk with all of the departments that would be part of creating it, so they are agreeable, that as soon as your approval is put on it, everything, including phones will go forward. They've given us a timetable of two weeks to complete."

"You are outstanding Tina. And so organized! So you figured I would probably go with creating this new position, didn't you?" He couldn't help but smile at her. He planned right from the start to do this thing. Anything to lighten her workload.

"Well, let's say, I hoped it would go through. There is a list of applicants waiting to be offered a secretarial position as well, so we'll have a pool of people to pull from to fill her current position."

"I like the way you think. Maybe I could hire you to sit on my lap while I work? I could give you a raise, and a few bonus's to boot." He wiggled his eyebrows at her.

"You're turning into a dirty old man, Michael."

"No, I'm turning into a man that is seriously contemplating becoming a very married man, Tina. My Tina! My special Christina!" he murmured as he took her chin in his palm and pulled her against his lips.

Tina didn't know what to say. He sounded as though he meant it.

Well, I guess we've solved that problem then. I'll walk over with you and we can tell Marsha the good news. And you need to start interviewing possible new secretaries. I'll send an official memo to start the construction of Marsha's new office."

As they walked toward his door she realized he was holding her hand tightly in his larger one. She pulled lose and looked up into his face.

"Sorry! I forgot. It's getting harder to not touch you." He laid a soft kiss on her lips before he opened the door.

Marsha was excited when she got the word, right from the big boss. She jumped up and gave him a big hug. Then she stepped back, embarrassed. "Oh, I'm sorry!" she told him. And he just laughed.

"That's okay Marsha. I understand. It's not everyday one gets promoted. Tina is going to start interviewing applicants for your current position, so she'll need your assistance in giving whomever she chooses to fill your shoes some training so the transition will go smoothly."

"I understand! I'll be glad to do that."

"As soon as the new room is ready, we'll be moving you in there, so you don't have long to get our new person trained. Good luck to you Marsha. I know you're going to do well." He nodded at her and stepped away.

Marsha came around her desk and hugged Tina. "Thank you, thank you, so much. I didn't even have to take a test to qualify. You sure you won't be sorry?"

"Not a chance. I know you're going to be great in the position. That's why I suggested you. When I told Michael that you would be the perfect one for the job he said, then why bother with a test. That's how much he trusts my faith in you."

"Thank you Tina. I'll try hard to be worthy of that trust."

"Silly girl. Go back to work. Pretty soon I won't get to order you around as much. I may as well do as much ordering as I can get away with while I still can." She was laughing as she said it.

"Well, I'll still be only your assistant. I'll let you boss me around, boss!" she laughed.

Tina was laughing as she walked into her office. She had wasted enough time. She needed to get back to her course outlines.

Chapter 13

Tina's afternoon went by very quickly and she decided to go home at her usual hour. At five o'clock she walked out of her office and into the elevator, along with most of her office staff. She arrived at her car a few minutes later and unlocked it, then climbed in. She closed and locked her doors and just sat there. She was elated for Marsha. Tina was certain Marsha would make an excellent assistant. But she felt as though she must be burning out. She didn't have as much energy as she thought she used to have, nor the interest in her work. She tried to think about that, attempting to understand why. Sliding down on her seat she rested her head on the headrest on the back of her seat. She thought of Jeff.

She wondered what he had done during his life and if he had been happy. By now he was probably long dead and buried. If not, he would be about one hundred and twenty something, since he was thirty five when she met him. She couldn't bring herself to think of him as gone. She pictured him just a couple of years older than herself and in the prime of his life.

She had thought he had called her name as she stepped into the hole in time, when she left him. She wondered what it was that he wanted to say to her at that moment. She almost thought about trying to get back to his time again.

He had been a good friend, just when she needed one. She was dubious that anyone in this time would have been so kind to invite a total stranger into their home. She pictured how tall he was, and how he had once called her sweetheart. She wondered if he had meant it, or if it was a gentle friendly nickname, tossed out at the spur of the moment.

Tina began to feel the beginning of a nasty headache coming on. She didn't know why, since she wasn't feeling stressed in anyway, and she was no longer at work. For some unknown reason she moved her hand up along the steering wheel and as she looked at it, it seemed to shimmer. "Oh my gosh!" she said out loud.

As she watched, her hand faded and started to disappear. She looked at her arm fearing she might be slipping through time again, even though she was no longer in the location where she believed the hole in time to have been located. "No, No!" she shouted, as her head pounded and she felt faint. Even though she missed Jeff, she wanted to remain in her own time. "No, No!" she whispered as her eyes closed and she drifted into darkness.

She didn't know how long she was unconscious, sitting there in her car. She thought she heard someone calling her name, but it sounded so far away she didn't think anyone was really calling her. Maybe they just were calling someone else with the same name, somewhere near by. She couldn't quite wake up. Then she felt the car door move, suddenly aware that her head had slid over against it.

The driver's door opened and she began to fall. She landed in someone's arms. Thank goodness for that. She would have hated to have landed on the cement. She could have hurt herself. She began to rouse and she lifted her hand to her aching head.

"Tina! Tina? Are you all right?" came the voice close to her ear. Blinking, she looked up into a familiar face. "Tina, Sweetheart, what's wrong?" came Michael's voice.

"Head hurts!" she whispered. "Just a very bad headache," she told him. "What is going on?" She couldn't understand how he opened her door, and who the two men standing behind him were?

"Sweetheart, you looked as though you were unconscious. You wouldn't respond to my calling you so I called for the parking attendant to bring his 'Slim Jim' to open your door. You scared me to death. What happened to you?"

"You don't have to shout Michael. My head feels as though it is splitting apart. What do you mean, what happened? Nothing happened."

"How can you say that? You were unconscious when I found you. I tried for at least ten minutes to wake you and you didn't even budge. Only when I opened the door did you open your eyes. Have you been having headaches often Honey? You really have been working too hard."

"Michael, you're not making sense to me. Why did you come to my car?"

"I went to your office and one of the guys there said you had just left and if I hurried I might catch you, so I did, only to find you passed out cold. That does it, you're taking the day off tomorrow. You'll soon have an assistant to help take some of work load off of your shoulders." He turned to the two men standing behind him and said, "Thanks guys for all your help. I think I can take care of this now. Thanks again!" They mumbled something and walked away.

Michael was squatted down next to her open door, holding her in his arms. He pulled her head against his chest and kissed the top of her head. "Honey, I'm not letting you drive like this. If your headache was that bad, I'm surprised you even contemplated driving."

"I didn't have it when I first got into the car. I sat here just thinking about some things when it hit me. No I wasn't about to drive like that. I'm not stupid. It just frightened me that it came on so quickly." She felt anger that he would think she might drive when she wasn't well. She knew she couldn't tell him about her hand shimmering out of view. Actually, she half way expected to wake up in 1912 again. Or heaven forbid, somewhere else in time.

She needed to be alone so she could think about this and maybe figure it all out. Was the hole in time looking for her? Was it following her, to slip her through time again? If so, how could she stop it? And why would it be searching for me specifically? All of the questions going round in her head made her head hurt worse.

"Okay Sweetheart, slide over. I'm driving you home. I'll get my car later."

Slowly Tina slid over onto the passenger side of the bench seat. And Michael slid in behind the wheel.

"Someone has short legs I guess," he said as he had to adjust the seat back quite some distance to be able to fit. "I like the idea you're short enough to fit under my arm but I can see I couldn't drive your car without some changes here," he laughed.

Michael leaned over to help her attach her seatbelt, then he fastened his own, started the engine and pulled out. Tina just laid her head back on the headrest because she really wasn't feeling too well. "Please drive slowly. I may just decide to throw up along the way. I'll let you know if we need to stop," she said hoping it wouldn't be necessary.

Now she was getting a little frightened. If the hole in time was moving, searching for her, she might very well be in serious trouble. She didn't have any idea how to stop it. It apparently moved from her office to the parking structure. Even though that really wasn't very far, it told her that it may not have closed when she returned through it.

She figured it had to be an inanimate object, so it couldn't have conscious thought and be able to search for her. Why would she think such a silly thing?

"Honey, did you hear me?" Michael was asking.

"What were you saying, Michael?" she said when she realized he had been talking to her as she had been thinking about the hole in time.

"I asked you if this has happened to you before, Tina?"

"Oh, no! I don't think so. I can't remember it happening before. Why?"

"You have got to quit working so hard. I think this is just stress and tiredness. Your system is telling you to slow down, Sweetheart."

"Ummm," she answered him. "Michael, I really don't feel like talking right now. I just want to get home before I throw up."

"I understand. I'm sorry. And I'll take the turns more easily so they don't make you feel worse. Just relax. I'll get you home safely and soon."

He pulled her car into her usual spot and shut it off. He helped her out of the car and into her home. When he closed her front door he picked her up and carried her upstairs to her bed. Placing her on the edge of her bed, he pulled off her shoes and asked, "Do you need to go into the bathroom, Hon? Are you going to be sick?"

"No, it seems to be letting up. I think I'll just lay here a little while. How are you going to get back for your car?"

"Don't worry about it. I'll just call and have the attendant bring it over here. Are you going to be all right?"

Tina looked up into his face. He looked worried and a little shaken. She laid her hand on his and said, "I'll be fine. It was just a headache and it's going away now." She began to get up so she could go get some medication to hurry the pain away, but he stopped her.

"No you don't little Lady. What is it you need? Just tell me and I'll get it."

"I just need some headache medication from the bathroom cabinet, and some water."

"I'll get it for you. Just sit right there." He stepped away and glanced back. "You're not going to faint are you?" He didn't want her falling and hurting herself.

"No, I'll be fine." She watched him as he walked into her bathroom. She hoped he would be able to find the pills. Her cabinet was rather cluttered. But in a couple of minutes he was back, two Excedrin in his palm and a big glass of water.

"When you take these two pills, Tina, I want you to drink the entire glass of water. You know a headache can be caused by not having enough hydration in your body. Maybe the water might help you."

"Sure, okay!" she replied. All she wanted to do was lie down and go to sleep.

"I'm glad you're feeling better, but I think I'll stay the night with you anyway. Is that all right with you, Tina? I promise, I'll stay in the guest room and be a good boy. No hankie-pankie, I promise. I just don't want you alone."

"That isn't necessary, Michael. I'm sure you had things to do tonight. I'll be fine."

"Yeah, I had a dinner date tonight."

"Oh, you better call for your car so you won't be late," she told him.

"Tina! Don't you remember? We were going to have dinner together tonight."

"I don't think I want anything to eat. But you better call for your car, so you have it."

"If I didn't know better I'd think you were trying to get rid of me." He stood and looked at her with a puzzled look on his face.

"I don't want to be a bother. I'll just rest a little while and get something to eat later, if I'm hungry."

"Nothing doing. I'm going to stay right here all night Just in case you need anything, or anyone. Preferably me, that is." He grinned at her as he said it.

She had polished off the two pills and all the water so she handed the glass back to him. He returned it to the bathroom and returned to stand at her bedside.

"If you'll go into the other room for a couple of minutes, I'd appreciate it. I'd like to change into my gown and robe." She looked up at him.

"Are you sure you don't need any help?" he asked, with an evil grin on his face.

"Definitely not. Now go away. Go make your call for your car."

He nodded his head and left the bedroom. She listened for his footsteps on the stairs. As soon as she knew he had gone downstairs she changed into her gown and robe, found her slippers and headed for the stairway.

Just as she reached the top of the stairs she met Michael as he was coming up.

"I had a sneaking hunch you might try to come down. Here, let me help," he said as he picked her up.

"You know, I'm beginning to suspect you like carrying me. Aren't I too heavy for all of that?"

"Not at all. You only weigh about an ounce. Besides, I like to hold you in my arms."

He put her on the couch, with a pillow under her head. "Would you like some soft music on? Or the TV?"

"No, no noise. I just want to relax and rest. It would be nice to feel your touch though. It's very soothing."

He lifted her head and the pillow laying the pillow along the back of the couch, placing it where it was close enough to grab if she needed it. Then he sat down, placing her head on his lap. He unbuttoned his shirt and took off his tie. He hadn't put on his suit jacket when he ran out of the office to find her, so he figured he would retrieve it later. He liked the idea of having her head on his lap. He laid his hand over hers on her waist. "How's that Sweetheart? I like to touch you too. You know, you're very calming to me. When I hold you, or just touch you, I feel so peaceful. It must be your sweetness coming through." She thought he was just talking but when she looked up into his eyes, there was tenderness there. Maybe he really did care. Why else would he be so caring and protective of her?

"Tina?" he said. "Do you believe that one person in a couple that care for each other, cares more than the other?"

"I wouldn't be surprised. Not everyone loves at the same level of passion, at least not all of the time. But yes, I think it's possible that one person may have stronger feelings that the other, even though they love each other. Why do you ask?"

"Oh, no special reason. I was just thinking."

"Michael, if you have things you need to do I wouldn't expect you to stay with me. I really appreciate that you offered, but I would understand if you needed to leave. I'm sensing something is on your mind, and I don't want to be a burden to you. A woman's headaches shouldn't interfere with your business or life."

"Tina! I don't want to leave you. Right now you're the most important thing in my world. I just want you well. I love being with you."

"Is there something on your mind, Michael? I just feel as though something isn't quite right here. Please tell me. We're close enough to each other to share almost anything. At least I think so."

"Tina, I don't know how to tell you this. It feels to me as though you don't feel as strongly about our relationship as I do. Here I am, acting all concerned about you and you're so tough, you're just taking everything in stride."

"You know Michael, I've been alone a long time and I'm used to taking care of my problems all by myself. I haven't ever had someone who really cared about me and wanted to take care of me. So I'm not used to it. It's always been I had to deal with whatever came up. It was a matter of 'sink or swim'. And that's what I've done. I'm a survivor. I've always believed that we have to live with the hand we're dealt."

"But Sweetheart, I want to take care of you. You deserve someone to love you and care for all your needs. Not to say you can't be your own person, but someone to share your concerns with, and whose shoulder you cry on. I want to be that shoulder for you, Tina."

"You are! I feel more drawn to you that anyone in a long time. Maybe you're just feeling the backlash of my fear of being seen as a couple at work. I just haven't ever believed it was right to mix business and pleasure, so I'm a little self-conscious about it there. No one has seen us as a couple there."

"That's true, but I want them to see us as a couple. Tina, when I'm away from you, you're all I think about. When I'm trying to get something done at my desk your face pops up in front of me. Why do you think I've been calling you into my office so often? I love to grab you as soon as you come in and just hold you. You feel right to me. I love your kindness to everyone you meet. You're the most compassionate personnel manager I have ever known. You even let my niece off the hook. I think you'd make a great mother. And I'd like you to be the mother of my kids, Tina."

"Michael! Do you know what you just said? You better beware or I just might take you serious."

"I wish you would. I want to go home at night and just be together. We don't have to go out all the time, or entertain a lot, or go to workshops or conferences or anything else. I just want to be an old married couple, with you. I want to be there when you have that headache. I want you to be there when I'm ill, to hold my hand and just give me that wonderful peaceful feeling that you have. I don't think you even realize how you radiate peace and it goes right into my heart. No one has ever done that for me before, Tina. Only you, my Christina, my Love."

"Michael, we haven't known each other very long. We don't even know if this attraction we feel for each other is real, or if it will last. When I get married I want it to last. Not get a divorce two years later when we realize things weren't working out. I want a husband that is willing to try to make them work out, always."

"I've always considered myself a stable person. I guess that's why I make up sixty five percent of the business. My brother is a spendthrift and would buy anything that someone tells him will improve the business, whether it actually will or not. I'm more methodical and I research things out more and then I make my decisions. Not up front."

"But wouldn't we be making this decision up front if we decided to get married so soon after we met? Wouldn't that be the same thing your brother does? I don't think we should rush into this. Let's take our time and really get to know each other first. There isn't any rush. We have lots of time. I know I'm very attracted to you Michael, and I believe you feel the same, but let's enjoy the moment first. And learn more about each other. You may discover you hate the way I brush my teeth, or the way I wear my hair."

"Yeah, I like your hair down. Up looks so formal and business like. Down, it looks for sexy and feminine, it makes me want to grab you and do this." He pulled her into his arms and bent her head back so he could ravish her throat, then her chin then her lips. When he finished with her lips he licked her bottom lip and then laid soft kisses across her cheekbones and her eyelids. "I love you, Christina. I think I'll always love you. You're my sweetheart, lover, my best friend, mother; just so much to me. I want to be with you, Honey."

"And I want to be with you too," she told him. Every time you touch me I seem to lose control. You seem to light a fire, just with your eyes."

"Good! At least we're getting somewhere. Now I know you like my eyes. And I like all of you. Your skins your lips, your eyes, your throat, your graceful hands. God help me, I just want to touch you and feel that wonderful feeling of peace."

"Michael, maybe you shouldn't stay the night. I don't want to put us in a position where we'll do something we'll regret later."

"It's nothing like that, Tina. Oh yeah, I want to eventually make love to you, but I think that is something that we should save until we get married. If we do it all now, there won't be anything left for then. But to touch and just spend time together means so much to me right now."

"I understand. I agree with you on all of that. Marriage is sacred and should be kept that way. But I do love your touch, and your caring. You'll never know how much it meant to me that you came looking for me in the garage today."

"Christina!" It was all he could say. He had to show her with actions how very much she meant to him. He had tried with words, but didn't actions speak louder than words?

He held her close against him and just rocked her. Like a child that had a bad dream and was hugging their teddy bear to have something familiar to hug and make the bad images go away.

Since she was no longer lying down she curled up against him where she could feel the beat of his heart. He laid his hand across her shoulder and hugged her gently. "Can you picture us as gray haired grandparents, watching TV in the evening? Our kids grown and gone and it's just us?"

"Wait a minute there. Let's just enjoy the couple part, then we can get to the parent part, and them the grand parent part. Let's not rush it, okay?" She laughed and he kissed her.

"Are you feeling better, Hon?" he asked. "I could order a pizza so you wouldn't have to fix anything."

"Maybe so, yeah! Do you like Canadian bacon and pineapple with extra cheese?"

"Sure! It sounds good to me. I'll make the call and you see if we need to order some Pepsi with the pizza or if you have some here."

The evening went by quickly and easily. They enjoyed their pizza in front of the TV and watched a movie until late. When he noticed her eyes growing heavy he picked her up and carried her to her bed.

"I'll make sure the doors are all locked and the lights are off, Honey. Don't worry! Then I'll crash in the guest room down the hall. If you need me in the night just call. I'll hear you. I love you Christina! Sleep well."

After he went back downstairs she freshened up, brushed her teeth and climbed into bed. It was nice having someone look after her, she decided.

Chapter 14

Tina woke in the night in a cold sweat. She had been dreaming about traveling though time and she had a niggling feeling that she had summoned the 'portal' to her. She sat up suddenly, gasping for breath. Its here! I brought it to me! It's here! How did I do that? Is it real? What should I do?"

She became aware she was crying. This darn portal had her frightened out of her wits. If she could summon it at will, she could pass through it in her sleep and not know what she did. And that sounded dangerous.

"Tina?" came the voice. Michael stepped into the doorway. "I thought I heard you crying. What is it?"

She hadn't told anyone about the portal. Except for Jeff, that was, and Mrs. Braxton. But they were in another time and probably dead by now. She suspected that if she told anyone they might try to use the power of the portal to control time, and money, and who knew what else. It was just too volatile to let others in on. A person without honor could cause unbelievable changes in the future.

Michael walked over to her bed. As he did so, she could see him shimmer. At first she thought to jump out of bed to grab him so he wouldn't pass through the portal to somewhere else, but decided she could see that only his arm was shimmering, meaning he wasn't going to go into enough of it that it would pull him out of this time. He sat down on the edge of her bed. Apparently he was sleepy enough he hadn't even noticed what had happened.

Her tears ceased but there were still some lying on her cheek. Michael wiped them away with his thumb. "What is it Sweetheart. Here, let me hold you." He gathered her against his chest and she immediately reached around his waist to hold on. Should she tell him? She was rapidly getting to the point where she was going to have to tell someone, because it was creating too much pressure on her.

"Michael, it was a bad dream. Just a dream! I'll be all right in a minute."

He slowly rubbed her back, and brushed her hair from her face. He laid kisses across her eyebrows and just rocked her. "I'm here, Honey. Everything will be all right."

Michael just held her until her breathing slowed and her pounding heart rate calmed. Then he laid her back on her pillow and laid a kiss on her forehead. "I think you should be able to sleep now. Just think of good things." He sat there a moment longer just looking into her eyes. "I'm glad I was here, Honey. Dream of me," he told her.

His suggestion seemed like a good idea so when she had told him good night, she closed her eyes and did just that. She dreamed of Michael, and what it might be like to be married to him. But somehow it just didn't feel right. He was caring, and attentive but he seemed to be wanting something more. Something that perhaps was beyond her ability to give him, and she wasn't sure what it was. But at least the ability to dream of a possible relationship with him allowed her to drop off into deeper sleep. She watched as he headed for the open doorway, ready to pounce if his form began to shimmer.

The following morning she woke early and got ready to go to work. By the time she wandered down to the kitchen Michael was there already, making coffee for them.

"How wonderful! I have my own coffee maker this morning. I feel spoiled!" She laughed and he picked up that she was feeling much better.

"Good morning Sweetheart. I woke up early so I thought I ought to make myself useful. I guess I didn't need to have my car sent over. Now we can't ride to work together. I seemed to have messed up there."

"That's okay. At least we had our transportation. You could have left last night if you had needed," she told him.

"Yes but I was needed here when you woke in the night. It makes me feel needed and that's a good thing. I'm just glad I was here for you. You see, that's what it would be like if you'd marry me. The only difference would be you'd have to sleep on the side of the bed, not in the middle, or you'd have to cuddle up to me, cause there would be two bodies on your bed. On our bed, that is," and he laughed at the thought of it.

Tina smiled at him wondering what that would be like. She remembered the one time they had slept together she had cuddled up to him.

They sat at her kitchen table for a few minutes enjoying the morning and their first cup of coffee together. Then they headed for the front door and out to their cars, to drive to work.

She went directly to her desk and put away her purse. Grabbing her cup she walked over to the coffee corner where a pot of coffee was already sitting waiting for her, and poured a cup. Returning to her office she began pulling out paperwork that needed her attention. She sipped her coffee until she had drank half of it, and then promptly forgot it. By then she was deeply entrenched in her current project.

She worked straight through lunchtime. Between taking care of things needing her input for her staff, and this paperwork the time flew by. By one thirty she was almost finished with the last part of her paperwork when she heard her com-line beep. Keeping her eyes on what she was doing, her hand picked up the telephone receiver and she automatically answered, "Tina Taylor!"

"Ah, the voice I love to hear. What are you doing Tina? You sound a little distracted?"

"And a good afternoon to you too, Michael. I'm finishing up some in-office paperwork. Why do you ask?"

"I want to invite you and your about to be new assistant, to a dinner on Friday night. It's suppose to be a big annual affair. I try not to attend unless I absolutely have to. But I guess this one I must attend. I understand the guest speaker is a billionaire that has lit the world on fire. He is making major investments in many corporations, underpinning them with a better cash flow and allowing expansion on a massive scale. Some of the companies that he's purchased stock in have grown by leaps and bounds in almost no time at all. I have an appointment to get a few minutes of his time after his speech, and I hope to get him interested in joining us in business. So, to make a long story shorter, I must attend and I decided I wanted to have you and Marsha along with me."

"Yeah, so you don't have to suffer alone. No thanks Michael, I think I'll pass on this one. It sounds dreadful."

"You can't do that to me, Honey. I need a date, and this would give Marsha an opportunity to get to meet some more people in this business. It would be a good chance for her to be seen and to see others. You can't tell me no."

"Well, if you put it that way I suppose we have no choice. Is it formal or just semi-formal? I'll have to let Marsha know so we both know how to dress."

"It's semi, so just a fancy dress would be fine. The guys will be wearing regular suits. You know, just like going to church clothes."

"That's an interesting way for you to put it, since you don't go to church. Do you?'

"Not lately. But I used to, before I became so busy, and before I found this lady that keeps me busy at all hours."

"Watch it! You make that sound bad!"

"Never that, Sweetheart. So it's Friday at seven, dinner, and dancing after the speaker does his thing. I'll send a limo to pick you both up and take you home, so you don't have to worry about drinking and driving. You can relax and leave the driving to us," he laughed.

"Okay, Michael. I'll tell Marsha. We'll be your cohorts in boredom."

"Thank you Sweetheart. Who knows, Marsha might even enjoy herself."

"Yeah, right! I guess I should be polite and say thank you for inviting us, but I'd rather say, don't do it again," she laughed. She was laughing with him about it, but she really would rather not have to attend. But business was business.

She completed the needed paperwork that had kept her busy all day and called Marsha in to deliver it to the necessary staff members. When Marsha came in to her office, Tina asked her to sit with her in the two chairs that were grouped together and sat adjacent to her couch. She wanted to feel comfortable rather than formally busy. This was to be Marsha's first official business dinner and she wanted to prepare her as gently as possible.

They both were comfortable in each other's company so there wasn't any stress between them. Tina kicked her shoes off and put her feet up on the coffee table in front of them. "Oh, that feels good," she said.

"I get the feeling you're about to drop something big on me. Just tell me before I get too scared here," Marsha said.

Tina smiled and wiggled her toes. Apparently you are going to get your first opportunity to meet some new faces and maybe make a few new contacts in the business. Michael has said we are to attend a dinner dance with him this Friday evening. There's some big-wig speaker that is investing in companies like ours that are ready to expand. And I believe that's where we are right now. Just like our adding you to the management staff. This business is growing rapidly, and eventually this office isn't going to be big enough for all the people we'll need. I'm sure our office will be moved so we can encompass an entire floor. That's the type of growth that I think is coming, Marsha. So Michael wants us at his side to meet this man and hear what he has to say."

"Oh my goodness. My first official business function! What fun! And it's a dinner dance too. Wow! Does Michael dance? Is he any good?"

Tina laughed. "Yes, he's a very good dancer. At least I suspect he would be, even tho I haven't seen him dance. But he's had to go to so many of these things over the years he grown to hate them. He only attends if he knows he can't get out of them, or if there is something that he may be able to get, by going to these things. And this is one of those. Apparently this fellow we're going to hear speak has the ability to make even money grow."

"Is it formal? How should we dress?"

"It's semi-formal. We can wear party dresses. And this can give us a chance to go shopping. I'd love to get something new for this. I can't remember the last time I bought something pretty. What do you think? Maybe after work we could catch something quick to eat and go over to the mall and see what we could find? There are so many specialty shops there, we ought to be able to find something."

"Sounds like fun. But I'll have to make a call to make sure my babysitter will stay longer. Even though my daughter is growing up, I don't like to leave her alone, especially in the evening. Oh, and I'll have to arrange for someone to be with her on Friday night too. Maybe I can make that one a sleepover arrangement, to make it easier. Well, whatever, I'll work it out. Just think, my first business dinner!"

Marsha was bubbling over with excitement, and Tina thought it would be fun to go shopping together. So when four o'clock rolled around both gals were ready to leave the office. Neither one of them had taken a lunch break so they left early, planning on counting their lunchtime at the end of the day. Normally that was not allowed for employees to leave early using their lunchtime at the end of the work day, but Tina decided to do it anyway, this once. Besides, it was for business stuff anyway.

They piled into Marsha's car and drove over to the mall, just a few miles away. When they arrived they found a neat little Mexican restaurant and went in to enjoy dinner before they went shopping. They figured an early meal would get them in and out before the rush, so they could have more time for shopping.

When they left the restaurant they hit several stores before they found just what they were looking for. Tina bought a powder blue dress of chiffon that ended right at her knees. She liked the straight across neckline that covered her collarbone. It was the back that shocked her. It almost didn't have a back to it. She knew she wouldn't be wearing a regular bra with this little number. Her back was bare almost to her waist. The creation made her feel feminine and sexy.

Marsha found a emerald colored sheath that stopped just above her knees and showed off her slim legs. Her dress was sleeveless and had a low neckline in the front. Because she was full busted she could wear such a thing and carry it off well. Tina felt since she was rather smaller busted so she wouldn't have worn such a dress, but she knew that Marsha looked like dynamite in it.

They managed to find matching shoes and were ready for a cold drink by the time they walked out of the shop. They wandered over to a lounge that was in the mall and went in. Finding a booth open they slid into it and just leaned back to relax. They ordered New England Iced Tea for each of them and laughed when they saw how tall the glasses were. They both knew that when they staggered out to the car that they would probably be doing just that. Staggering!

Marsha dropped Tina off at her car and Tina saw she was laughing as she drove away. She just hoped that Marsha made it home safely. If she had an accident on the way home, Tina would never forgive herself.

Tina slid into her vehicle and started for home. When she got there she found a certain Jag parked close by. As soon as she got out of her car she couldn't help but smile. Michael was walking toward her. He must have come by to see her and just waited for her to come home. Now that was love, she thought. Most men hate to wait on a woman.

She reached into the passenger seat to get her packages just as he reached her side. "Where have you been Sweetheart? I was beginning to worry."

"Marsha and I had to go shopping for dresses for Friday night. And we decided to have dinner while we were out. Then we stopped to have a drink and got a little soused. Can you tell?" She weaved a little as she stood there.

"I think I can, yes!" He grinned at her. And he couldn't help but wonder if since she felt a little tipsy if she was going to be less inhibited as well.

He took her packages from her and followed her into her townhouse. Laying the packages on the chair by the door, he gathered her into his arms and kissed her. "I haven't been able to do that all day, and I've wanted to."

"Well, now's your chance," she said as she leaned into him.

Uh oh! he thought to himself. This evening is going to be a challenge. She would be very easy to end up in bed with tonight. And he wanted to, actually, but he had given his word to her. And he knew he had to stand by it. So nothing was going to happen this evening.

"Do you want anything to eat?" she asked.

"No Sweetheart. I had a late lunch about four, and I'm still full. Thanks anyway. Were you hungry for something?'

"Not at all!" she told him. "We went out for Mexican food and I ate and ate and ate. I can't seem to stop myself when it's Mexican. I love that stuff. The only problem is that it loves my body too. If I ate it very often I would weight a ton."

"I can't picture you weighing a ton. Not even near it. But you know what? I would love you no matter what you weighed. Cause I love the you that's inside."

"Silly man. If I got fat you'd probably get tired of me very quickly and I know it. Every man wants his woman to be attractive."

"Yeah but you have to remember that beauty is in the eye of the beholder. And I'm the beholder, Hon. I'd love you no matter what."

"Thank you," she said softly. "That means a lot to me."

They curled up on the couch and kicked off their shoes, and spent the evening watching summer reruns of last winter's programs. At ten thirty Michael stood and pulled her to her feet.

"Well, Sweetheart, I guess I have to head for home. I don't have any good excuse to stay over tonight." He pulled her with him toward the door, where he kissed her goodnight.

"Stay safe going home my special Sweetheart," she said to him. Her use of the endearment surprised him, but he chalked it up to the alcohol in her system.

"You just go to bed and rest well, my own Christina. Remember how much I love you. Maybe when I get home I'll call you, just to let you know I got there safely. Would you like that?"

"Yes, my Love, I would. Please be careful," she said.

"Naturally! Just like you were extra careful driving home tonight even though you had been drinking. I worry about you Darling. Next time call me, and I'll come and get you. I don't want you drinking and driving."

"Let's see what's the expected saying here? Oh yes it's, Yes Dear!" She grinned up at him so he had to kiss her again.

Michael went to his car and slid in. He arrived home safely and quickly and reached for his phone. He called her number and she picked it up on the second ring.

"Hello," was her soft answer.

"Are you ready for bed, Sweetheart?"

"Yes, I've showered and brushed my teeth and I'm ready to hit the sack. I feel as though I could sleep for a week."

"You better not, we have a dinner date on Friday. I just wanted to let you know I'm home and missing you. Go to bed Sweetheart. Sleep well."

"I will, Michael. You do the same." And they hung up and she went to bed. As soon as her head hit the pillow she was out.

Chapter 15

Friday seemed to come quickly for Tina. She and Marsha were going to skip lunch again and leave early so they could get home to rest up for the evening. Marsha had brought celery sticks and Jicama for them to munch on, and they planned on having coffee or water, at their desks while they worked. They figured that would keep them going energy wise. They didn't want to eat much because they planned on going crazy over dinner.

Tina headed for home thinking about the evening ahead. She really wasn't looking forward to it. But she was excited about her new dress. She hoped that Michael would like it. And she also hoped they wouldn't have to stay very late. She recalled Michael saying that he had an appointment with the unnamed gentleman after his speech ended. It might be possible that not too long after that that they would be able to get away. She figured she would just have to keep her fingers crossed.

Michael called to tell her the limo would be picking up Marsha first, then arriving at Tina's home at six thirty. Michael would have been picked up first so he and Marsha would be riding together to Tina's. Then they would go directly to the hotel for the dinner and speaker. After the speaker came the dancing, in which Tina didn't plan on partaking.

And true to his word the black limo pulled up in front of her townhouse right at six-thirty. Michael got out laughing at something Marsha had said. Tina was standing at her door waiting for him as he turned and spotted her. He smiled and seemed to turn a little pink as though he had been embarrassed. Tina wondered what Marsha and he could have been talking about that would cause such a thing. Maybe it was a dirty joke?

Michael approached her in the doorway and pushed her back into her home. She looked up surprised he was doing that. But as soon as they were out of sight of the limo he took her into his arms and kissed her silly. Then he looked her over, admiring her new dress. He even went so far to tell her he liked her new shoes as well. Then he planted a small kiss on the end of her nose before taking her by the elbow to escort her to the car. On the way out she grabbed her handbag and they were off.

He sat between the two women in the back seat, joking and talking about how wonderful this fellow was suppose to be and how he had rescued so many companies. Even though Michael didn't feel his company needed rescuing he was interested in some financial backing. Tina could see he was excited about a possible opportunity opening up through the efforts of this unknown man.

Michael reminded the chauffeur that they might be leaving earlier than most of the others attending so he should not allow the limo to get boxed in. Then, with a woman on each arm he escorted Tina and Marsha into the hotel banquet room.

Michael was excited about the possibilities for this evening. He not only had two beautiful women all to himself, he had an appointment with 'The Man'. He was very hopeful he might be able to persuade the fellow to invest in Hart and give him some extra cash flow in the process. Yes, he thought, it could be a very profitable evening anyway he looked at it.

They located their table assignment and introduced themselves to the others at the same table. It was only minutes until their table was filled and dinner was being served. There were individuals from many different walks of life attending. So comments varied and conversations were both interesting and boring for Tina. She noticed Marsha was making small talk with the gentleman seated next to her, as well as joking with Michael.

Just as the dessert was being served and the final pots of coffee were being brought to all the tables a gentleman stepped to the microphone and began to speak of the attributes of the guest speaker. Apparently he was arriving just in time for his talk, and hadn't attended the dinner portion of the evening. Tina turned her chair a little so she could more comfortably watch whatever was happening on stage.

A tall fellow stood just off stage next to the curtain, unseen by most people in the room as yet. Then suddenly the person talking identified their speaker by name.

"Won't you welcome Mr. Jefferson Marlboro, Ladies and Gentlemen?" He began to applaud and apparently that was the signal for the gentleman in the sidelines to come forward. Tina couldn't breathe. Jefferson Marlboro? But he's dead? How could it be? Maybe this was his son or even his grandson? Tina had to concentrate just to get air into her lungs. She waited and watched.

The man began to speak. The voice was the same. He looked just like her Jeff. But it couldn't be, could it?

Then it hit her. Was it possible that he too came through the time portal? He wasn't introduced as Jefferson Marlboro the Second, or the Third. Tina had to force herself to breathe in and out. She just hoped that Michael wasn't noticing her distress. She glanced around to see him in her peripheral vision and noticed he had his arm across the back of Marsha's chair and was joking with her. Marsha and he were laughing softly.

No, she realized he wasn't concerned about herself at the moment at all. He seemed to be having a great time joking with Marsha. Tina began to feel uncomfortable with the sudden comradery that seemed to be developing between Marsha and Michael.

Returning her view to the man who was their speaker for the evening she tried to recognize him. He had the same dark hair and eyes. But she was far enough away from him to not be able to tell if it might be only his relative. This was one time she wished she had a front row seat. Usually she hated being so close that she got a crick in her neck looking up at the speaker. Not so tonight!

He began speaking of the importance of good relationships and their importance between employers and employees. Then Tina turned to look at Michael and Marsha to see if they were listening. They were, finally. Michael smiled at her when he noticed she had glanced back at him. He was like a kid, excited and almost couldn't sit still. She attributed it to the anticipated meeting with the speaker in just a short while.

She could see that this Mr. Marlboro was scanning the faces in the crowd. As his eyes drifted to her area he seemed to pause. Then, very quickly, he picked up the thought again and continued on with his talk. Much of his subject material was similar to the workshop material she herself taught. He touched on management's awareness of employee needs and how to strengthen it. Then he drifted off into other areas of expertise such as insufficient staffing and over staffing problems. Tina quit listening. She suspected this was her Jeff, come through the portal. And if it was it would explain his pause when his eyes caught hers.

She began to think the talk would never end. She wanted to get up and walk outside for some fresh air, but she was afraid to do so, for fear Jeff would notice her. So she sat quietly, no longer listening to the acclaimed speaker, but listening to the soft joking around that was happening behind her between Michael and Marsha.

Fear entered her heart for the relationship between herself and Michael. Somehow he seemed to be tickled by anything and everything that Marsha had to say. Was he enamored of her? If that was the case, why wait until now? Why was he acting so strange this evening? Was the pressure getting to him and he was acting out? She didn't know for certain, but she did know she wanted away from Michael. She just didn't want to see him acting this way. Not after he had said he loved her and wanted to marry her.

If this was to be his behavior, then she was not interested in marriage. She wanted an up front, honest, all encompassing relationship that had honor and complete trust in it.

Finally the speaker concluded his talk and the audience applauded loudly. Then they were on their feet with more applause. As Jeff left the podium Tina excused herself to go to the ladies room. She had to get from air. She was having difficulty breathing in this crowded room. She headed for the hallway that led to the restrooms so it would appear she was truly going to the restroom, then ducked out a side exit door to a small patio. She grasped the iron railing along the low wall and held on for dear life. She wasn't sure what was going on here, but at the moment she couldn't deal with the two men in her life at the same time.

She stayed there for several minutes until she was able to take a deep breath. Then her heart quit pounding so hard and she felt better. She wasn't sure what was going on between Michael and Marsha, but she felt certain she was ready to cut

Michael lose. If he wanted to flirt with Marsha, than by all means he could do that, but not on her time. She no longer wanted to have a personal relationship with him if he was going to act stupid with another woman, especially in her presence.

She just wished she could speak with Jefferson. She needed to know if it was the same man. She remained where she was a few minutes longer. She hoped that Michael's meeting with the man was occurring now, so she could get out of there soon. At last she took a deep breath and reached for the door handle. She opened it and went back inside. She approached the table to find Marsha talking with the gentleman that had been sitting beside her during dinner. Michael wasn't anywhere to be seen.

Tina glanced around to try to see if the speaker was circulating around the floor talking with people. She didn't see him. So she assumed that he and Michael were deep into their meeting somewhere in the building. She walked over to the bar and ordered a glass of white wine and stood sipping it along the wall where she could watch their table for Michael's return. Then she heard the music start and Marsha stood along with the man that she had been talking with and headed for the dance floor.

That seemed to be the signal for Tina to return to her chair. She sat down and just sipped her drink. She tried to understand the emotions going on at the moment. She just couldn't figure anything out right now.

One of the men she knew from another table came over and asked her to dance. She thought about refusing, but then changed her mind and decided, why not. So she stood and moved with him onto the dance floor. The music was slow and dreamy and as Tom gathered her into his arms she went with him, swaying with the music and just trying not to think about much of anything.

"That was quite a powerful speaker, don't you think?" Tom asked her. He was moving slowly through the dance and was easy to follow.

"Yes, it would seem so," she replied. "Have you heard him speak before?"

"No, but several of the personnel people in the companies around town were looking forward to his visit. I understand he's let it be known he was interested in possibly purchasing stock in some companies in town."

"Oh!" she answered. "So he has so much money he can afford to do some investing?"

"It was rumored. I don't think my boss will take him up on it though. But you never can tell. It almost seems as though this guy was looking for something special. I may be wrong, but it's just a hunch I have. He apparently is asking a lot of questions about companies with large personnel staffs. I guess time will tell. Oh, speak of the Devil,…" Tom quit talking and looked over at the man who had just walked up to them.

Tina looked up into familiar dark eyes. And he was looking at her as well.

"May I cut in?" he asked.

"Of course, Sir," Tom said quickly, stepping back. "Talk to you later Tina."

"Okay Tom. Thanks for the dance." Jeff moved forward pulling Tina close as he began to dance with her. He looked down at her, silently waiting for her question. It didn't come. She simply moved closer and he accepted that for now. He laid his cheek beside her forehead and held her as they moved slowly on the floor.

Jeff could feel her trembling. He hadn't meant to frighten her, only find her and tell her how he felt about her. He had waited until the following day after she went through the portal to make his decision. He couldn't sleep. In the morning he contacted his attorney and told him what he wanted done. It would guarantee wealth would be his in the form of Jefferson Marlboro the Third. He talked with Mrs. Braxton and told her of his plan. Then, later in the afternoon he returned to the hole in time and passed through.

He had decided he needed Christina in his life, even if he had to travel through time to get to her. He wanted her back. His only fear was that she might not want him. If that was the case then he would let her walk away from him.

Jeff didn't know for sure whether she was glad to see him or not. She looked shaken. When he had seen her in the audience, even though he had been hoping at every speaking engagement to find her, he hadn't really expected to see her tonight. He could see in her face that she recognized him, or at least she thought she did. Now he had to find out where she lived and her phone number. But just for the moment all he wanted was to hold her close. He had hoped that since he was the guest of honor that no one would cut in on their dance.

He had completed the prearranged meeting with one of the company owners in town, and hoped that he might find her through meeting with such employers. She was the reason for his speaking engagements, and many meetings. Locating her was his entire program, and now he had. He wasn't about to let her just disappear again.

"Christina!" he said softly to her.

"Yes?" came the soft whisper. She sounded as though she was in shock. He remembered she had been trembling when he had first taken her into his arms.

"Christina, I had to come and find you. Tell me where you live and your phone number so I can call you after this is over. I have to talk with you."

She slowed her movements and looked into his dark eyes. As she tipped her head up to see him, he could see tears, unshed, in her eyes. Then her face went down again.

"Oh Christina, my Love. I didn't mean to make you cry. I realized you were too important to me to let you go." He pulled her more closely to him. He laid a soft kiss on her temple. "Look at me Christina."

Again her eyes came up to peer into his. He wanted to drown in her eyes. I need to talk to you. Please, Christina. How do I get hold of you here? You aren't going to just walk out of my life again are you?"

"You know I'm not, Jeff. Do you have a piece of paper you can write on?" she asked.

"Yes!" He stopped dancing and pulled out a small notebook and pen from his pocket. He wrote her address and phone number on it. "You are with someone tonight?"

"Yes," she answered. My boss and my new assistant. He brought us in a limo."

"I have to speak with a few people before I can get away. I'll call you as soon as I get back to my hotel room. Will you wait up for me?"

"Yes! You know I will. I want to talk with you too. I just want to get away from all of these people." She looked into his face and felt something strong pulling at her heart. He was so dear to her.

The music stopped and he stepped back dropping his hands. "Until later, Christina!" he said softly and turned her to walk her to her table.

"It's all right Jeff. You don't have to walk me to the table. It might cause questions that you might not want. We'll talk later tonight." She reached a hand out to him and he took it. Raising it to his lips he kissed it, then turned it over and kissed her palm as well.

Chapter 16

Tina walked back to the table. Marsha and Michael were sitting together talking softly. Tina almost felt jealous. It was as if in just a couple of hours the two of them had become best friends and possibly something much more. And it was the much more that concerned Tina. For a man who had said he had committed his heart to her he appeared to be ready to give it to Marsha as well.

As Tina arrived Michael glanced up at her. She had expected him to pull out her chair to seat her but he made no attempt to get up. Instead he returned his gaze to Marsha and continued talking with her.

Tina pulled her own chair out and sat down. She turned to Michael and asked, "Did you have your meeting with our speaker?" She didn't want to sully his name by using it in front of Michael.

"Yes, I did. He'll be visiting my office tomorrow afternoon. He sounds as though he may be interested in learning more about Hart. Maybe the cost of our new position we've just created won't be coming out of my own pocket after all."

"Well if that's taken care of, I suppose you're probably ready to get out of here?"

"Not really. I though we might get some dancing in before we left." With that he turned to Marsha and asked her to dance.

Marsha smiled widely at him and stood up. He rushed around the table to her and said to Tina without even letting his eyes leave Marsha's face, we'll be back shortly Tina."

Tina's feelings were rapidly being crushed. But she couldn't show it in front of Marsha. No one knew about her and Michael's relationship, so how could Marsha feel guilty over getting between Tina and Michael if she didn't know there was a Tina and Michael relationship? It was impossible. So Tina simply said, "Take your time and enjoy yourselves."

She pulled her lipstick out of her bag and began to put some on. As she slipped her tube of lipstick back into her handbag her friend Tom returned.

"Looks like you've been left all alone. May I join you?" Before she even answered he pulled out the chair next to her and sat down.

She purposely waited until he was seated to say, "Sure have a seat," and she started laughing. Tom laughed too.

"You are too much, Tina. Hey, let's dance. You aren't wore out yet are you?"

Tina looked over at the small dance floor and saw Michael and Marsha were dancing very closely. So she said, "Sure! Why not? And what's this wore out business?"

Tom grinned at her and gave her his hand as she stood. He led her onto the dance floor. He put his hands in the proper places for dancing with a friend but she suggested he put both hands on her back while she put her hands around his neck. This brought their bodies much closer together than they would have been if he had held her the way he originally was going to do. He paused and looked into her face and said,

"You surprise me. Somehow I didn't think you liked to cuddle close."

"Sure, why not. I'm in the mood tonight. Let's enjoy ourselves. It's not often we get the opportunity to dance together."

That was all the encouragement he needed. He pulled her up against him and she laid her forehead against his cheek. She was so much shorter than Tom that her cheek didn't even reach his. She noticed as they danced by Michael and Marsha, that Michael's head came up and he had a surprised expression on his face.

When the dance ended Tom asked if she would stay on the floor with him for the next one, and she did. As the next dance started Michael took Marsha to the table. He seated her and turned toward the dance floor. Suddenly he was beside Tina, tapping Tom on the shoulder and cutting in.

"That wasn't very nice," Tina told him. "You had a dance partner. What happened?"

"Maybe I don't like another man dancing with my future wife. I can get rather jealous sometimes." He was holding her closely and looking down into her face.

"Maybe you should have thought about that before you asked someone to dance that wasn't the lady you think you're going to marry. I would have thought you would have wanted to dance with me the first time on the floor. But I guess I was mistaken. Maybe I was mistaken about a lot of things."

"Tina! What are you saying? Are you upset that I danced with Marsha before I danced with you? Why? You know I belong to you, heart and soul."

"Well don't look now but your heart, and maybe your soul were having too good of a time with your new Assistant Personnel Manager. And your Personnel Manager was left all alone to fend for herself. But as soon as someone paid her any attention you come running. Is there something wrong with this picture?"

"I'm sorry Sweetheart. I guess I just got a big head, having two such beautiful ladies on my hands."

"Well this lady would like very much to go home and not be on your hands, or in your hair. I thought you said you hated attending one of these things? But now it seems as though you aren't in any rush to leave. I think I'll just have the chauffeur drive me home, then come back to pick you two up. I suspect you and Marsha have a lot to talk about and don't need a third party around."

"Oh God, Tina, I didn't mean for this to go this far. She and I were joking around. I thought it was safe because you and she are friends and you and I were secure. But I didn't think I was hurting your feelings. Forgive me Honey? We'll all leave right after this dance. I don't want to jeopardize our relationship. Please Honey, don't be mad at me. We'll drop Marsha off then go to my place so I can pick up my car. Then we can go to your place."

"No Michael, we'll reverse the way the chauffeur went earlier. You'll drop me off first, then you and Marsha can do your thing. I don't think I want to be a silent partner to all of this. You'll be free to spend time with the lady you want to spend time with." With that said she dropped her hand from his and stepped away from him, headed for the table.

Michael followed her back to their chairs. Instead of sitting down he looked over at Marsha and asked, "About ready to call it a night?"

Marsha's face registered surprise but quickly covered it with, "Yes. Of course. I have a babysitter with my daughter, so I guess I ought to be getting back. But Marsha knew she had told Tina that the babysitter was sleeping over so there wasn't a problem. Yet she didn't mention that.

Michael reached into his pocket and found the small pager and pushed the button twice. That was the signal for the chauffeur to bring the car up so hopefully it would be there when he and his two ladies came out the door.

Both women grabbed their handbags and turned to leave. At that moment Tom walked up to Tina.

"Ill give you a call Tina. Thanks for the dance. See you Michael, and your lovely date. Talk to you later, Tina. Good night."

Michael grabbed Tina's arm and stepped over to Marsha. He grasped her arm as well and started for the door without a word to Tom. Both women looked up at their boss and saw a look of absolute consternation on his face. He walked them quickly to the exit and stood with them for the two or three minutes it took for their limo to get up to the loading area. As soon as the chauffeur opened the door Michael put Marsha in first, then Tina. He followed her in, wanting to sit beside Tina, and only Tina. He knew he was in trouble. He had been in seventh heaven having two gorgeous gals with him and he had treated the love of his life shabbily and hurt her feelings. She was the last person in the world he would want to wound in any way. She carried his heart within hers, even if she didn't know it. So now he was going to have to pay for acting so stupid.

Marsha chatted with Tina all the way to Tina's house. The chauffeur opened the door and Michael slid out, turning to grasp Tina's hand to help her out. Softly he whispered to her, "I'll call you as soon as I get to my place."

"Don't bother, I'll be in bed already. I don't think I'm in any mood to talk to you tonight, Michael." She turned and walked toward her door, opening her purse to get her key out. He didn't even walk me to my door, the louse! She waved at the two of them as she entered her townhouse.

Tina locked the door behind her and walked through the darkened room to the stairs. She thought she could tell just where the first step was and proceeded to jam her toe into the back of the step. "Oh!" she cried out. "Darn that Michael anyway."

She went up the stairs and to her bedroom. She didn't even feel like turning on any lights. She didn't want to see anything but forgetfulness. She slipped out of her clothes and tossed them on the chair. Finding her gown under her pillow she slipped it on and went to the bathroom to brush her teeth.

Falling into bed Tina found she had the beginning of a headache. She rubbed her temples and was getting ready to curl up on her side to try and go to sleep when the phone rang.

She reached over to the phone on the table next to her bed. Picking up the receiver she said, "Hello"

"Christina? This is Jefferson. Were you in bed?"

"Yes, I just laid down. Are you in your hotel room now?" she asked him

"Yes! I just wish I was where you are. Christina, there is so much I have to tell you. I don't suppose I could get a cab at this hour. Can I see you first thing in the morning? I could be there right after you get back from your run!"

"Oh Jeff, I'm not sure I'll be going for a run in the morning. I seem to have a terrible headache. I think it might be from the wine. And all of the excitement! But please, come over as soon as you're up. Just give me a call so I know you're on your way so I don't take off to the grocery store and miss you. Oh Jeff,…" Her voice broke and she almost cried.

"Maybe I ought to come now. You don't sound so good. Maybe if I just hold you, Tina you'll feel better."

"I'll be all right. I just need some sleep. But Jeff,…I'm glad you came through. I can't wait to see you, and touch you to make sure it's really you."

"I know what you mean Christina. I want to touch you too. You don't know how long I've been searching for you. You just relax so that headache goes away. That reminds me of when you came through the hole in time. We have to talk about that too, Tina. Rest and get rid of the headache and I'll be there early in the morning. And Christina, …I have missed you."

"I've missed you too. And I've thought about you often. The worst part was thinking you were probably gone from this world by now. I couldn't stand the thought of that. Stay safe and I'll see you in the morning, Jeff."

"Sleep well my precious Christina. Dream of me. Good night!"

Tina lay on her pillow thinking about the portal in time. She realized it hadn't closed up after she passed thorough it. She wondered if it was still open. As she pondered over that possibility she began to feel her headache getting worse. She lifted her hand to bring it to her temple to rub it and she noticed her hand was shimmering. Quickly she sat up in bed. That scared her. She had only thought about it and it seemed as though by only doing that, just thinking about the portal, her thoughts brought it to her. She knew it was beside the bed right now because as she moved her hand toward the right side of her bed her hand and arm shimmered again as though it was entering the portal. She hoped it wouldn't suck her in to it. This could be dangerous, she thought. She forced herself to think of other things, then placed her hand by the right side of her bed again to see if the portal was still there. It was gone. So apparently she could summon it to her by just thinking about it, and she would know it was there by the headache and moving her hand around her until it shimmered, showing her the location of the portal.

Tina laid back down on her pillow as her phone rang again. She picked it up and said, "Hello?"

"Tina, Sweetheart! I'm glad you're still awake. I had to call you. I need to talk to you, Honey. Would it be all right if I come over?"

"Michael! It's late! And I'm not sure I want to hear what you have to say. What could you possibly have to say that could make the situation any better?"

"Just for a few minutes? I just have to see you, Hon. You don't know how sorry I am about tonight. Say it's all right I come over. I can be there in a couple of minutes."

"A couple of minutes?" She laughed. "That would mean you had to be at the curb. No Michael, I know your place is across town and it would take too long to get here. I'd probably be asleep by then."

"Go to the door, Sweetheart. Just go to the door."

"All right. I don't understand, but all right."

"You won't be sorry, I promise, Hon."

Tina slid out of bed and headed for the stairs. She flipped on lights as she went. She decided she didn't want to smash her toe again.

She approached her front door and turned on her porch light so she could see if anyone was out there. When she looked through her peep hole Michael stood on the other side of her door. She shut the light out and opened the door.

Michael stood looking at Tina. She was the most beautiful woman he had ever laid eyes on. How could he have gotten so carried away so as to hurt her feelings? He didn't know. All he knew at the moment was that he had to make it up to her. He couldn't bear the thought that one evening of acting silly could cost him so much. He never dreamed that she would be jealous of Marsha, just because he was over zealous with the hope of Mr. Marlboro becoming part of the company.

They just stood and looked at each other. Finally he said, "May I come in?"

Tina said "Yes. Come in." She reached for his hand. Suddenly he had tears in his eyes and he rushed to her, pulling her into his arms. He felt as though he wanted to take her into himself. To become one with her. He kissed the top of her head and slid his hands down her upper arms. He lifted her chin with his fingers and as he peered into her eyes he told her, "I'm so sorry, Honey. Can you forgive me? I was just feeling so good, I guess I just took you for granted. I didn't mean to hurt you. You're the best thing that ever happened to me. Tell me you forgive me, Baby."

"Okay, Michael. I forgive you. But don't ever do it again. Do you have any idea how I felt? It wasn't just one thing. You kept joking around with her and didn't include me so it made me feel like an outsider. Then you danced with her before even thinking of dancing with me. And when I came back to the table you didn't get up like you normally would have done, to seat me. You ignored me and made me feel as though I was no longer important to you. I won't put up with that kind of treatment again. And when you brought me home, you didn't even care if I got into my home safely. You usually would have walked me to my door. Tonight you didn't leave the limo door, as if what was in the limo was more important to you than I. How do you think that made me feel?"

"I admit I messed up several times. But like I said, I didn't think you were that unsure of our commitment to each other that it would bother you like this."

"Are you telling me that you think this is my fault?" She pulled free of his arms and stepped back. "You're saying I'm to blame for all of this? Michael, I can't believe you're saying such a thing. Maybe you're not the man I thought you were. I thought I had a man in love with me that gave me unconditional love; that wanted to put me first, before job or other women. I wanted a relationship with a man that cherished me, like I thought I cherished you. Now I'm not sure there is such a thing in this world. Maybe I was wanting more than I had a right to demand or expect. And if that is the case, if I have to accept second best, and be with a man that will allow me to slip into second place in his heart every once and a while, then I don't want that man in my heart. I don't think I deserve treatment like that. I've never lied to you, or cheated on you or purposely hurt you in any way. And those are the attributes that I require in the man that I give my heart."

"I promise Sweetheart not to ever hurt you like this again. I never dreamed my actions were hurting you this evening. Not until you walked away from me on the dance floor. I thought we were more secure in our relationship than that. I guess I just wanted to make Marsha feel included, since you've raved about her ability on the job and since we were a couple this evening and she was alone. Since she was so important to you I didn't want her to feel like a fifth wheel. And I ended up hurting the one woman who means the most to me. I'll try to be more protective of our relationship in the future. I don't want to lose you, Hon."

"Come in Michael. We can sit for a minute or two and just talk, before I send you home."

"You frighten me, Tina. You sound a lot like my mother. You say you'll be sending me home, like I was a bad little boy." He looked at her, and all she could see was that little boy in a man's body that was doing his very best to get him self out of trouble.

Tina couldn't help but smile at him. She felt very much like his mother at that moment, and she just wanted to hug him and forgive him. But she wasn't his mom, she was the woman that he had said he wanted for his wife, and no wife wanted to be treated the way he had treated her this evening. But she couldn't help herself. Maybe it was the mother in her that made her do it. She stepped forward grabbing his shirt in her fist.

She tried to look tough as she looked him in the eye. "Okay Mr. Thorpe, one more chance for you. Now don't mess up!" Then she lifted her lips to his and kissed him.

Those were the words he needed to hear. She was going to trust him once more. She forgave him. And he would try harder to be worthy of this very precious woman. "Thank you my Sweet. I promise you won't be sorry you forgive me." He wrapped his arms around her, pulling her tightly against his body.

Tina could feel his trembling. He really meant it, that he was sorry. Now she was glad she had forgiven him. She dropped her head down against his chest. "Michael, I'm so tired. I feel just drained. I think I'm going to send you home now."

"Yes Dear. I'll go now. You don't know how much your words mean to me. I'm glad we talked. At least now we better understand where each of us is coming from. Now I think I'll be able to sleep. Tomorrow is Saturday. Will you have dinner with me?"

"No, I don't think so. I think I need this weekend to do some figuring. I've got a lot on my mind right now Michael. Would you give me a little time to think things out?"

"Yes, of course. Whatever you need, Hon. I'll just go to the office and take care of a couple of things. And I have a meeting with Mr. Marlboro at two o'clock at my office anyway. I'll call you later Sunday, if that's all right with you."

"That would be fine. Go home and rest," she told him.

She walked him to the door and kissed him goodnight. She waited until he was in his car and she saw that the car's headlights came on. Then she waved and stepped back into the house. She locked the doors and started shutting off lights on her way back to bed.

Climbing into bed she thought about the portal, then immediately changed her thoughts to Jeff. She wondered if the portal came to him when he thought about it. She needed to talk to him.

The morning brought her the phone call she was expecting. She was still half asleep when she reached for the phone. "Hello?" she whispered.

Jeff laughed at her. "So you're still in bed?" He knew she was. He pictured her there and wished he could be beside her.

"Morning!" she managed to say. "What time is it?" She blinked her eyes trying to adjust to the light coming in the windows. The sky seemed overcast so that the sun hadn't broken through yet.

It's six thirty. I thought you usually got up early to run. What happened?" he asked.

"I just didn't feel like it this morning. Jeff,.." she paused, not sure how to tell him. "We need to talk."

"I know, Christina. How about if you get around and I'll come over and make the coffee. Mrs. Braxton taught me how. I can't guarantee it will be as good as hers, but I think I make a pretty good cup."

"That sounds wonderful. Do you have a car, or will you be taking a cab?"

"I have a rental car. It's quite a change from the one I had when you and I first met. I'm still amazed at some of the things I'm seeing here in your time. Or rather, should I say, our time now."

She found out where his hotel was located and gave him directions to get to her place. When she got off the phone she went quickly to her shower and turned on the hot water.

She felt certain that they needed to discuss the portal, among other things.

She enjoyed washing the smell of cigarette smoke out of her hair from the previous evening. The warm water running over her scalp felt comforting. She hurried around and was just coming down the stairs when she heard her doorbell ring.

She opened the door and there stood the most handsome man. He stood six foot three or four at least and she just stood and looked at him in wonder that she was actually seeing him. He was truly real. She couldn't move. Then tears began pouring from her eyes and she had to reach out to him. He gathered her into his arms.

"Come here, Sweetheart. It's all right now. I'm real! You can feel me!" He hugged her tightly and kissed the top of her head.

Tina couldn't get the tears stopped. She knew she was soaking his shirt but she didn't care. She somehow felt certain that he didn't care either. Finally her tears stopped and he took her by her upper arms and leaned her away from him.

"And now your eyes are all red. But I'm happy to see them anyway. Can I come in?"

"Oh, I'm sorry Jeff. I just got carried away. Of course, come in. I want you to see my home. Remember, I told you it wasn't anywhere as big as your home, but I like it."

"If it's yours, then that's all that matters. Just finding you means so much to me. You have to know, that was why I came through. It was so frightening, but I figured that if you could do it, then I could do no less. I had to find you, Christina. Once you were gone I knew I couldn't live without you. You were too important to me. I had to have you in my life again. Even if you decided you didn't want a personal relationship with me."

She wasn't sure how to answer his comment about a personal relationship, so she didn't address it.

Tina had her tears under control now and she grabbed his hand and pulled him in to her home. As soon as the door closed behind him she dragged him to the kitchen. She began pulling out her coffee and pointed toward her coffee maker. Are you sure you know how to do this?" she asked.

"Absolutely! Just take a seat while I do my magic." She sat on one of the tall stools she had sitting at her tall counter, and watched him work. He shed his jacket, loosened his tie and rolled up his sleeves. He stepped to the sink and rinsed his hands and grabbed a paper towel to dry them. Then he began to make a pot of coffee.

He moved around her kitchen as though he felt very comfortable there. She liked that. When he finally threw the switch to start the coffee brewing he turned to her and smiled.

Jeff very much wanted to know if she loved him. He already knew his heart needed hers. But he would keep his word. If she told him that he could only be her friend, then he would settle for that. He didn't have to get married. He had already moved into his posterity. He didn't need children to carry on his name, he was doing it personally. By all rights he should be dead now. He was actually one hundred and twenty seven years old.

Tina returned his smile, which somehow caused his feet to start moving toward her. He stood directly in from of her and reached out to take hold of her arms in both of his hands. He wanted very much to hold her, but she didn't give him the feeling that it was on her mind at the moment. So he waited.

"Jeff!" she started. "Sit with me. I have to ask you something."

He sat in the stool next to hers. He could hear the coffee starting to bubble and perk. The kitchen was beginning to have the smell of fresh brewed coffee. He kept his hands on her arms. He felt as though he needed the contact with her. He still didn't feel completely sure he was actually with her again.

Watching her face felt so right to him. He liked the way her face relayed all that she was thinking. He could see that there was a problem. He wanted to help her solve it and relieve her from the pressure of it. So he waited for her to find the words she needed to tell him.

"Jeff, I know you went back to the hole in time so you could come here. I'm supposing you went to the same place we did when I returned through the portal. Is that correct?"

"Yes! That's correct. I went there with the distinct purpose of coming through time to try to find you."

Have you thought about it since then?" she asked.

"Thought about what? Do you mean, do I regret coming through time to you?"

"No, I mean, have you thought about the portal since coming through it?" She watched his face to see if he might give away that he now knew it could be summoned to wherever he was at the moment, but nothing crossed his expression that might give that information away.

She wasn't sure how to get the information out of him, so she decided to just be direct and tell him what happened last night. She couldn't help but wonder how he was going to take it that she summoned it to her just last night.

"Let me tell you what happened to me last night. I've been thinking about this for a while and last night I had a pretty scary thing happen." She could see confusion on his face. Perhaps he wasn't aware of her concern. "You see," she started. "You see, I was thinking about the portal last night before I went to sleep and it came to me."

"What came to you?" he asked.

"The portal!" She waited for his reaction.

"What do you mean it came to you?"

"I was thinking about you returning to it when you came over, and my head began to ache. Remember how I fainted and had that awful headache after going through it?"

"Yes! I remember being concerned that you were actually unconscious for quite a while. I was a little worried for a while there."

"Did you have a headache when you passed through?"

"Just a dull ache. I didn't black out like you did. And the pain passed within minutes. Why?"

"Have you thought about it since?" she asked. She was hoping he would just blurt it out that he found out when he thought about it, it would summon the thing to him, but he didn't say anything about it.

"I don't think it was the same for you as it was for me," she told him. "I don't know how to tell you so you'll understand. So just watch!"

She closed her eyes and thought about the portal. In only a moment she could feel the pain starting in her temples. She reached up and rubbed them. Then she felt his warm hands over her own, trying to help her sooth away her suffering. Apparently he could tell she was in pain. She opened her eyes and looked at him. He was watching her very closely. It was there in his eyes. He wanted to take away her pain but didn't know how.

She moved her hand around where she sat to locate the portal. Directly in front of her, her hand began to shimmer. Immediately her eyes went to his. "Did you see that?" She wanted to know if he saw her hand shimmer, which was the sign that her hand was entering the hole in time.

"My gosh, Christina. What's going on?" He looked at her, waiting for an explanation.

"I've summoned it to me. Can you do it?" she asked.

"Do that? No! I don't know how. How did you do that?"

"I didn't know I could until last night. I was just lying there thinking about it when the headache started and I just happened to move my hand across the blanket on the side of my bed and I saw my hand shimmer. It scared the stuffing out of me. I was afraid it was going to suck me into it. Then I tried to get calm and think of other things, and it just went away. Try it and see if you can summon it. Give me a moment to clear my head and think of something else so it will leave."

She looked at Jeff's lips and thought about how good they would feel on her own. Suddenly she realized her headache was gone. She moved her hand in front of her and there wasn't any shimmering. The portal was gone.

"Okay,' she said. "It's gone. You try to summon it."

She watched as he closed his eyes and thought about the hole in time. He waited for the headache to come but it didn't. Finally he opened his eyes and waved his hand all around his body looking for the portal. Nothing happened. Apparently he could not summon it.

"I don't think I can do what you just did. Do you think it was because you've gone through it twice and I've only gone through it once?"

"I don't know. But I can't help but wonder what passing through it does to our bodies. It could actually be doing damage that we don't know about. It could affect our brain or even our organs. We just don't know."

"This is amazing, Christina."

"Yes, it is. And I'm not sure if I'm glad I can do this. Actually, I wish it would go away and leave me alone. It's a little frightening. I could dream of it in my sleep and get up to the bathroom and just walk right in to it and simply disappear. But, I suppose, wherever I went, if I thought of it there, I could summon it and it would come back. It appears whatever time

I am thinking of just before I summon it, is where it takes me. I had been thinking of 1912 when it swept me to you. I'm just grateful it didn't take me to the deck of the Titanic itself."

"Christina, this is something that we should share with a scientist. I'm sure they would want to study this, to see if other people could do the same as you."

"I agree with you that we should let someone wiser than we are know about this. But I'm afraid someone without honor might attempt to use it to their own advantage. And perhaps even alter history. Or they might attempt to use it to gain power. Thinking about such a thing makes me wonder if the world is ready for such a thing. Perhaps the government might be a better place to start with this knowledge. Someone we trust." The last thing she wanted to do was allow someone to use this ability inappropriately.

"Actually, I suspect not everyone will be able to call the portal. As you see, I can not, yet you can. There must be a reason for that, but we may never know what it is."

"You may be right, Jeff. But to whom would we take this information? I wouldn't know where to start."

"Since I've come to this time, Christina, I have met some very interesting and powerful people, simply because they wanted their hands on my money, giving them more power. Along the way I have met some men in government that might be interested in this discovery. Once we share this with them or whomever, I would suggest we require a legal document drawn up releasing us from the actions of others in regard to this discovery. That way, if anyone uses the portal for power or their own gain we have something in our possession that exonerates us from their actions."

"I agree! That sounds like a good idea. But how do we do all of this, Jefferson?"

He looked at her in surprise. He couldn't help but smile at her.

"What is it? Did I say something silly?" she asked.

"Did you hear what you just called me?" he asked. "I thought you didn't prefer my long name. I thought you preferred short names that were easy to say and remember. Do you know what I think? I think you're beginning to feel much more comfortable with me, to the point that either name is now comfortable for you to use. And I like that. I'm hoping that you will soon feel comfortable enough with me that we might become better, closer friends." He continued to smile at her with what looked like a secret smile.

"I do feel comfortable with you. I love being with you. Truly! You're actually my very best friend. Why wouldn't you be? You cared for me when I couldn't care for myself, and you didn't have to. You didn't even know me, yet you cared for me. You have no idea how much that means to me. Most people would just have taken advantage of my situation and used it to please themselves, but not you. That's one of the things I love about you."

"Thank you, Christina. Your words warm my heart."

"So where do we go from here? Can you contact someone you think would be trustworthy to share this with?"

"Yes, I think so. There's a gentleman that is looking into para-normal things in relation to history. He studies how it has been used by different peoples in the past. He works at one of the large colleges. I'll make a point of contacting him and set up an appointment. And he probably will want to bring in other scientists, or government officials that may want to look into this."

"I just don't want to be thought of as a freak. You know, sometimes they lock up people who say they can do such things. And there was a story once about a man who had so much power he could do all sorts of things just with his mind, and they froze him and sliced up his brain to study it. I don't want to give my life for this craziness. I just want to share it, then be allowed to live my life, whatever I choose it to be."

"I understand. Nor would you want to become a government safety concern, or be in jeopardy of being kidnapped by unscrupulous characters from other countries. Perhaps we ought to not include the government in this and just stay within the scientific community. I don't want this to take over our lives." The more she thought about it, the more invasive it appeared to possibly become.

"Never fear, I think I can handle that end of it. Let me talk with a certain gentleman and we can take it from there. Now, we need to just enjoy this coffee I've made. You do want some don't you?"

"I can't start my day without it! So you say Mrs. Braxton taught you her talent?"

"Yes, a little part of it, that is. A good basic cup of coffee." He walked over to the pot that had finished brewing and poured some into the two cups he had sitting on the counter. Picking them both up he returned to the stools and placed one in front of Tina. "I seem to remember you like it black."

"Yes. If I'm going to drink coffee, I'd like it to taste like coffee, not milk, or sugar or other flavors. But I suspect the majority of people around here would disagree with me."

"That may be true. From what I've seen, there are a lot of flavored coffees available. I've notice there are a couple of major companies that sell pretty much, just coffee drinks, and have made it into a big business."

Tina sipped her coffee, then looked up at Jeff. This is really good! What did you do? When I make it, it isn't this good."

"Sometimes the smallest thing can make such a difference," he told her, smiling.

"So tell me this small difference that you did this morning. I thought I watched you make that pot of coffee, yet I didn't notice you do anything special."

"Ah, but I'm sure you did see, only your conscious mind didn't expect it, so you didn't absorb the fact. Do you see what is setting on the counter next to the coffee maker?"

Tina looked over toward the pot of coffee that was being kept warm and then to what sat next to it. There sat a salt shaker.

"Salt? You put salt in my coffee?"

"Just the tiniest amount. Just enough to absorb any bitterness that might have been in the machine or pot." He couldn't help but grin at her. He liked sharing secrets with her.

"And that was all it took to make such a good cup of coffee?"

"Sometimes!" he told her. "And sometimes just a dash of cinnamon will do the same thing, but add a special festive flavor. I like it like that at Christmas time."

"Wow! This is amazing. I'll have to remember this. Or keep you around to make my coffee for me."

Jeff couldn't help but smile because that was just what he wanted to have happen. He would gladly make coffee for her every day of her life if it meant having her to share his life with. "You see how valuable I am. Now I'm indispensable. You need me Christina!" And he laughed softly.

"I guess you're right. She leaned over and gave him a kiss on the mouth. But as soon as their lips touched sparks seemed to start to fly. He gathered her into his arms, pulling her against him. She slid off of her stool and was pulled up against him to stand between his knees. His arms were around her and his lips were taking her to the sky. There seemed to be fireworks going off all around them. Then he released her and they floated back to earth.

Tina stood quietly before him just looking at him. She blinked slowly trying to understand what had just happened.

Jeff left his arms around her loosely, allowing her to recognize what was between them. He didn't speak. He wanted to hear what she was thinking. He hadn't meant for the kiss to get so out of control, but it had happened anyway. Surely she had to know now how he felt about her.

Tina moved forward as though she didn't want the moment to end. She moved as though she wasn't really aware of what she was doing. She was just following instinct. She moved her left shoulder forward, than her right, as though she had actually taken two steps toward him, but her feet hadn't moved. Her head came down onto his chest and he tightened his arms around her. Again she snuggled against him. His hand came up and rested on her back, the other on the back of her head. And he just held her.

Tina let her arms go around Jeff's waist and she squeezed him. She was like a little kitten that wanted to get closer. And he wanted to accommodate her.

They stayed like that for a couple of minutes, before she seemed to wake up and pull back. As she did so he could see her face turning bright pink. She was embarrassed for kissing him and then cuddling with him. She had started it, not him. He knew she had to feel she had done something wrong. That it was the man's place to pursue a woman, not a woman's place to do what she had just done. She seemed very shy.

"It's all right Christina. It felt so good to me too." He didn't know what else to tell her, except that he wanted to carry her upstairs and make love to her. Real love, not just sex. And he wanted to meet her in the church and change her name to his, so she would always be able to cuddle with him, and never feel guilty about it.

"I'm sorry," she said softly as she pulled back further. "I don't know what came over me. I just meant to give you a little kiss for making such great coffee, and then,…"

"It's all right Christina. I wanted it too. Couldn't you feel it? I've wanted to kiss you ever since you left me back in 1912."

"But that's crazy! Why would you want to do that?" She just couldn't fathom why her best friend wanted such a thing from her. It didn't enter her mind that they were attracted to each other.

"Christina! Do you have any idea why I came through the portal?"

"Because you wanted to see all the things I had told you about, and wanted to try it for yourself. And maybe, to see if you could be successful here as you were there?"

"Yes, you could say all that is true. But before all of that, I came for you. I tried to call you back, just as you shimmered away from me. I guess you didn't hear me. I suddenly realized I didn't want to lose my best friend."

"Am I that?" she asked. "I hadn't thought of it from your point of view. I just thought you were only interested in helping me, and then learning more."

"I learned enough about you the short time I knew you, that I wanted to be around you always. As your best friend, or as something more, if you were interested, Christina." He simply looked at her, watching her reaction. She obviously hadn't considered anything more than just a friendship with him.

"Jeff?" she said softly. "You make rockets go off in my head when we kissed. You made me feel differently. I've trusted you right from the start. Now, I wonder if there is something more for us." She felt stunned by this sudden knowledge. She just assumed she would return to this world and marry Michael. But after last evening she had doubts about that. So was she acting on the 'rebound' here? She didn't want to rush into something and be sorry later. But she did so enjoy the feeling Jeff gave her when he pulled her into his arms. She liked the feel of his hard chest and his strong arms holding her secure.

She reached out to take his hand in hers. He wrapped both of his large hands around her little one. Her eyes drifted to his lips and her other hand reached up to touch those magical lips. She slid her index finger across his bottom lip, causing him to smile at her. She looked into his eyes and saw infinite patience and caring. She thought she saw acceptance there as well.

Jeff opened his mouth and drew her finger into his mouth. He sucked on it, causing a tingling feeling to go right up her arm and straight to her heart. Then she watched as he moved forward to place his lips on hers. That was when her arms went around his neck and she pulled him closer.

As the kiss ended, gentle though it may have been, she felt power coming from him. He made her feel safe, and as though he was going to take care of things and keep her safe and protected. And now she knew she wanted that. This was a good man, a man of honor, that she could put complete trust in. And she would.

"Yes!" she told him.

"Yes, what?" he asked her.

"Yes, I trust you, Jeff. Only you! So what are we going to do about this mess?" She sat back on her stool and looked him in the eye with absolute confidence in whatever he was going to suggest.

"I'll make a call. Then we'll go see this gentleman I know. We'll take one step at a time with this."

"And you'll be with me all the way?"

"Yes! There's no doubt about it. We'll see this through together." He smiled at her. He felt certain she was beginning to love him. He knew she already trusted him. And that meant a lot. No matter what, they would see this through together. He would protect her as best he could through whatever madness may arise. And he felt certain it would try.

Chapter 17

Jeff made the phone call to his associate about the portal. The man didn't really want to believe that such a thing was possible. After a little discussion about taking this unbelievable find to another man who would be happy to expand the study and get some of the accolades for the findings of this amazing historical portal, he agreed to meet with Jeff and Tina the following afternoon at his office.

Sunday after noon at three o'clock found the two of them in front of one of the oldest colleges in the state. They climbed out of Jeff's rental car and walked into the impressive looking old red brick building. They both knew this might be a bit difficult for Tina, but she said she was willing to do this as long as Jeff was beside her. They had agreed not to mention that Jeff had also come through the portal, because it would invalidate his credentials otherwise.

Walking down the hallowed hall Tina began to feel nervous and her stomach was roiling. She vowed to her self that she would see this through and not be sick or faint. But she could see it was going to be difficult. Jeff squeezed her hand and smiled at her just before he opened the office door. Then they walked in. Neither knew how much trepidation the other was feeling at the moment.

The gentleman behind the desk stepped forward and grasped Jeff's hand firmly. Jeff turned to Tina and introduced her.

"This is my dear friend Miss Christina Taylor, Doctor. She has been the happy, or rather, at the time, unhappy individual that traveled through time and space, and located the portal in time."

"Good afternoon Doctor Bernard. It's a pleasure to meet you. Thank you for agreeing to see us on a Sunday. It would be difficult to get away from my work during the week."

"And what type of work do you do, Miss Taylor?" He expected to hear she was a scientist of some sort.

"I'm the Personnel Manager at Hart Personnel Development Corporation." She was proud of her work and it showed in her face.

Doctor Bernard paled for a moment. He wasn't ready to hear that her employment had nothing to do with her discovery. He was shocked.

"Are you all right, Doctor," Jeff asked immediately seeing the man pale so suddenly.

"Yes, yes, of course! I was simply surprised that this lovely young woman wasn't actively engaged in scientific study in an adjacent field when she made this momentous discovery. To be working in a field that has absolutely nothing to do this finding amazes me."

"It wasn't as if I was looking for a tear in time, Doctor. It just seemed to find me. Or rather, I seemed to stumble into it. I actually found it in my office while working at my desk," she informed him.

"Do tell? How amazing! Please, come in and sit with me. We must discuss this thoroughly. I want to know all of it."

Jeff seated her in one of the two wooden chairs in front of the doctor's desk, then sat in the chair beside her. He reached over and placed his hand over hers as the doctor returned to his seat behind the desk.

"Well, young lady, tell me what you were doing when this amazing phenomenon occurred." He placed his hands together on top of his desk and eyed her suspiciously.

"Actually I was just doing my job. I was working on some paperwork that I needed to get finished as soon as possible and I was looking forward to doing it." Tina lost eye contact with the doctor and glanced down into her lap. Seeing Jeff's large hand lying over hers gave her confidence.

"Yes, and had you had any premonition of something present around your proximity?"

"Not that I recall. I had noticed shimmering of light waves and distortion of whatever was within my vision. That had happened twice before but of course I wasn't aware at the time of what they represented. You see I was having a terrible headache when that happened."

"And did you have a headache the time that you actually entered the time warp?" he asked.

"Yes, I did. But you see, at the time I wasn't putting all these things together. I was struggling to just stay conscious and functioning. I really had no idea what was taking place."

"And what did you do as the papers in front of you shimmered?"

"I began to feel as though I was falling. But I couldn't see how that could be possible since I was sitting in a chair at the time. But as the feeling became more pronounced I started to grab onto anything that I could to try to stop it."

"And when you found you couldn't stop it, were you aware of movement of any kind? Were you able to see anything, such as a tunnel, or lights, as you moved through time?"

"I don't recall any. I think I fainted. The pain in my head was so unbearable that I believe I fainted. The other two times that I had an encounter with what we now are calling 'the portal', I fainted, or almost fainted. The pressure in my head was enormous."

"I see. And when you arrived at your destination, were you aware at that point? Were you awake and conscious when you arrived?"

"No, I don't think so. I don't remember landing there. When I awoke, I was seated on the ground, but I was so ill I almost couldn't think straight."

"Did you receive any insight as to where you were going before or during your travel? Was there any premonition of anything about to occur?" He leaned forward in his chair, as if to glean more from her words.

"Before it happened I had had a thought about the year 1912. I had thought about what it might be like to live there, at that time. I suspect that was what made the portal take me there. As I sat on the ground trying to wake up and rouse myself enough so I could think clearly I could hear the sound of an automobile coming toward me on a dirt road. I couldn't see it, but I could hear it. It took me a while just to get on my feet. I think I may have fallen again after I stood. I remember being very dizzy."

"And what happened when the,…automobile approached you?"

"I heard, because I couldn't focus enough to see clearly, I heard the engine stop and a man came up to me and asked me if I was all right, and what was I doing out in the middle of no where."

"And then what happened?"

"I'm not sure. I remember feeling terribly cold. Perhaps he wrapped something around me. I'm sure he could see I was shaking and chilled. I remember reaching up to him, for him to help me up from the ground. I think he picked me up."

"And then,.."

"Well, I assume he put me in his car. I think he may have laid me down, because I don't recall seeing anything, or even feeling the movement. I suspect I passed out."

"And when you came to, Miss Taylor, where were you?"

"I was in a bed at the gentleman's home. His housekeeper was with me. Apparently I was out for several hours. I remember being very weak and lightheaded."

"I see. And how long were you a guest in this gentleman's home?"

"I believe two days. The first day, after I was feeling better I requested he take me back to the area where he had found me. We sectioned it off and began to pace it in rows, covering the entire ground area to try and find the exact spot of the portal, if it was still there and open."

"And were you able to locate it, Miss Taylor?"

"No! We didn't find it. We discussed the possibility that that wasn't the right spot. So the next day we went there again, and paced off an adjacent area just like we had done the day before in the other area."

"And were you able to locate it that time?"

"Yes, we did. Actually I had told him of the shimmering so we watched each other for any signs of shimmering, or partial disappearance, and he almost walked right into it."

"And then what did you do?"

"I rushed over to him, and thanked him for his kindness, and stepped into the portal. My headache came back full force and I ended up back in my office, at my desk, at almost the same moment I left. I checked the time and the date immediately to be sure."

"And did you share this information with anyone at work?"

"Are you nuts? No, of course not! I'm sure they would have thought I was having a breakdown."

"Forgive me Miss Taylor, but have you had a break with reality?"

Tina looked at him in shock. Then the shock turned to anger. "Mr. Bernard, I did not come here to be insulted. I wished to give this information to someone who would appreciate knowing about the possibilities of time travel. If you wish to insult me, then our meeting is over." She stood, ready to leave.

"Please, Miss Taylor, I had no intention of insulting your honor. I'm sure you must realize that this is very hard to believe. It would seem an impossible thing to be able to do. Please, sit down. Let's discuss this calmly. I had to ask you that, because if you had ever had a break with reality in the past, it could have created an illusion that might appear real to you. But since that is not the case here, we should proceed further."

Jeff had been quiet the entire time sitting with his hand covering hers. "Doctor, Miss Taylor informed me that last night she realized she could summon the portal to her. I think it might be beneficial to discuss that also."

"Let me understand this." He looked at Tina. "You're saying that you did not summon the portal to you the first time, but now you are able to do such a thing?"

"Yes, that's true Doctor. Would you like a demonstration?"

"You mean you could do it now, here?"

"Yes, absolutely! Give me a moment. But you must remain still. I would hate for you to disappear into time."

Doctor Bernard gave a nervous chuckle. "I would hate for that to happen as well."

Tina looked over at Jeff. He nodded at her calmly and gave her hands a gentle squeeze. Then Tina closed her eyes to shut out the world around her and thought about the portal, and the wonderful friend she had found in 1912. In only a moment she felt it. Her head began to throb and she opened her eyes. As she looked around her she stood. She swept her hand in large circles around her to locate the exact spot. When she had moved to the end of the doctor's desk she found it. Waving her hand she saw it shimmer and start to disappear. She looked over to the pale man sitting behind his desk and said, "Here it is, Doctor."

"My God! You weren't joking! Please, be careful there. Don't fall in, young woman."

Jeff had watched her closely. He saw the redness in her eyes, showing how much pain she was in when she summoned the portal. And as she had began to disappear into the portal he grabbed her clothes and quickly stood up to stand behind her, with his hands on both sides of her waist. He was not about to let her slip through time away from him.

The good doctor looked as though he was about to have a heart attack. He was standing at the corner of his desk, afraid to step too closely to the hole in time, for fear of falling into it. He swung his hand through the shimmering light and saw his own hand shimmer and disappear. He pulled it back quickly. He stepped back to his chair and collapsed. He believed!

"Get it out of here," he whispered. "Make it go away!"

Tina thought about how wonderful it felt to feel Jeff's lips on hers and she immediately began to feel the pressure in her head letting up. She now knew that thinking about something other than the portal would allow it to drift away. She had no idea as to where, and wasn't sure she cared. Slowly she stepped back to her chair, sat down and placed her face in her hands. She rubbed her temples to get some more relief. The effort was very stressful. Now all she wanted to do was sleep until the pain and exhaustion dropped away.

Jeff huddled close to her, constantly keeping his hand on her. He knew that just feeling his touch helped her get relief.

And it seemed to calm him as well. It was as if she was a part of him, and when that part hurt, he hurt as well.

"I think I should take her home now Doctor. She needs to rest. This is extremely hard on her. We'll talk again." He leaned over the man's desk to shake his hand and turned to lift Tina from her chair. He could tell she was so weak she would not be able to walk to the car. He pulled her close to his chest. She felt good there, where he could feel the fever radiating from her from the strain. He knew that soon she would be chilled and needing warmth, and lots of sleep.

The doctor rushed to open the door for them and walked with them to the main exit which led to the sidewalk. "Is she going to be all right?"

"Yes, but doing this takes it's toll on her. She'll need some time to recover. I hope you'll think about the possibilities here. I'm looking forward to hearing from you after you have spoken with your colleagues on this matter. Thank you for your time, Doctor."

"Yes, yes, by all means, Mr. Marlboro. This is stupendous! I can't wait to talk to some of the other doctor's and scientists in the field. I'm sure they'll want to see this for themselves. I'll be in touch with you."

Jeff carried her to his car. He had a little difficulty unlocking the door while he held her in his arms, but he refused to ask her to stand in her weakened condition. He now knew what to expect, and that included a very strong possibility that she would pass out, and he was not taking any chances of her falling.

Jefferson Marlboro was a very strong man. His six foot four frame was solid with muscle. He was accustomed to using his strength at his home, and since traveling to this time, he continued to work out, even though it was in his own gym with machines helping him to use his muscles as he had used them before to maintain his property. He gently laid Tina on the back seat and covered her with a blanket that he had brought, specifically for that use. He also had a pillow for beneath her head.

Jeff tucked the blanket around this very special woman, talking softly to her, but uncertain if she was hearing him.

"It's all right Darling. I'm here with you. We're going to go to your place and let you rest. I'll drive as carefully as I can to make it as smooth a ride as possible. These new automobiles are so much smoother riding that the one I carried you in the last time. But I promise to take very good care of you. Just relax and rest. I'll have you home soon. Rest, my Sweet. How I hate to see you hurting like that. Just rest."

He closed the door and walked around to the driver's door, sliding in quickly to start the engine and get moving. He liked the idea of having seatbelts. That was one thing his automobile back in 1912 didn't have, and he remembered thinking about it when he had placed her in the vehicle before. Funny how need made man create things.

He moved quickly into traffic and headed for her townhouse. He hoped she wouldn't be ill on the way. He seemed to recall she had told him before that she had been sick to her stomach. He made his turns gently, hoping to not create any adverse vertigo.

Before too long he was pulling into her driveway and parking his vehicle. He knew that she preferred he leave his vehicle in an adjacent parking spot, but he wanted to get as close to her front door as he could, to carry her inside quickly. Besides, she wasn't about to be driving away in her own car this afternoon. So it shouldn't be a problem that he had blocked her vehicle in. She might not even make it to work the following day.

Jeff searched in her purse for the key to her front door. He opened it and tossed her purse onto the nearest chair. Then he returned to the car to carry her in. He pushed the door shut with his foot and continued up the stairs to place her on her bed. He didn't have a housekeeper to undress her so she might be more comfortable, so he just removed her shoes and covered her with the blanket from the foot of the bed.

Jeff sat on the edge of the bed and held her hand. He reached over to brush her hair from her face. Slowly her eyes came open. She was looking directly at him.

Jeff hoped she could see all the love shinning out of his eyes for her. He wanted to wrap her up and keep her free from pain and fear. But he knew he couldn't do that. At least, not yet.

"Thank you Jeff. Once again you've proven yourself a special friend. I know I couldn't have done this without you with me."

"I want to be more than just a friend, Christina. Certainly you must know that by now. But we can talk about it later. Right now I just want you to rest. Do you need some medicine for your headache?"

"Yes, that would help. There's some Excedrin in the medicine cabinet in the bathroom." She closed her eyes as soon as she quit talking. He suspected she was still feeling quite ill.

Jeff headed into the bathroom and found the medication. He filled a glass with water and walked back to her side. Setting the glass and two pills on the table by the bed he helped her sit up so she could take the pills. She weaved as though she was drunk and he tried to steady her. He was afraid the extra vertigo might make her more ill.

Jeff held the glass to her lips after she had put one of the pills in her mouth. He held the glass for her even though her hand was there, he knew she probably could not hold it by herself. After the second pill was down he laid her back on the pillow and returned the glass to the bathroom. He grabbed a washcloth and rinsed it in warm water. Returning to the bed he washed her face gently and patted it dry with a soft towel he had seized as he left the bathroom.

He watched as her eyes opened slowly. He could still see some red in the whites of her eyes, reflecting the high level of pain she was experiencing. He sat beside her and just held her hand. As he sat with her he heard her doorbell ring. He thought about ignoring it, but then remembered he had not locked it when he had brought her in. Tucking the blanket around her he went to see who might be at her door on a Sunday afternoon.

Just as he reached the bottom of the stairs the front door opened and Mr. Michael Thorpe stepped in. Michael looked up, surprise showing on his face. "Mr. Marlboro? What are you doing here?"

"I've just laid Christina on her bed. She's quite ill. I might ask the same of you, Sir. Do you know Miss Taylor?"

"Yes, very well. She works for me. But I was unaware that you knew her. You say she's ill? I don't understand. She didn't seem like she was a sickly person. But these past few days something just seems to keep bothering her. I want to see her."

Michael started for the stairs as though he was familiar with Christina's home. And that concerned Jeff. He began to wonder if this man had a special relationship with his Christina. And if that was the case, this man was his competition for her affections.

Jeff followed Michael up the steps and into Tina's room. He didn't think it was proper for her employer to feel he could simply walk into her bedroom, but he held back at the door and watched him as he approached her bed.

"Tina? Are you all right? I just came by to see if you wanted to spend some time together. What's happened?" He reached down and took her hand in his.

Jeff watched as Tina's eyes opened. He saw the surprise when she saw Michael standing beside her bed.

"Michael? What are you doing here?" she asked.

"Sweetheart, I just came by to spend some time with you. You don't look well. Do you need a doctor?"

She cracked a small grin. "No, thank you. I just saw one. And that's the problem."

"Are you saying there is something seriously wrong and the doctor just sent you home? What are you talking about, Tina?" He sat down on the edge of her bed.

Tina's eyes drifted around the room until she spotted Jeff standing in the doorway. She raised her eyebrows as if to ask, should we tell him?

Jeff walked over to the open side of her bed. He took her hand in his and gave her a small smile. "Perhaps, since Mr. Thorpe appears to be a special friend of yours, as well as your employer, you might want to divulge to him what we did today. It's up to you."

"What you did today?" Michael shouted suddenly. "What does that mean? Tina? Did you go off and get married or something? Tell me, I have a right to know." By now he was on his feet, and Tina could see he was very upset.

Wanting to calm him she tried to lift her head, but found she couldn't and it fell back to the pillow.

"Please don't upset her," Jeff said calmly. "Do you want me to tell him Christina?"

She looked at Jeff. "He might as well know now. He'll find out eventually. Please sit down Michael. I have to tell you something, and I doubt that you'll even believe it."

Michael sat again on the side of her bed. Still holding her hand he waited. He glanced angrily at Jeff, then back at Tina. "It's all right, Tina. I'll listen. Tell me what you have to say." He was expecting to hear that they had gone off and gotten married. Why else would he be in her home?

"Do you remember the morning that I spilled the coffee on my hand?" she asked.

"Yes, I do." He felt as though whatever she was going to tell him was something he didn't really want to hear.

"And you recall that I fainted?" she continued.

"Yes, Tina. I remember you weren't well and I brought you home."

"I'm not sure just how to explain this," she said in a whisper. She pulled her had free from Michael's and rubbed her forehead. It hurts so badly. Jeff?" she said, looking at him.

Jeff pulled a chair up along side of the bed and sat down. He didn't feel right sitting on the edge of her bed with Michael there. He looked at Christina, then at Michael. "Of course I wasn't there but I understand you were. She almost fainted, I understand."

"She did faint. I caught her just before she hit the floor. So I took her into her office and laid her on her couch. And that was when she came to."

"Yes, well, apparently that was one of the times she may have called the, ..the.."

"The what, Man? What did she call? What are you people talking about?"

"The portal! I called the portal," Tina told him. "And when I do, either on purpose or accidently, it gives me a terrible headache and I usually end up fainting."

Michael looked at Tina with a puzzled look on his face. Then at Jeff, but neither of their expressions explained what they were talking about. "What the heck is a portal?"

Tina looked at Jeff again. She was almost afraid to tell Michael for fear he would think her mad.

"Michael, Christina has found a tear in time. Each time the portal, or tear in time came near her, or she came near to it, it caused her to have headaches and faint. Michael, Tina has traveled through time back into the past and returned. We went to see an esteemed scientist and doctor in this field and he asked her to produce the portal. She did, and I brought her home ill."

"You two are joking! You must be making this up. What you speak of isn't possible."

"It is not impossible. It, up until now, has simply been unknown to us. Christina just happened to be the first one to discover such a thing, and slipped through it. The day in the office she fainted she had somehow called the portal, and that was why she became so ill."

"What a lot of hogwash this is. Why don't you two just tell me the truth that you two fell in love and got married and didn't want to tell me about it?"

"Sorry old man, but that isn't what this is all about. She really did slip through a tear in time and traveled back to the early nineteen hundreds. And then, two days later, she found the portal again and returned," Jeff told him adamantly.

"If that's the case, why didn't she just summon it right away, the same day and return?"

"First of all, she was too ill. Secondly she wasn't aware at that time she was summoning the portal to herself. And thirdly, she didn't know how to summon it. When she came across it on the second day she slipped back through."

"I can't believe this. It can't be true. Tina, tell me this is just a big joke." He looked at her with unbelief in his eyes.

"I guess there's only one way to convince you. Just like I convinced the doctor this afternoon. Michael, would you move for me please?" As soon as he left the edge of the bed she tossed the blanket off of her and swung her feet over the side of the bed. After rubbing her temples once she rested her feet on the floor. Immediately Jeff stepped up beside her and grabbed hold of her arm.

"All right Christina, but this is the last time today. You need your rest. I'll hold on to you. We don't want you slipping in to it."

"Thank you, Jeff." Tina closed her eyes and thought of the portal. It was only seconds and her head began to pound. "Oh!" she cried out and grabbed her head. She began to lean forward to try and move away from the pain but Jeff had her arm held fast in his hand, and it was a good thing he did because as soon as she leaned forward her body began to shimmer and disappear.

"Christina!" Jeff shouted and pulled back on her arm bringing her out of the portal before she could totally disappear. "Stay back from it Michael or you might slip through into another time and we wouldn't be able to get you back."

"I'm going to be sick!" Christina said and Jeff lifted her feet from the floor and ran carrying her to the bathroom. He left her leaning over the sink because she was pushing him out of the room. She was embarrassed that she was probably going to throw up and she didn't want either of the two men she cared most about to see her so ill.

Pulling the bathroom door shut behind him Jeff stepped back into Tina's bedroom with Michael. He looked up at Michael just as Michael sat down hard on the edge of Tina's bed. Jeff stepped quickly over to Michael's side. Are you all right?" he asked.

"I will be. I think I'm in shock. This is unbelievable! Just unbelievable!"

"Yes, it is hard to wrap your mind around such a thing. But you know, every great discovery in science was probably called unbelievable at first. The thing that bothers me is how it devastates Christina. This is too much for her, to do it twice in one day."

Jeff sat there shaking his head. He didn't know how to deal with such a thing.

The bathroom door opened and Tina stepped slowly out. Jeff went to her immediately lifting her up in his arms and taking her to the bed to lay her down. Michael jumped up quickly from the edge of the bed to give them room. Just as Jeff was lowering her to the surface of the bed she fainted and her head dropped back. He laid her gently on the pillow and brushed his thumb across her forehead. She was burning up at the moment. He knew it would only be a few minutes until she started to chill. This had to be a terrible strain on her body, he thought.

Michael walked around her bed to the other side so he could stand beside her. "This is really draining her, physically and emotionally. No wonder she's been fainting. I can't help but wonder if such stress on her body might also shorten her life span. A body can't take all of this and not have a reaction."

"That's very possible, I would say," Jeff replied. She wanted you to see it, knowing she wasn't in any shape to go through it again today. But knew you wouldn't believe her unless she demonstrated it."

"And how did you get mixed up in this?" Michael asked Jeff.

"We've been friends for a long time. I guess she just felt it was natural to come to me about it."

Tina was through radiating heat and now was having chills. She moaned and Jeff covered her with the blanket again. He sat on the edge of her bed and rubbed her arms and hands to try to warm her up. Again Tina moaned. Then her head moved and her eyes slowly opened. "Oh," she complained. "My head!"

"And you've just had two pills for pain. It wouldn't be wise to take anymore just yet. I'll get you a cold washrag for your head, Christina." Jeff got up to get the cold compress, hoping it would help relieve some of the pressure for her.

Both men stayed with her well into the evening. Neither one wanted to leave her this way. She finally went to sleep and Michael and Jeff sat in the living room, just wanting to be close in case she needed them.

"I'm not leaving her like this. I'll sleep on the couch and you can have the guest bedroom, Jeff. She can't be left alone when she's so ill. Now I understand why the other day she took an entire day to recover. Poor Tina! She is really suffering through this."

"Yes, she is. And I'll not leave her either. By ten o'clock it was apparent she wasn't going to wake up to eat something so both men agreed to go to bed, but keep an ear open for her needing some help in the night.

Jeff walked up the stairs to the guest room and Michael made sure the front door was locked. He went to a hall closet and found a couple of blankets and a pillow. He kicked off his shoes and stretched out on the couch in the living room.

Jeff walked into Tina's guest room. It made him feel like he was home. The colors were almond and dusty blue and he could almost sense her presence there. It felt peaceful to him. With all of his wealth all he really wanted was to be close to her. If this Michael was the man in her life, and she chose to marry him, then he would chose to try to be their friend. He could not live his life without her in it at least to some degree. He slipped off his shoes and sat them near the side of the bed in case he needed them in the night. He tossed his jacket over a nearby chair and slipped out of his slacks and shirt.

Going into the bathroom he splashed water onto his face and rinsed his mouth out with water. Then he went over to the bed and stretched out on top of the blankets. He hadn't eaten all day, but somehow he wasn't hungry. He felt warm enough not to want to cover up. As his head rested on the soft pillow he remembered how her eyes looked red when she demonstrated calling the portal for the doctor. They could not ask this of her too often. It would kill her. And he would not allow that to happen. If she married him he could protect her behind private security in her own large home and grounds. She could come and go but he was certain she would have to have protection around her at all times.

Perhaps this wasn't such a good idea to share the knowledge. But it seemed too late for that now.

Slowly his eyes closed, but he slept very lightly. His mind and his heart was tuned to the other bedroom. Any sound at all and he was going to go to her.

At two o'clock in the morning she roused and began to cry softly. She was on her side when Jeff came in.

"Are you all right?" he asked. He was just zipping up his slacks.

'Yes, I think so. My headache is gone but I just feel like crying. I'm not sure why. I guess maybe it's just the emotional strain of it all. I don't think I can do this very often."

"No, I don't think you should. It's too much of a strain on your system." He didn't want to say on her heart or her brain, but he suspected that if she continued to call the portal very often it may cause her to have a stroke, and could kill her. He felt certain that her blood pressure was off the charts.

"Are you hungry? I can go see if there is something to eat in the kitchen."

"Jeff!" she spoke softly to him. "I feel very weak, but I know I'd really like a cup of hot chocolate. Could you help me down the stairs so I could fix it?"

"I can go fix it. Just tell me where it is and I'll go make it."

"No, I need to do this for myself. I just need help on the stairs."

He could see she was going to be adamant so he said okay. She tossed the blanket back from across her and sat up. She slid her feet to the floor and as they touched the floor and she tried to stand, she began to collapse. She didn't even have the strength to stand up. Quickly Jeff gathered her into his arms and hugged her to himself.

"Christina! Sweetheart!" he said before he could stop himself. Oh well, he told himself, if she questions his love name for her he would tell her it's what he calls most women. That way if he slipped and used it again she wouldn't be so quick to question it.

Jeff laid a soft kiss on her forehead and carried her to the kitchen. As they passed through the living room Michael woke up. He jumped up, slipping into his slacks quickly and followed them.

Jeff put Tina on one of the high stools and made certain she wasn't going to topple off before he stepped away. She told him where the hot chocolate mix was and he pulled it out. After setting the teakettle on to boil, full of water, he started pulling three cups from the cupboard. "I remember when I was young, we used to make it with milk," he told her.

"Yes but now the mix had dried milk in it so it's easier. Especially if you were hiking or out camping in the woods, you can't always carry a carton of milk with you." She told him.

"Yes, I suppose you're right, Christina," he replied.

The three of them sat at the counter enjoying a mug of hot chocolate. Christina was happy and all seemed well at the moment. So by two thirty they were all back in their beds, drifting back to sleep.

Chapter 18

Everyone was awake around six thirty. Tina was feeling more like herself and was the first person showered and dressed. She was in the kitchen making coffee when Jeff came in. They could hear the water running in the shower, which told them that Michael would be down soon. As Jeff looked at her he wanted to gather her into his arms and just keep her there. But of course, he knew he couldn't. Not yet, anyway.

Tina was pulling out cereal and spoons and bowls, so they could have breakfast. She asked Jeff to pull out three napkins, and together they had the kitchen table set for breakfast by the time Michael came in.

Tina turned to him and asked, "Ready for that first cup of coffee?"

"For sure! What are we having for breakfast?" He could see the table was set. Then he saw the boxes of cereal on the counter. "You know, sometimes I have cereal for dinner, for a change. I guess I'm still a kid at heart." He grinned at Tina and was surprised when she told him that she did the same thing sometimes.

Jeff grinned right along with them, not knowing what to say. "The honey nut cereal sounds good to me. He grabbed that box and began to open it. He dumped cereal in his bowl and sat the box on the table.

"That's one of my favorites," Michael said. "Hand it over Jeff."

Jeff slid the box closer to Michael who proceeded to fill his bowl with the cereal. Tina stepped up to the table with the carton of milk in her hand, as Jeff jumped up to get the pot of coffee that had finished brewing.

"Coffee?" he asked Michael who nodded an affirmative, so Jeff filled his cup. He knew Tina wanted some so he filled hers next, then his own and returned the pot to the heating unit. He sat down again after seating Tina. "This is rather nice to have someone to talk to over breakfast," he said. "I remember one time when Christina came to my house and we enjoyed breakfast together. She insisted on eating it in the kitchen rather than the dining room, so we did. And after that, I never had breakfast in the dining room again." He looked at Tina and she looked surprised. Then she couldn't help but grin at him.

Michael got the definite impression that he was missing something, but hesitated to ask.

Looking at Michael, then at Jeff she said, "that was when Jeff discovered sitting in the morning sunlight gave a special feeling to breakfast. And the atmosphere in the kitchen is always much more friendly. She winked at Jeff across the table, and he gave her the most spectacular smile that she wanted to go over to him and kiss him. But she didn't move.

As her thought sunk in she felt embarrass for even thinking that and felt the warmth creeping up her cheeks.

"I think we caught her in a secret thought there," Michael said noticing her high color. He wondered if it had anything to do with an attraction she might have for Jeff. He hoped not.

Breakfast didn't take very long and soon everyone was putting their bowls on the counter for Tina to rinse off and put in the dishwasher. When everything was cleared up she dumped in some soap and pushed the button to start the wash cycle.

"Well, I guess it's time to get to work. This is later that I usually go in," she said looking at Jeff.

"Oh, what time do you usually start work?" he asked.

"Usually at eight o'clock, but lately I've been trying to get some extra things out of the way, so I've been going in early."

"What is early?" Jeff asked.

Michael came up with the answer for her. "She's often in before I am," he said. "Usually six thirty or so." Looking at his watch he said, "Yeah, she's usually there now."

"Is he paying you overtime, Tina?" Jeff asked.

"Absolutely! That is, when I remember to put my time card in the machine when I come in early. But I'm not worried about it. He pays me a good salary and he's a great boss. He makes a good friend too," she smiled at him as she said it. "And sometimes I get to have breakfast with him," she laughed.

Michael looked over at Jeff. "Would you say this is boss harassment, going on here?" he grinned and asked.

"Could be. And she looks like she's enjoying it too," Jeff grinned at Tina.

Tina couldn't help but laugh out loud. She felt so much better this morning. She had had her two best friends at her breakfast table and had enjoyed every minute of it.

They all drifted toward the living room where Tina grabbed the blankets Michael had used and began to fold them up to put back in the closet. As she stood on her tip toes to slide them up on the top shelf Michael stepped up behind her, reaching for the blankets. "Here, let me do that for you. How did you get them up there the first time, anyway?"

"I stood on a stool. I'm a thinker, you know!" And she laughed. Both men looked at each other agreeing that they could see she was back to normal and they were glad for it.

Tina went to put on some lipstick and locate her purse. As she returned to the living room they all headed for the front door. "Seems funny that we have three people all going to work and three cars outside. I guess we're the typical commuters. One person to a vehicle."

Tina handed her key to Jeff who had come out the door last, so he could lock it for her. Then she hugged both of her handsome men and turned to walk to her car.

Jeff called out to her before she got in her driver's seat. I'll call you later, Christina. I'm sure we'll be hearing from the doctor very soon. Let me give you my phone number so you can reach me. He pulled out one of his cards and wrote his private number at the bottom. He hated the feeling that he had to just let her walk away from him. But there wasn't anything he could do about it.

Michael already had his car running and was waiting for the others to start theirs so they could all pull away at the same time. Somehow he didn't want Jeff staying alone with her.

Everyone left at the same time, with Jeff backing out of her driveway first, and waiting for her to do the same. When she pulled away, he did too. Michael left last. There was something about Jeff that made Michael uncomfortable.

Tina headed for the office while Michael went home to change clothes. Jeff headed for his home in Los Angeles to change and check in with his secretary. He hadn't decided whether he was going in to his office or not. His goal was to be with Christina, and he needed to figure out how that could be accomplished, and if it was something that she wanted.

Jeff finally decided to go in to his desk. He wanted to arrange for a large home to be built on a large parcel of land, larger that the one in which he resided now. He wanted to have it along the coast with many acres of his own property around it, so in the event he had to sequester Tina to keep her away from the press or to remain secure, he could do so. And He wanted the finest security available. So it was time to start the ball rolling on that. It had to be built immediately so she could move in within six months. He knew he would pay dearly for that privilege, but he felt the cost would be worth it.

Jeff thought even if she decided not to marry him that Tina would eventually need to have a place of peace to escape to, and this hideaway would be that place. Even if it had to include Michael. He and Michael were able to get along with each other so far. Jeff decided that if he had to take Michael to get Tina even as a friend, he'd agree to it.

Chapter 19

Tina sat at her desk thinking about what had transpired over the weekend. Now Michael knew about her little trip. He had yet to ask if she was gone on company time, but perhaps he hadn't thought it through that far yet. She chuckled to herself. Even though she went on company time, she didn't miss a minute of work.

She wondered what Jeff did during the day. She thought she remembered hearing him mention an office, but she wasn't sure. And how did he get so established in this time, financially? Had he set up some investments before traveling through time? She suspected he had. She didn't mind, as long as he wasn't one that affected the future.

As she sat pondering all that had transpired, when her secretary buzzed her on her com-line. "Yes, Marsha?" she answered.

"A Mr. Marlboro on line one for you."

"Oh, I'll take that call. Thank you!" She punched the button to open the line and said, "Hi Jeff! What are you up to?"

"I'm up to you Sweetheart. That is of course, if you want me." He wanted to spell it out for her but he didn't think it would be proper until she gave him some sign that she felt the same as he did. But he figured he could drop a few subtle hints though.

"Jeff, I have to tell you how much I appreciate your caring for me again. Seems like whenever I'm in trouble you show up. There's something very special about that. I hope I didn't interfere with any of your plans."

"Don't be silly, you couldn't interfere with my plans." He thought to himself, that's because you are my plans. Instead he said, "I want to be with you and help you Christina. I just want you to know that. I called to ask you what your plans were for dinner tonight."

"I don't have anything special planned. I just thought I would go home and relax and have whatever I found in the cupboard for dinner. Does that sound interesting to you?"

Lots of things began going through his mind. He would love to go home with her and relax. Just the two of them. And he could put a picture of himself in her cupboard so she would find him in her cupboard. Perhaps they could have each other for dinner. But he said, "Sounds interesting. How about I pick you up right after work and we go for a little ride before dinner?"

"Okay! That might be nice. I love to leave the driving to someone else. Then I can sit back and just enjoy the scenery."

To himself he thought, I'd love to be your scenery. You will certainly be mine. I could look at you for hours and not get bored. To her he said, "That's fine then. I'll pick you up at your house at five if that's all right with you."

"Yes, I'll be sure to be at home by then. I'm looking forward to it Jeff. We haven't been able to spend anytime together since you've come over, and I really would like to do that. Just the two of us, just like before." She wasn't sure what made her say that, but her heart seemed to let it pour out there. She did want to be alone with him. She enjoyed their time together in 1912, even though she was a little scared she might get stuck there.

"I'm glad to hear you say that. I'll see you at five then."

"Yes! See you then. Bye!" When she hung up the receiver she felt as though she didn't want to let go of it. As though she didn't want to quit talking with him. She gently shook her head to clear her mind of cobwebs, and decided she needed to get back to work.

At five o'clock Tina was feeling a little excited about being with Jeff. It was less that a minute after the hour when the doorbell rang. She rushed to answer it. Jeff was standing there looking tall and handsome. She was so glad to see him that she couldn't even speak. She just smiled and reached out for him. He grinned at her and stepped inside, taking her into his arms. He wasn't sure if she just wanted a hug, or something more. He sensed it might be more, and he prayed it was more.

As soon as their bodies touched his heart began to beat harder and he felt as though he couldn't get his breath. He hugged her tightly against his chest wishing she would show him how she felt about him.

Tina loved the feel of his arms around her. It made her feel safe and cared for. As Jeff tightened his hug she snuggled deeper against his chest. She laid her head over his heart. She could hear it beating strong and hard. She loved his strength and size. He was so tall it made her feel small rather that large and gangly. She hated feeling that way. But there wasn't anything to do about it, since she felt she truly was gangly.

The hug lasted a long moment, but she enjoyed it. Then as he began to release her she tipped her head up to look at him. And as though it was planned his lips came down to hers. Their touch created sparks and she reached up encircling his neck with both of her hands, drawing him closer.

Jeff deepened the kiss. He didn't know what she wanted but he suspected she was drawn to him without her conscious mind being aware of it. His hand came up to hold the back of her head in place as he ravished her mouth. He rubbed his tongue along her bottom lip and as she gasp for air he pushed his way into her mouth. He touched tentatively everything that was Tina. He tasted her teeth, lips, tongue, everything. The deeper the kiss became the harder it became to breathe. Finally he withdrew his tongue and teased the edges of her mouth with it. Then he left butterfly kisses there. He could hear her heavy breathing, and could feel the tremor that went through her body. And he treasured it. She didn't know what a gift she was giving him.

Tina followed his lead in the kiss. She couldn't have stopped if she had wanted to. She felt as though she was falling into him and loved every minute of it. When he laid the butterfly kisses on the edges of her mouth she felt as though the two people kissing had become one. And she liked the feeling.

Finally Jeff lifted his head and looked longingly into her eyes. God woman, surely you must know how I feel about you, he thought. He wanted to kiss her again, so he did. But this one was more chaste and gentle. Laying a path of light kisses across her cheekbones he headed for her eyes and her temples. He left soft kisses all across her beautiful face. Then he started along her jaw, dropping down to her throat. He pulled her upward, lifting her from the floor as he kissed her all the way down to her collarbone. Lifting his head he again peered into her eyes. He couldn't speak. The passion in his heart was so encompassing he just hoped she could feel it all the way to her heart. And he hoped that her mind got the message almost as quickly as her heart. He slowly let her slide down to the floor along the front of his body.

Tina gasped for air. She couldn't remember feeling so wanted and desired. She couldn't speak, so she raised her hand to his cheek and left it there as a gentle embrace.

Jeff took her hand in his own, and kissed her palm. He found her other hand and kissed that palm as well. He didn't want to leave any part of her out, within reason. He decided that the day he married her, if he was so fortunate to be given that sweet blessing, he would kiss every inch of her.

He picked her up and walked over to one of the large, overstuffed chairs that sat close to her couch. Dropping into it he placed her on his lap. As soon as he settled onto the seat cushion she snuggled down a little and laid her head on his chest. Jeff kissed the top of her head, smelling the sweet smell of her shampoo. It made him think of strawberries.

Some time later they seemed to wake up. They had sat quietly, with him cradling her close, on his lap. When Tina lifted her head and looked up at the clock on the wall she saw it was six o'clock. They had sat together, without even talking for almost an hour. And they both sensed the peace that seemed to flow between them.

"Oh, I didn't realize how long we sat together," she told him. "Didn't you say you wanted to go for a ride? Do you still want to?"

"Uh ummm," his answer came out softly. He hugged her gently and said, "Yes, I think we should. There is something that I want to show you. Shall we go?" he asked.

"Ah humm," she replied.

"You talk just like me. Perhaps we have more in common that you thought."

"Ah humm," she answered again. He tilted his head down to look at her and they both grinned at each other.

Tina got off his lap and he stood up. She grabbed her purse as they walked through the living room and toward the door.

She handed him her house keys after he opened the front door and escorted her out. Turning, he locked her door and handed back her keys.

Jeff drew her under his shoulder, causing her to walk with their sides touching. He wanted to keep her close to him, and he felt a need to touch her.

Tina liked the feeling she was getting in their touching. Again the thought came to her that he made her feel safe.

He put her in his car and went around to the driver's side. As the vehicle began to move he reached over and took her left hand in his, and proceeded to drive using only his left hand. They traveled silently for several miles. Finally he swung north along the coast and picked up speed. They traveled for almost an hour when he turned onto a small road leading up into the hills. It seemed as though wherever they drove on this street, she could see a great view of the ocean. She had always dreamed of a home with an ocean view from her breakfast nook. She wanted to sit in the morning sunshine and watch the waves roll in. But that was just a dream and she knew it.

The sun was dropping from the sky and after traveling a short way Jeff pulled the car over and stopped. They watched as the sun slipped closer and closer to the sea. They released their seatbelts and he pulled her over toward him, on the bench seat. Gathering her under his arm they watched as the golden sun slipped into the ocean. The clouds were darkening and as the last golden light disappeared he leaned down and kissed her.

When the kiss ended he asked, "What do you think of the view?"

"I love it," came her quick reply. There weren't any homes within sight.

"I'm thinking of purchasing this property to build on," he told her. "It's a nice section. I think I'll level some of it along the top. It looks as though it should remain a nice quiet area for some time into the future." He didn't tell her that the reason it would remain a quiet area was because he was going to purchase all the land within sight, and more. He anticipated over ten thousand acres. Then, when and if developers came to create homes along the ridge, they would not be able to build above him nor near him. It would make a perfect safe hideaway for Tina. He planned on even installing a helicopter pad further up the hill. He would put in servants quarters so that whoever worked for them would live in. And there would be an office for him and one for her as well, for whatever she chose to do in it. There would be a pool and spa, and perhaps even a couple of holes for golf. But he needed to know if she liked it.

"This would be a great place to build a home, with a breakfast nook right where it could get the morning sun, while I could watch the waves," she laughed. She figured he was just dreaming about building a home here.

"You know, the little lesson you taught me about the comfortable feeling of having breakfast in the kitchen stayed with me after you left 1912. I was serious when I said I no longer had breakfast in the dining room any more. You're the one that caused that change." He smiled at her.

Grinning up at him she felt happy that she had made his morning a little better. She just wished they would have more time together, but she didn't see how that could happen. And now that he was in 2004, he seemed busier that before. He wouldn't ever find time for her.

"Are you serious, Jeff? You're thinking of building here?" She expected him to say, no he was just dreaming.

"Yes, absolutely! I wanted your input as to what you thought of it."

"And you can afford to buy this land?" she asked.

"Yes, thanks to you. I made a few investments and put together some financial planning for the future before I came over. I would say I am financially secure at this point," he said.

"Then you should 'go for it'," she told him.

"Could you explain what that means, Christina? It sounds positive, but I'm unclear just what you mean by it."

"I mean you should do it. This place has a wonderful view, and it looks as though there would be a breeze most of the time. I think I would suggest you put up those plexiglass shields around the patio though. And install patio heaters as well, so you can enjoy being outside at night without getting too cold."

"Excellent idea, Sweetheart. As I have the house drawn up I'd like you to look at the drawings. Perhaps you might have some more ideas to suggest, before we actually start putting up the house. Would that be all right with you?"

"Sure thing, Jeff. I'd love to help. I just figured you would be so busy, you probably wouldn't have time for the likes of me any more."

"That will never happen, Christina. You really don't know how much I appreciate your input on this project. Without you, it wouldn't even get off the ground."

'I seriously doubt that. You would have found someone to help. I'm just grateful that you asked me."

"Christina, can I ask you something rather personal?"

"I guess so. What would you like to know?"

"How serious is your relationship with Michael?" he asked sheepishly, not wanting to upset her.

"I like him a lot. And I think he feels the same. Why do you ask?"

"To put it bluntly, in my day a man didn't try to date someone who is already spoken for. So if you are serious about him, and are thinking of getting married, then I'd just like to know that."

Tina clasped her hands together in her lap and looked down at her hands. "No matter whether Michael and I get married or not, you will always be my dear friend."

"Yes, well, I appreciate knowing that, but I guess what I want to find out from you is whether you want to marry him." He realized she wasn't getting the message that he wanted to know if he could court her himself.

"Perhaps some day," she answered him. "Why are you asking, Jeff?"

"You really haven't any idea, do you Christina?" he said feeling rather exasperated.

"Not really! I feel as though you are trying to tell me something but I'm not sure what that is. Won't you just spell it out for me? We're close friends. There isn't anything that we can't talk about."

"Okay, Christina. I want to know if I can court you myself?"

Christina sat stunned. She looked up into his face wondering why she hadn't seen it before. The special kisses and the fireworks when they touched! He wanted to know if she cared for him as a man. "Jeff!" she said, "I thought you knew how I felt about you. You're the reason I haven't been able to decide about what to do with Michael. When I'm with you, you make me feel safe. That's something that I don't get when I'm around Michael. You're the one that makes the fireworks go off in my head when you touch me. Yes, I like Michael a lot, but not as much as you."

"Do you mean it Christina?"

"Of course I mean it. But I figured you weren't interested in me in that way. So I figured I would just keep on dating Michael until something happened to make me make up my mind as to what I should do. And I think that has just happened."

"Christina, Sweetheart, don't you realize you were the reason I can through time? Only you!"

"I didn't know. I thought perhaps you just wanted to see the future and all the things I had told you about. And since you had some previous information that you could be financially secure rather easily. But it never entered my mind that you were interested in me. You hadn't said anything when I was back there."

Tina sat forward on the seat so she could face him and see his expression. With her left leg drawn up on the seat and that foot under her bottom she faced him. "You're telling me that you care for me?" she asked.

Before his answer was spoken she saw it in his eyes. He was in love with her. With her! The ugly duckling from 2004.

"Yes, Christina! It's more that that. I think I'm in love with you!"

"Oh my gosh! I felt your caring and it warmed me. It literally warmed me. When you held me, it felt so right! But I never guessed you felt as I do."

"As you do? Are you telling me you love me too, Sweetheart?" His eyes looked large in his face and were beginning to sparkle.

"Yes, Jeff. I was just thinking as we drove across this little road that you seem to be busier now than you were back in 1912 and that you wouldn't have any time for me pretty soon. And it broke my heart. I know it's probably wrong, but I guess I was holding on to Michael as second best. I just didn't want to be alone any more. I hadn't expected to find that you felt as I do."

Jeff's hands came up to her face and drew her to him. As their lips touched the fireworks began for both of them. Then his arms enclosed her drawing her up against his chest. She leaned into her left knee and stood up on it on the seat, putting her head higher than his. She wrapped her arms around his head and held him close as she kissed him.

As the kiss ended she sat back down on the seat and dropped her hands into her lap. Then she began to laugh. "Do you realize it took almost a hundred years to get us together?"

He started to grin too. "I guess it did. I hadn't thought about it. Christina, I want to ask you here and now. Would you marry me?"

"You bet your boots I will!" she told him. "There hasn't been anyone like you in my life, and I don't think there ever will be another like you in my life in the future. I go to sleep thinking of you, Jeff. That is when I don't have that awful headache going on. I love you, Jeff!"

"And I love you, Christina. You realize I want to build this house for you?"

"But why?" she asked.

"In case you haven't figured it out yet, when the word gets out about your ability at time travel, people are going to want to get to you. That means the news media and other scientists, and all the quacks as well. You're going to need a place where you will be safe from those folks. And also from people from other governments. There's always the possibility that someone may want to kidnap you to force you to give them the knowledge of how to travel through time. You're going to need a safe haven where you enjoy living your life but are safe. And I was planning on supplying that for you. Even if you married Michael this could have been your home. And his as well. I just wanted to keep you safe. Of course, there's always the possibility that he wouldn't want me doing that for you. But now that I know that you love me, there isn't any problem. Mr. and Mrs. Jefferson Michael Marlboro will be the primary residents here."

Tina leaned forward and kissed him. Then she leaned her forehead against his cheek. "Just us, Jeff. Just us!"

"Christina, you make me so happy! I want to start construction on this place right away.

I want to be able to move in soon. I can't wait to make you mine!"

"Does this mean I can quit my job too? You know, I don't think it would be proper for me to continue to work for Michael after dating him and encouraging him to think we might get married."

"It would make me very happy if you quit your job, Sweetheart. If you want to work, you could always work for me in any one of my businesses."

"Did you say businesses? How many do you have?"

"Well, I would have to check, but at last count I think fourteen. But I'm in the process of purchasing some others now, so anything is possible. You know we could even create something for you, if you wanted. But right now, I just want to hold you close. I can't believe you really love me, Christina."

"Silly man! I do!"

"I guess that means we ought to go have a cup of coffee to celebrate. Let's go! Let me help you fasten your seatbelt Darling." He leaned over and grabbed the belt hanging by her door, draping it across her and snapping it in place. "There! Now I know you'll be safe."

Jeff grinned at her as he fastened his own belt and turned the car around. He hurried down the hill and turned toward Los Angeles.

"Where are we going? And why do you want coffee? I'm surprised you don't want champagne!"

"We'll have that on the next round. Right now I want coffee. And I know just the place!"

Chapter 20

Jeff drove as though he knew just where he was going, which he did. The early evening showed signs of clouds gathering as the shadows lengthened.

They drove across Wilshire Blvd. and slowed as the traffic became heavier. Then Jeff turned into a small parking lot and slipped his car into a parking stall. Shutting off the engine he reached over to take Tina's hand in his. "Come on! Let's go get that cup of perfect coffee!"

He climbed out and walked around to her door to pull her out. As she stood he moved forward causing her body to come up against his as her feet hit the ground. She actually had her feet between his as she looked up into his face, wondering why he seemed so jubilant. She blinked once as she saw his lips coming toward her own. Then he was kissing her. And what a kiss it was. It felt like a celebration all by itself.

His arms went around her wrapping her in a cocoon of warmth and safety. She couldn't help but snuggle a little against his chest that felt so solid against her. When the kiss ended all she could think of was that she wanted more.

Jeff pulled his lips back from hers and when she opened her eyes he was grinning at her. "Come on! I have a surprise for you!"

He took her hand and gave a small tug. They started across the parking lot toward one of the many "Bronco's" coffee shops. Only this one looked a little larger than most. Why would he take her to a coffee chain, she wondered. Why not just go to a regular restaurant? She didn't know, but she figured he must have a good reason.

They brushed through the door just as a couple was leaving a table and he sent her to grab it as he got their coffee. He walked up to the counter and ordered two tall black coffees and was speaking to the guy behind the counter about something. As Jeff turned toward her with his hands full of their cups of coffee he glanced up to see who was coming from the back of the store. He quickly sat their cups on the table in front of her and opened his arms. Tina wondered what was going on? Just that quick an older woman rushed into his arms and hugged him. Tina watched them as he laid a gentle kiss on her head. Then he took her by the upper arms and turned her toward Tina. When Tina saw who it was she was out of her chair so quickly she almost tipped it over. And just that quickly she was hugging and being hugged as well. The woman was none other than Mrs. Braxton.

When the hug ended she looked at the woman that was suppose to be dead and long gone. What was she doing here? She wanted to know how she came to be here, and how did Jeff know?

"What are you doing here?" Tina asked. She didn't mean to sound rude, she just wanted to know. She really was delighted to see her.

"I came with Jefferson!" she told her quickly. "I take it he hadn't told you. You look wonderful. How have you been? Is everything all right?"

"Everything is better than all right, Mrs. Braxton. She agreed to marry me!" Jeff told her with a huge smile on his face.

"Oh, I'm so glad!" She grabbed him again for a hug. Then she turned to Tina and asked, "You aren't angry that we came are you?"

"No! No! I'll be eternally grateful he came to find me. And I'm so tickled that you came too. But wouldn't your family have missed you terribly?"

"Not really! You see, they were all busy with their own lives, and didn't live anywhere near me. So it would just be like I died. Which I probably would have done before too many more years anyway. But this way I was able to be with Jefferson and do just what you told me about."

"What I told you about? What was that?" Tina couldn't recall any such thing.

"You told me that there was money to be made because of all the different ways people like their coffee. That it was a big business in your time. So here I am, and you were right. It is a big business. I now have twenty seven stores and the possibility of creating more. I still can't get over how much business there is in just making coffee." Mrs. Braxton smiled broadly at her. She looked as though she really was enjoying life.

"The future Mrs. Jefferson Marlboro is such a smart one," Jeff told Mrs. Braxton. "I'm lucky she came to me. And now that I've found her I haven't any intention of letting her go."

Jeff pulled Tina against him, hugging her. He was so happy to finally tell Tina who had come over with him. But he hesitated to tell her how ill Mrs. Braxton had become, through the process. At one point he was afraid that it might kill her, going through all that pain and illness. But after a couple of days she began to come around, feeling stronger each day until she was back to normal.

So now Jeff had his two favorite women together and he decided life was going to be good for all of them. He knew when he gave Mrs. Braxton the money to start her business that she would do well. They sat together for hours figuring out how to start her business after visiting one or two small coffee shops watching for what they did right and what they had done wrong. Mrs. Braxton vowed not to make the same mistakes they had made, and that was how it went. In no time at all she had a second shop, and then a third, and things just kept going so well that she began to branch out into all of the nearby communities until she had covered the state with 'Bronco' coffee. She even sold her own brand of coffee, made by one of the major brands with her label. She experimented with flavors and many of them became very popular. She was in big business to stay. Her 'Bronco' coffee was a familiar name now all across the state.

Mrs. Braxton sat down with Tina and Jeff and told her a little about all that they had done to get her business up and running. She told Tina that at first she lived with Jefferson, but after her business took off she wanted a place of her own. So he bought her a townhouse, about the size of Tina's. But it was all on one floor so she wouldn't have the strain of climbing stairs as she got older.

Mrs. Braxton shared with her that years ago her son had wanted to be a rodeo star as he was growing up, riding wild bronc's and becoming well known. And that was how she got the name for her company. She used 'Bronco' in honor of her son's earlier desire to be come famous at the rodeo.

Time passed quickly and suddenly it was getting late. Tina glanced at her watch and realized it was going on ten. Mrs. Braxton noticed and said that it was time to close up. She excused herself, giving Tina and Jeff hugs before she left them. She made them promise to come back, and to visit her at home so she could fix dinner for them.

Walking out to the car Jeff pulled her close and she put her arm around his waist. Tina couldn't remember when she had felt so content.

Just before he put her into his car he leaned against the vehicle, pulling her against him. With his arms firmly around her he asked, "Well, what do you think of our Mrs. Braxton now?"

She couldn't help but smile at him. "I'm so proud of what she has done! She is an amazing woman. And as I remember, she was an amazing cook as well."

"Yes, that's true! When we sat and talked about my coming through time to find you, and all of the things you had talked about from your time, she said she wanted to come through with me. She insisted that she wouldn't have anything to do after I left, what with her family so far away, and busy with their own lives. She said she would just sit around waiting to die. She sounded so forlorn that I couldn't refuse. She looked a little frightened when she thought about how ill you had been and that it had been caused by moving through the portal, but she has a lot of spunk, that woman. And she asked to come with me. She said that her life was with me anyway. So I finally gave in, and told her when I was going back to find the portal again, and she went along. As soon as we found it, we held hands and stepped through. And when we landed, because that's just what happened, we landed on our bottoms in the middle of a park. I was grateful it was early in the morning so no one was around to see us, thank goodness.

I managed to make contact with the attorney's office that was related to my attorney from 1912, and made arrangements to get some money so we could establish a place to live. Mrs. Braxton was ill for a couple of days from the experience of coming through the portal, but after two days she was herself again.

We had to go shopping for clothes and lots of things. But actually, I think she was enjoying herself the whole time. I think she likes to shop.

"Once I had an idea as to how much funding I had available to us, I purchased a home and invested in her first coffee shop. She paid me back very quickly, even though I told her she didn't have to. But she said what was right, was right. So I accepted the money and put it into a trust for her, only she doesn't know it yet."

"You're a good man, Jeff. It's almost as if she is your mother."

"Yes, I think of her that way. My own mother passed away long ago, so it's been just Mrs. Braxton and myself for a long time."

Tina began to laugh. "You can say that again," she said. "A long time!" She giggled until he kissed her on her neck. Then her temperature began to rise and she wanted to kiss him. She pulled on his shirt and he looked down at her. She went up on her tip toes to place her lips on his and he came away smiling at her.

After the kiss ended he put her into the car and walked around to the drivers side. Sliding in he leaned over and kissed her again gently. "I love you, Sweetheart!" he told her.

They drove slowly back toward her townhouse. Jeff walked her to her door and accepted her key so he could unlock the door to let her in. He followed her in and closed the door behind him, and locked it. Tina heard the click of the lock, but wasn't worried. If there was anyone she felt safe with, it was Jeff.

They curled up on the couch and Jeff put his arm around her, pulling her close. She liked the protective way he kept her close to him. Laying her head on his shoulder she thought to herself, this is something I would like to do often after we're married. She very definitely wanted to keep their love alive.

As they rested quietly he told her about his ideas for their new home. He didn't want to frighten her, but he did want to make her aware that when the knowledge got out about her ability to call the portal and pass through time that she need to be kept safe and protected. He asked for her ideas and desires for the new house on the hill. He knew since they were going to have it built that any special changes she wanted could be incorporated in the original design, such as a breakfast area off the kitchen that caught the morning sun. By midnight he said he had to head for home and reminded her that she had to go to work the next day. So they said a reluctant good night at her door and he kissed her gently.

The week went by quickly and almost before she knew it, it was Friday evening all ready. Michael had asked her out for dinner twice during the week but she declined, saying she had things she needed to do. So he said he would probably call her over the weekend to possibly get together. She finally had to tell him that she had plans with Jeff for Saturday and she had several things she wanted to get done on Sunday.

Michael wasn't very happy about the amount of time she was spending with Jeff but he figured he didn't want to upset her to the point that she broke it off with him, so he acquiesced and didn't complain. She hadn't told anyone yet that she was getting married to Jeff.

Saturday morning Tina heard a knock on her door at eight thirty. She was languishing in bed and was enjoying having the opportunity to sleep in. But she knew she had to answer the door. Slipping out of bed she grabbed her robe and went barefoot to the front door. Opening it she found Jeff standing there.

"Sorry I didn't call first but I just decided to surprise you. I guess you weren't up yet, huh?"

"I was awake but just not up. Come on in. How do you get up so early on a Saturday? I'm surprised, as busy as you seem to be that you wouldn't enjoy getting to sleep in once and a while."

"Yes, that's true most of the time, but I started thinking about you and then I couldn't go back to sleep. I just wanted to be with you. There's something very special about being able to look up and see you close by. Or to be able to touch you as often as I would like. But to do that I have to be with you, so here I am!"

"You're so silly sometimes, but I love you for it," she told him. "Come on in. Have you had some coffee already?"

"Only one cup. I could always use another one." She led him to the kitchen where he helped her start a pot of coffee. She began to pull out cups from the cupboard and sit them on the counter near the tall stools that she loved to sit in. Then he slid into one of the stools to wait for the coffee to brew, pulling her with him. She stood between his knees and he turned her to face him. Slowly her hands went around his neck and his lips sought hers. The kiss deepened and he pulled her even closer. When she raised her head they peered into each other's eyes, the love between them shining brightly.

"You know, it's interesting that when I traveled through time I went back in time rather than forward. Most people, I would think, would be interested in what is going to happen in the future."

"I guess that would be true. But, of course, I got to look into the future."

"Well, you're special. I'm glad that you came after me, Jeff. I knew I was drawn to you when I was in 1912, but I didn't know until I came back here how very much you meant to me."

"Maybe sometime we ought to consider visiting the future, just to see what changes are going to take place?"

"Tina, I'm not sure that may be wise. I suspect that if you travel through the portal too many times, or too often, it may have dire consequences."

"How about now? It's Saturday and we don't have to be anywhere today. What do you think?" The more she thought about it the more fun it sounded to her, especially if Jeff was going to go with her.

Just that quickly her head began to throb. Her eyes got large as she looked at Jeff. She stretched her hand out in front of her and it shimmered and disappeared. Just because she had been thinking about it, the portal had appeared and waited before her.

"I don't know, Christina. I don't think we should play around with this thing. I wouldn't want anything to happen to you. I suspect that time travel puts a great strain on your body, Sweetheart."

"Let's go forward in time and just take a quick look? Now that we know how to call the portal to us we can come back quick and easily," she said.

"Against my better judgment, Christina. And we're not staying long."

Leaning forward she pulled his hand and they slipped into the portal. Everything shimmered and then they were falling. Jeff pulled her tightly against him as they fell. He wasn't about to be separated from her and they end up in different times. Especially since he couldn't call the portal himself.

She had been thinking about 2125 just before she had leaned into the portal, so she figured that was where they were headed. Suddenly they hit the ground, rolling one over the other, because Jeff refused to release her. Then they were stopped, lying on the grass in what looked like a cemetery.

There were statues all around, which Tina suspected marked several graves. Sitting up she grasped her head. She felt dizzy and lightheaded. She rolled over onto her knees prepared to throw up. But it didn't happen. She felt grateful it didn't.

Jeff sat up and glanced over at Tina. "Are you all right?" he asked.

"Ummm," she answered, afraid to speak just yet. She put her hand on her stomach and waited for it to settle down. Slowly the churning came to a stop and she lifted her eyes to his.

Jeff could see the red in the whites of her eyes, which signaled the presence of a headache. He gathered her more tightly into his arms hoping to help relieve her suffering. She laid her head against his chest as his arms went around her. He gently rubbed her back and the back of her neck. Her muscles felt tense and tight. He worried that she might require several hours to recuperate. That was something he hoped wouldn't happen, since he wanted to return to 2004 within the hour. He figured they could see enough in one hour to satisfy their curiosity.

They sat on the grass for a few minutes more till they started feeling better. Jeff only felt a little dizzy but it was Tina he was concerned about. She held her head with both hands for several minutes. When she lifted her head to look at Jeff he could see the headache appeared to be letting up, so he stood and reached down to help her up.

"What a place to land in," she said as she looked around. "A cemetery!"

"It seems unusual that there would be so many statues though. I can't remember any cemetery I've been in that has so many," he told her.

"Yeah, it does seem a little strange. Let's walk!"

Jeff grasp her hand in his and started along a row of statues. They followed the row until they reached the fence line, and followed that until they found the front gate. Exiting the cemetery they discovered they were on a concrete sidewalk along an empty thoroughfare. Walking to their right they wandered along until they seemed to be entering a residential area. Each home had a fence of some sort around it.

One house had a brick wall that was only waist high. The next house had a wooden picket fence. The very next one had a tall eight foot high plaster wall that they couldn't see over. And so it continued. When they approached the gate to the home with the tall wall around it they peered in through the iron gate to see what looked like a small cemetery. As Jeff continued to look at the tall white statuary he said, "You know, they look similar, don't you think?"

"Now that you say that, I think so. They actually look like faces of brothers and sisters and other family members. Why would they want to go to all that expense just to remember their loved ones, when a photograph would do just as well?"

"I can't imagine. It'd be nice if we could ask someone."

Just then they noticed a gardener clipping the grass that was growing around some of the statues. He glanced up at them and Tina waved at him to come over. He stood and walked slowly toward them as they stood outside the gate.

"Good morning! Could you tell me, why this family has so many statues of what looks like relatives in their yard? Is this a private cemetery?"

"Of course not! This is their memorial garden. They don't have as many as most families, but I find it impressive," he told them.

"Do you mean many people have memorial gardens?" she asked.

"Of course! Don't you?" he asked her.

"Well, we're not from around here, so this is new to us. Are you saying most people have a memorial garden?"

"That's right! If you're going to be moving in around here I would suppose you will probably have one too. Everyone does. It's the best way to remember each and every member of one's family. Even the ones that haven't died yet."

"Oh! That's interesting!" Jeff said. "Thank you so much for the information and your courtesy. Have a good morning!" Both Tina and Jeff raised their hand to wave goodbye to him and he did the same. He turned to return to his clipping, and Tina and Jeff continued down the sidewalk.

Looking at the different homes they noticed some families had their memorial garden near the front gate, apparently so it would be visible to passersby, but other families seemed to want more privacy for their garden and it was only partially visible around the back of the house.

Isn't it funny that they would go to all that effort just to remember their forbearers?" she asked.

"To me it seems a little absurd and a waste, but I suppose it's important enough to them to want to do it. Personally, I would prefer pictures or movies of my loved ones that I could look at and use the funds that all of this would cost for something more practical. But who's to say what's in fashion. We've come a ways into the future, so their ways are apparently not our ways. I'm sure you saw me doing things in my time that you don't do, Christina."

"Well, yes, I guess you're right. Let's walk toward those tall buildings over there and see what we can see?"

They wandered for another ten minutes and entered what appeared to be a business district. Many of the buildings were several stories tall with unusual shapes on top. Some had what appeared to be the shape of an onion, which was painted a bright gold. Others had glassed in areas that looked like giant sunrooms. And many tall buildings had what appeared to be their own water towers placed somewhere on their roofs.

They noticed that several of what looked like office buildings had turnstyle type glass doors in their entryway, rather than ordinary single doors. "Now that looks as though they chose something that had been done in the past. Perhaps they felt it would control the flow more easily," Jeff said.

They had stopped walking and Tina was looking up and down the street they stood beside. It gave the feeling of being haunted since there wasn't any traffic at all.

"Look at that, Jeff. It seems they have a concern about safety too. Look how many cameras are stationed along the street. I wonder if they have a problem with keeping the law here?"

Jeff scanned the area around them and discovered seven cameras, just within his sight. That many made him wonder why there was such a need. It was just like the old saying of 'Big brother is watching' had come to life. "Apparently the police have a need to observe the populace here. Maybe the people of 2125 aren't to be trusted."

"Or possibly, the police, or the government isn't," Tina shot back at him. "You know corruption in government could cause such a problem too."

"Well, whatever it is, we're not going to stick around to see it. It appears this generation of folks has their problems, just like every other generation."

Tina stood at the curb and looked up and down the street. "You know, it almost seems as if they are under Marshall Law, or something. Or maybe there's a curfew in effect. Otherwise there ought to be a few cars for those people who go to work early. And it seems as though there ought to be some people on the street as well, yet it almost looks abandoned. This is a little scary!"

"I think I would agree with you. I suspect we should be leaving here, Christina. I don't like the feeling I'm getting."

Just at that moment Tina noticed some movement down the block from them. A vehicle with yellow flashing lights on the roof was rapidly approaching them. Suddenly a loud speaker burst on their hearing with, "Stay where you are. You have broken the law! Stand and answer to the law!" Tina and Jeff looked at each other. They didn't want to be caught by the police in 2125, especially if they were supposedly breaking the law.

Jeff grabbed her hand and they turned and ran. They ducked into the narrow walkway that led between houses where there wasn't a street. This double row of houses faced each other just as though there was a street in front of them, but there was only a narrow walkway. And it wasn't wide enough for the police car to follow them.

Running down the block and seeing only a walkway made Tina think of some of the beach neighborhoods in Venice in 2004. There were several such "streets" there. All vehicles, except for bicycles, had to go on adjacent streets. She thought, at least this will give us a chance to get away. They rounded the next corner and as they did she looked up at the light posts to see cameras, turning in their direction. They were being 'tracked' by the police.

"Jeff, the camera's are on and they're tracking us. It looks as though no matter where we go they can see us, even if the police car can't follow us."

"Then we need to get to where there aren't any cameras, if there is such a place. Then we need to return to our time, Christina. I think we've seen enough of this place." They ran around another corner and Jeff stopped. Tina stopped beside him, looking up at him to understand what he had in mind. "Look at the sun Christina! It rises in the east! Lets head for the beach area. Maybe there won't be as many cameras there. That means if we want to go west then we have to go this way," he said, pointing to his right. Grabbing her hand again he gently gave a tug and began to run across the street that they had come out on. As they were in the middle of the street they both glanced down the street and saw the police car approaching with lights flashing. This time they had a siren going as well. Looking around they could see people's faces appearing in windows as they tried to see what all the excitement was about.

"I think your jogging practice is going to payoff today. Let's go!" He led her down alleys, and through parks. They ran through walkways between more houses where there wasn't any street, and on and on. As they listened they could hear more sirens joining the search for them. Tina's heart began to pound in her chest.

All the time they ran they didn't see one person on the street. But they did see a few behind glass windows, watching. It looked as though people were afraid to even be in their own yards. What kind of curfew did these people have to live with here, she wondered.

They had run over two miles already and Tina thought she could smell the ocean. Jeff paused at the entrance to an alley, looking both ways on the street they were leaving. Three blocks down he spotted a police car headed their way. He gave a tug and they were off again, running in the center of the alley because there were cardboard boxes with people in them, watching them as they ran by.

"Now we know that 2125 has problems with vagrants and street people, just like 2004," he said as they ran.

They were almost out of the alley when a young man stepped out into their path, not more than twenty feet from them. "Here! Over here!" he called to them.

Jeff didn't hesitate. He ran right up to him.

"Come on," the young man said. "You can hide in here. Hurry!" He turned and stepped into the ground floor of what appeared to be the back of a large red brick building. It looked as though it might be an apartment building, built many long years ago. As soon as they stepped inside the door was pushed shut and almost as soon as it was, they heard sirens coming through the alley. The police were very close by.

Tina leaned against the wall to catch her breath. Jeff stood next to her.

"Come on. You can't stand there. They have heat detectors that will show them your body heat. Since you've been running, it will be higher than normal for people who have been staying inside, so they'll know it's you. Come on!"

Tina's stomach was beginning to roil and she was becoming seriously scared. "This is a nightmare! I've never been chased by the police before."

"Maybe this is what we get for visiting this place," Jeff told her.

The young man was jogging up the hallway so Jeff and Tina took out after him. He rounded the corner of the hallway and started up the stairs.

"Why are we going upstairs?" asked Jeff. "They could trap us there. We need to put some distance between us and them."

"Come on, I'll show you. We have our own road of travel here. Follow me!"

They felt as though they had already committed themselves so they followed him.

He led them up five flights of stairs and through a door, out onto the roof. He ran over toward the edge of the roof where a long plank laid. It looked as though it had a cable of some sort hooked into the end of it and the cable was strung across the abyss below to the building across the street.

Standing near the knee high wall around the edge of the building, the young man shouted to another young man on the next roof. "Tito! Pull man!"

Jeff and Tina watched as the young man on the other roof turned to two other young men who rushed to help him pull the cable. Slowly the long eight inch wide board began to go over the edge of the roof toward the building on the other side of the street. They were amazed to see that the board was long enough to actually reach from one roof to the other across the narrow street below. As soon as it was in place Tito stepped up on the board and raced across to where Jeff and Tina and their helper stood.

"What's happening John?" he asked.

"The police are after them. I called them inside so we could help them."

Turning to Jeff and Tina, Tito asked, "Where are you trying to get to so early in the morning? Don't you know that the curfew law is strictly enforced around here? Why are you even out now?"

"We aren't from around here," Jeff told him. "We didn't know about the curfew. And while we're on the subject, why aren't there any people on the street? Don't they have to go to work early here?"

"Where are you from, Mister? The curfew law is all across the state and has been for years. No one is allowed on the streets before six in the morning, or after six at night."

"Sounds like L. A. isn't a very nice place to live now," Tina interjected.

"Perhaps," answered Tito, "but it beats living where the weather gets cold. With the changes in the weather patterns all across the nation, it can get well below zero where the snow falls. I'll take this place any day, to that."

"So there's been serious weather changes in this century. Interesting!" Tina said.

"This is no time for lessons on history Christina," Jeff told her. "How can we get to the beach from here? And are there cameras on the beach as well?"

"There are cameras everywhere, Mister," answered the young man that called them into the building to help them. "I'm John MacIntyre," he said holding out his hand to Jeff.

"I'm Jefferson Marlboro, and this is Christina Taylor," he told the two young men.

"How did you happen to be on the streets at this hour?" John asked.

Jeff looked at Tina. "That's a long story!" he told them. "We really don't have time to tell it right now. Can you get us to the beach, or some place where there aren't any cameras?"

"There are cameras on the beach too," Tito told them.

"Is there someplace where you can take us where we can't be seen by any camera?" Jeff asked.

"You mean outside? It has to be someplace outside?" asked Tito.

Jeff looked at Tina. "Well, I guess it could be inside, couldn't it Christina?"

"Actually, yes. It could be inside. I guess we just didn't think of that. But yeah, it can be inside." She looked at the two young men. They appeared to be about twenty or so. They looked healthy and viral as though they had been using a lot of muscle in their daily lives and were very strong. Their biceps fit very snuggly in their long sleeve flannel shirts. And it appeared all of the four wore jeans and working boots. They looked as though they might be dock workers.

John turned to Tito who said, "We could take them to my place. And then they can decide what they want to do from there."

"Yeah, that sounds good," John answered.

"Okay, lets head over there than. Come on," John told Jeff and Christina. He turned toward the board and started across the manmade bridge.

"I don't know if I can do that" Tina told him. "I'm afraid of heights!"

"It's this, or go back down to the streets. And I wouldn't recommend that." John looked at the two of them.

"Okay! I'll try!" She and Jeff walked over to the board.

"Don't look down at the street, Christina," Jeff said. "If you have to look down at all concentrate on where you're placing your feet only. Not on what is beyond the board."

"Okay! Yeah, sure!" was her reply. She really didn't want to even try, but it seemed she had no other choice at the moment.

John stepped up on the board, reaching out a hand to Tina. She laid her hand in his and stepped up. Jeff had her other hand, so she figured between the two men they would make sure she kept her balance.

"Look at me," John told her. He was comfortable walking on planks since he had been doing it for years. He could walk a plank without looking down at all. He drew her eyes to him and Tina just looked at him with fear in her eyes. "Don't be afraid! We've got you. You won't fall. Just follow me." John walked backwards across the narrow eight inch blank and before she knew it, she was stepping off the other end onto the next roof.

Jeff followed her trying not to look down as well. He too watched John in amazement, that he could walk backwards across such a narrow bridge without fear. Tito followed Jeff across.

As they walked across the next roof John stepped up beside Jeff. "You two almost act as though you came from another time. Why do you need to make sure you aren't anywhere near a camera?'

"We're new here, and just got into town. We just thought we would visit for an hour or so and then head home where it's much quieter."

"Uh huh! Well, Tito's place is in this building so we'll go there so we can talk. That is, if you're willing to tell us more why you didn't know how Los Angeles is being run. If you're not far from home, then you should have known how the law is here in California," Tito said.

Tito headed for the adjacent roof that butted up against this roof and stepped across. He led them to the door that led into the building and down a steep set of stairs to the third floor.

Glancing around as if to check for anyone watching them, he unlocked the door and walked into his apartment. It had several computers set on desks around the walls. There was a couch and two chairs off to one side, with what looked like a TV standing in the corner directly across from the couch. There were a couple of units that looked like VCR's or DVD players sitting on shelves below the TV.

As the last man in the door turned to close it Tina heard a beeping noise come from the TV set. She turned to see John pick up a remote control from the top of the set and push a button on it. Immediately the TV screen was filled with the face of a young man.

"John! What's going on? The cops are going crazy out there."

John positioned himself in front of the TV set, and sad down on the couch. "They were trying to catch a couple of people, Mike. We found them though and they're with us now."

"What? What if they're spies for the cops? Now they know where one of us lives. That doesn't sound wise to me."

"They're not spies. I would have known. They just needed to find a place without cameras, is all. They're safe with us. Don't worry about a thing. I'll get back to you later. Watch your back, Mike." John pressed another button on the remote and the screen went blank.

"What was that?" Tina asked. "You can talk through that unit, just like using a phone?"

"A phone? I haven't really seen one of those. I've heard of them. They have a couple at the museum. This is the normal way to talk to your friends here, unless, that is, you're face to face." John's face lit up with a grin. He looked like a little kid at the moment, that had just shown his favorite toy. "Why don't you have a seat?" John offered.

Tina sat in one of the chairs, and Jeff sat on the arm of the same chair. He didn't want to be further from her than arms reach at any time.

"Okay! There's something funny about your not knowing about the curfew when it's been in effect for years here. So tell us, where are you really from?" John asked.

Tina looked up at Jeff and decided to tell them. She decided that once they were gone back to their own time there wouldn't be anything these young men could do about time travel. And if they talked about it to anyone, people would probably think they were crazy anyway, so why not tell them.

Just then John's head came up. "Hey! Wait a minute! What did you say your names were?" he asked.

"I'm Christina Taylor and this is Jefferson Marlboro. Why do you ask?" Tina asked him.

"As in Christina Taylor, the discoverer of time travel?" John said.

Tina was so shocked that she jumped to her feet. Jeff stood with her, grabbing her shoulders and pushing her behind him, he said, "How do you know that?"

Tina peered around Jeff's arm, then stepped out from behind him. "It's okay Jeff. He isn't going to hurt me."

By now John was on his feet as well. He began to pace across the room. His hand came up to the back of his neck and he rubbed it as though he had a headache. "We were told it didn't really happen. That it was all just a farce to trick people. But some studies were made and there was speculation that there was a possibility that such a thing was possible. But they taught us in school that it wasn't possible."

John walked back to the couch. "Please! Sit down! What an opportunity this is. Are you really THE Christina Taylor from 2004?" he asked.

Tina nodded her head affirmative. "I forgot that we were in the future, where it might be known what we did, Jeff." She looked up at him like a little girl that had gotten caught with her hand in the cookie jar.

Sitting back down again Jeff told the two young men, "It's true! Christina traveled into the past to 1912 where she found me. When she returned to 2004 I followed her, along with my housekeeper. We established ourselves there and I located Christina. We met with a scientist and scholar and demonstrated the ability of traveling through time for him. But we're just at the point of the study being started. It was a spur of the moment thing that we decided to come to 2125. But it looks as though you people are living under Marshall Law here. Why is that?"

"I'm sure you remember the Watts Riots? Well, we've been having the same problem here. It's been so bad that the streets are no longer safe. Finally the police decided to install a permanent curfew until the problem ceased to be. Only it never did. Gangs rule the streets and no one, not even your grandmother, is safe anymore. And that's the way it's been for years, all across California. People have gone crazy! They go out in gangs and break into stores, stealing everything they can carry, then burning what's left. It's been going on for so long that people almost don't know any other way of life."

"That's sad," Tina said. "I wouldn't want to have to live that way."

"So tell me, how were you able to travel through time?" John was looking at Tina with such interest that she felt as though she was a celebrity.

"Actually, I fell into it. Literally! There must have been a tear in time and I just happened to be there at that moment. It just pulled me in. That was when I went back to 1912. And it was a while before I could figure out how to get back to my own time. I was back for a while before I realized that I could call it to me."

"So it's real!" John said softly. "I always thought so. You say you can call the portal to you?"

"Yes! That's how we came here. I just called it to me, thought about where I wanted to go, and stepped through."

"And since you've traveled through time also, can you call the portal to yourself as well, Jeff?" John asked.

"No! Afraid not! Actually I'm glad I can't. I don't think I would want that responsibility."

"But how were you able to follow her then from 1912 to 2004?" John looked puzzled. I don't understand.

"You see, when I decided to try to follow her I went back to where we had found the portal so she could return to her time. At that point we thought the portal remained stationary. We've since discovered she can call it to her, so it's moveable. Anyway, I and my housekeeper, went to where Christina had stepped into the portal and were able to find it. So we stepped through, hopping it would take us to 2004, which it did."

"Have you tried to call it to you?" John asked.

"Not really. I didn't think I could." Jeff told him.

"You mean you've never attempted to call it? You just assumed that you couldn't?" Tito asked.

"I guess you're right. I hadn't considered it."

"And this was why you wanted a place without cameras? So you wouldn't be seen going into the portal?"

"That's right! No sense in causing more problems." Tina answered.

"So why not try it now Jeff? I understand you just wanted a safe place to return to your time, so why not do it here and now?" John asked.

Jeff looked at Tina. His expression asked her what she thought about him trying to call the portal. She nodded her head yes.

Jeff reached over and took Tina's hand in his. Then he closed his eyes and thought about the portal and that he wanted to go to 2004. In only moments his head began to ache. He reached out and waved his hand all around them to locate the opening in time. As his hand passed in front of Tina his hand shimmered and began to disappear. He quickly pulled it back.

Looking again at Tina, Jeff smiled. "I guess I can do it too," he told her, "not that I'm sure I wanted to really be able to do it."

Tina and Jeff stood up. John and Tito did the same.

"Can I go with you?" John asked.

"Why would you want to?" asked Tina.

"This is not the kind of life I want to live, Christina. There's no peace here. If I go back to 2004, I could find a peaceful life and begin to create a real life for myself."

"But it would be totally different. Everything would be different for you."

"Yes, but I think I would very much like to live in a world where I know my grandmother could walk to the corner store without being shot. And what about kids? If I ever get married, how can kids ever have a normal life living in a place like this?"

"Then that means you and others like you must take a stand and start cleaning up your own city block. And when that's done, clean up the street. And when that's done clean up the town. Until the entire state is free of this terrorism," Jeff told him.

"Another thing that must be considered, John, is whether or not you or your descendants might be important to the future history of our land. If you, or your child, or grandchild was someone that was to be president, or something important, you wouldn't want to upset history by changing that. You have to think of that. By moving to another time you could upset the balance of history."

"I don't really think that anyone in my family will become president, or even governor. Or anything else important. That just isn't possible."

"What if I just travel back with you, then return to my own time. That way I can visit your time, see how your government handled the riot problem and return here to apply what I've learned?"

"Well, perhaps!" Tina replied. "But you realize the possibility that you will then be able to call the portal. And you will have to remember that you could upset history and world control if you interfere with anyone in another timeline. Frankly, are you honorable enough to hold fast to not disturbing time or history?" she asked him forthrightly.

"I have no intentions of trying to rule the world or change anything. I just want to find my little piece of the world where I can live peacefully. I swear this is true!"

Tina looked at Jeff. She didn't want to give such awesome power to anyone that might misuse it. Jeff looked into her eyes and saw her concern.

"He is a man of honor, Christina. If he wasn't he wouldn't have gotten involved in saving us. He didn't know us, and didn't owe us anything. Yet he put his own life in jeopardy to help us."

"So you think we could safely give him this ability? To travel through time?"

"The decision is yours, but I think he's a good man, Christina." Jeff said.

"You realize that if you sleepwalk you could end up anywhere? The way I discovered that I could call the portal to me was in my sleep. Something woke me up and as I moved I just happened to notice that my hand shimmered and became invisible, meaning it was entering the portal. If I had just gotten out of bed without thinking, I could have traveled anywhere. And since I hadn't any thought as to where I was going, who knows where I could have ended up. The responsibility is awesome. And a little fearful as well. Not to mention that it will give you a royal headache and make you sick for a little while."

"I think I can handle that," John told her. "I believe myself to be a man of honor, Christina. But if you have any doubts, that tell me no. I trust your judgment in this," he told her.

Tina again looked at Jeff. They stood at the portal and waited for her decision. She waved her hand before her to see if it still was there, waiting for them. Her hand shimmered and started to disappear. Jeff grabbed her wrist and pulled her back.

"Don't do that unless I'm holding on to you Sweetheart. I don't want to have to find you again. And this time, I wouldn't know where to start." He grinned down at her, and she returned his smile.

"All right!" she said. "I hope I won't regret this!" She moved around where she figured the portal waited, to grab John's hand. With one hand in Jeff's large one, and her other in John's, she was ready to go. "Any last words to Tito?" she asked.

"I'll be back, Tito! Just you wait and see!" With that he nodded at Tina and she stepped into the void. Her body shimmered for a moment and disappeared. As she moved forward she pulled both John and Jeff with her. Suddenly she was falling. It lasted only moments and she hit something hard. With both of her hands in theirs, she was unable to roll free when she hit, and she felt a pain in her hip. Then she was lying down and all went black around her.

Chapter 21

Slowly the darkness receded and Tina began to be aware of Jeff's tender touch. He had pulled her up into his arms and was rocking her as if she was a baby. She could hear his voice.

"Sweetheart! You need to wake up. Christina! We're back!"

As she opened her eyes she saw they were back in her living room. She blinked twice to get things in focus and searched for the clock on the wall. It was only two minutes after they had left.

Looking around the room she saw John looking out of the window with his back to them. He turned as he heard Tina moan. She reached for her head and rubbed her temples. Her head ached, but not as bad as when she traveled into an earlier time.

Tina noticed she was on the couch, and so was Jeff. She couldn't help but wonder where John had landed. She distinctly remembered landing on her back. So she asked.

"Did we land on the couch?" she asked, looking at Jeff.

"Yes! Actually, I landed on top of you. I hope I didn't hurt you."

"No! No! And where did John land?" she inquired.

"Would you believe, on the floor? How did you manage to land on something soft, while I landed on something so hard?" John asked with a grin.

Tina couldn't help but chuckle. "It was because when we left, we left from the couch. I've found the portal usually returns you to where you started the adventure. Because you hadn't started here I guess it just 'dropped' you in the same area where it dropped us off."

"I see," he said. "I think!"

"How do you feel?" she asked him, suspecting he would have a horrendous headache.

"Outside of a nasty headache I seem to be fine."

"That's normal, at least for me that is. I usually feel ill with a really bad headache when I travel. Last time it took me two days to get back to normal. But when I come home the pain seems to be less. Maybe that's my welcome home gift," she laughed.

Sitting up Tina felt a little bit dizzy and she leaned back against Jeff's shoulder.

"I think you ought to take it easy for a little while, Hon. This doesn't get any easier with repetition." He looked at her with such tenderness in his eyes that she wanted to kiss him right there, even though they had company. So she did!

It was a chaste kiss since they weren't alone. Then she stood up and turned to head into the kitchen to make some coffee. She staggered a little and immediately Jeff was with her, holding her elbows to support her.

"You're still a little woosy Sweetheart! Maybe you should just wait a few more minutes. Sit here!" He led her over to one of the high stools at her tall counter where they liked to eat.

"Okay! Just give me a minute here and I'll be fine. I just wanted to make some coffee for us."

"I can do it!" he told her, proceeding over to the heart of her kitchen. She guided his movements so he would find all that was needed. She watched him wondering if his head hurt like hers did. Then he came over to sit next to her. Turning his swivel stool to be able to look at John he asked, "Are you ready for a cup of coffee, John?"

"What? What was that?" he asked. He hadn't really been listening. Firstly, because he felt he was interfering with their caring for each other, and secondly because he couldn't wait to go outside. Freely go outside when he chose to do so. He looked forward to such freedom.

John turned from the window and sauntered into the kitchen. Slowly he looked around the organized, clean room and looked at everything. He touched the toaster, pushing down the handle and feeling the sudden heat rising. He quickly snapped the handle back up. Then he looked at her blender. "What is this thing?" he asked.

"It's a blender for mixing things. I like to make ice cream shakes in it," she told him.

He turned toward her and asked, 'What is an ice cream shake?"

"I mix frozen ice cream with flavoring and milk and whip it up in there. Then I just pour it into a tall glass, pop in a straw to drink it through and enjoy. Maybe I can make us some later."

The coffee was beginning to perk and the room filled with the fragrance. "Oh Jeff, what did you put in that? It smells heavenly!" Tina asked Jeff.

"Just one of Mrs. Braxton's many surprises. I added a dash of cinnamon to the grounds. It's one of my favorite flavors."

"It does smell good!" John mentioned. Methodically he was opening and closing every cupboard door, looking to see what was in each. "You really have a lot of stuff, Christina."

"Yeah, women are like that. They like to have whatever they need on hand, so when they actually need it, it's there." She couldn't help but smile. Sobering she asked, "So in your time I suppose some things are hard to get?"

"You might say that. There isn't much room for unnecessary items outside of basic food supplies and paying the bills. Most people are lucky to have a steady job."

"I know that has to rough. But I'm glad you came back with us. I think you'll enjoy how it is here. Maybe you might even want to stay."

"Maybe!" he said, without sounding decisive.

As the coffee finished brewing Jeff stood, went to the cupboard and pulled out cups for them. "How do you take your coffee, John?"

"Hot and black. Just the basic way!"

Jeff poured their drinks and handed John's to him. "Careful there, it's pretty hot." Then he put a cup in front of Tina and one on the counter in front of where he had been sitting. Going around the counter again he returned to his stool and sat. He sipped a little from his cup and looked at his watch. "It's still morning, so after we finish our coffee, maybe we ought to take John for a ride so he can see the city."

John looked at them and smiled. "That sounds good to me," he said with a smile on his face. "I'm looking forward to this. I still can hardly believe I can go outside whenever I please."

A half hour later they were out the door, headed for Jeff's car. He opened the door for Tina while John climbed into the back seat. Jeff quickly went around to the driver's side and slipped in. He started the engine and they were off. They cruised through her complex first just to show him where she lived, and that it was a 'gated' community for security. Then they headed for downtown where he could see all that went on down there.

As they drove John was very quiet, his eyes scanning everything. He recognized the large Union Station building and city hall, for neither had changed much. Finally Jeff asked, "Is there anything that you know of that you'd especially like to see?"

"Just everything! I don't know of anything special."

So they drove out to Orange County and drove around Disneyland and over by Knottsberry Farm. He enjoyed seeing the replica of Independence Hall that sat there. Then they drove around Los Angeles Airport so he could watch the planes landing and taking off. They parked on a high hill along the beach overlooking the airport, and he seemed fascinated watching the planes. Slowly they drove back toward Tina's place where they climbed out and silently walked into the house.

They all were feeling the effects of their travel and were exhausted. And after a three hour trip around the city they were all ready to take a nap.

Tina showed him the guest room and private bath and told him, "You can rest as long as you want. This will be your room while you stay here. We're going to lie down for a little while and take a nap in my room. I'm exhausted and my headache hasn't gone away yet. Call if you need anything. Then, when we get up I'll fix some dinner for us."

"Thank you Christina! You don't know how much this means to me. It's like a miracle. I'd like to stay a little while if I may."

"Of course! You're always welcome here. You helped us when no one else would, and we're glad to return the favor. I've discovered there are good people in the world, even if I had to find them in different times." She chuckled to herself.

She gave him a little hug, which seemed to surprise him, and then turned to walk to her bedroom.

Jeff was just turning down the blankets for her and he sat on the edge of the bed and pulled off his shoes. "You don't mind if I rest here beside you, do you? I just want to hold you in my arms for a while." His eyes looked tired to her, but he radiated calm and strength. Again she felt peaceful and protected with him there.

"This is where you belong Jeff. Beside me always! We're going to be man and wife aren't we?"

"Yes, as soon as we can manage it. Come here woman, I want to feel you against me. It's been a long day, or at least it feels as though it has. I think this is the first time I have ever been chased by the law. Kind of opens your eyes as how easily things can go wrong in life."

Tina slipped off her shoes and sat on her bed. Then she laid down and rolled onto her left side so she could face Jeff. "You know, I think you're the greatest man I've ever known. And I don't want to lose you. You're one in a million. Not many would do what you have done for a woman. I love you, Jefferson." She smiled into his eyes and she could see how very much her words meant to him. His eyes filled with moisture and he reached out to her, pulling her against his hard chest, just where she loved to be. She very quickly fell asleep against his chest hearing the reassuring sound of his strong heartbeat.

Two hours later Tina woke still encompassed in Jeff's strong arms. She smiled to herself, knowing he would always be there for her. Slipping backward out of his arms she laid on her back and looked at the ceiling. What a day this had been. What a life she had been blessed with. To travel through time twice, and find the man of her dreams, to see the future, even if it was bleak, and to have visited the past were gifts that she would cherish all of her life.

She turned her head to look at Jeff as he slept, warmed her entire being. His long dark lashes lay on his cheeks looking sexy. She wished she had such full lashes. The width of his shoulders intrigued her and made her feel feminine and well protected. She liked the size of his hands and the strength in them. His arms were solid and his entire build spoke of strength and power. His expression was relaxed as he rested, but when he was awake he appeared stern and capable. He was a natural born leader. His ability to evaluate and arrive at solutions quickly impressed her. She knew he was an intelligent man. And she was surprised he wanted her. He could have someone much more beautiful and desirable than herself, yet he wanted her enough to follow her through time. She didn't think there were many men that would do that.

As she looked at him his eyes opened and he smiled at her.

"Do I pass muster, My Love?"

"I was just thinking about how lucky I was to have you in my life. You're so much more than I am, you could have someone so much better, yet you care for me. I don't think I could ever stop loving you for that."

"You're the only woman for me, Christina. I hope you know that. You came through time to find me. How could I do less than search you out and find you again? You are my world! Yes, I've managed well financially here, but it was just so I could do for you. So I could give you things, and keep you safe. My world revolves around only you. I could lose everything else tomorrow and still be happy because I have you with me, where you belong. I think you know that now, don't you?"

"Yes! We belong to each other. I feel as though I need to be near you a lot of the time. It's as though we're part of each other now and I don't want to be apart."

"That's how I feel too, Hon. When I wake in the morning and you're not beside me I feel bereft as though part of me is missing, but as soon as I see you, or hear your voice things get better. The day is brighter, and everything seems right in the world. There won't be a day that I won't love you Christina!"

"You're so good for me, Jeff. You make me more stable and strong. You're the first one I think of if I have a problem or don't feel well. It's you I want to take care of me when I'm ill. I'm sorry about that, but it's true."

"That's what people who love each other are suppose to do. We've both learned what loneliness is, and it's hard to live with. I won't ever go back to that. Even if something happens to you, God forbid, and I lose you, you will live on in my heart, so I won't be alone anymore. You're here, in my heart," he said, taking her hand and pressing it against his chest over his heart. He held her hand there long enough for her to feel how strongly it was beating.

Tina smiled at him and leaned closer to touch his lips with hers. And when they touched she felt his warmth surrounding her. She closed her eyes and rested a little while longer.

Another half hour passed before they finally got up. Tina took a shower and put on fresh clothes. Then Jeff showered as well. He slipped back into the clothes he had been wearing and walked downstairs to find her in the kitchen. She had pulled out some ground beef and made a meatloaf and was just putting it in the oven to bake. She washed large potatoes so they would be ready to go into the microwave later so they could enjoy baked potatoes for dinner. Then she searched through the refrigerator for some fresh vegetables, washed them and prepared a pan for cooking them, leaving the veggies on her cutting board lying on the counter until time to put them in the pan on the stove.

Jeff helped her set the table with plates and flatware and three hot pads for putting the hot dishes on. Then Jeff looked in the frig for a bottle of red wine. In the back he found one and gently placed it on the counter. He pulled out the cork and let it breathe so it would be ready for dinnertime.

It wasn't long before John came into the kitchen looking as though he too had decided to take a shower. His hair was wet and looked as though he had finger combed it, giving him a very masculine appearance.

Tina walked into the living room and turned on the TV. She watched John's face as the picture came into view. He immediately sat right in front of it, almost as if he expected to speak to someone. She couldn't help but smile when Jeff explained that it was only for entertainment and edification, that it was not a communication tool.

Jeff handed him the remote control and the three of them watched TV as John switched channels until he found something interesting. When dinner was ready they had a quiet meal in the kitchen. Finally they walked out onto Tina's small patio with their glasses of wine in their hands. Jeff sat in one of the chairs at the glass table and stretched his long legs out in front of him. John followed suit and Tina slipped demurely into one of the other chairs at the table. The sun was just going down and as they watched, stars began to appear. Tina knew the stars they could see were only the brightest ones, which could be seen even in the city lights, but she enjoyed the peace of it anyway.

No one had spoken for a few minutes when Tina heard her neighbor open her glass sliding door onto her own patio. They watched as Jacquelyn Woodley stepped out into the night.

"Jackie!" Tina called out after she saw that her neighbor was alone. "Come and join us for a glass of wine?"

Jackie looked up and smiled. Her eyes rested on the handsome guy known as John. After a moment she stepped off of her patio and onto the grass that was open between the two patios. She walked over to Tina's with a questioning look on her face. She couldn't take her eyes from the soft brown ones in the handsome face.

As she approached John and Jeff stood to be introduced. Tina liked the politeness of their act.

"Hi Tina! Are you sure I'm not interrupting anything?"

"Of course not, silly. I want you to meet someone special. Jackie this is John, who is visiting me for a short while. John, I want you to meet my good neighbor, Jackie."

Jeff remained still as John stepped over to take Jackie's hand in his own. He watched as he suspected these two people looked perfect together. Maybe his future wife was a matchmaker here.

"It's a great pleasure to meet you, Jackie," John said, bending down to kiss her hand.

Jackie was both pleased by his old world formality and a little embarrassed. "Oh, you make me feel as though I should curtsey. How charming and gallant! Where did you find this wonderful handsome man Tina?"

"You might say I had to travel through time just to find him. Come and sit with us. I'll get you a glass of wine," she said, stepping back inside.

"Please sit by me," John told her. He pulled out the other chair and pulled it closer to his own. Taking her hand he seated her in it. He couldn't quit smiling at her.

Immediately Tina returned with Jackie's glass of wine. She sat it down in front of John so he could hand it over to Jackie and as he sat it down, Jackie's hand reached for it. Their fingers touched and they looked at each other silently.

The moment passed and Tina introduced Jeff to her as well. Tina hadn't had a chance to talk with Jackie since Jeff had come back into her life, so Jackie didn't know who he was.

Jackie took Jeff's hand and he shook it gently and released it. Tina and Jeff sat down and watched as the sparks seemed to jump from John to Jackie. Looking over at Tina, Jeff smiled a knowing smile and Tina nodded her head slightly in agreement. The two other people with them already looked like a couple.

John had Jackie's hand in his and they were locked into each other's eyes. Tina decided they might like to be alone.

"Jeff, there's something I would like to show you in the living room. Could you come with me?" she asked, with a sly smile on her face.

"Of course, Sweetheart. If you two would excuse us?" he said to John and Jackie as he stood.

The two barely acknowledged his words and Tina and Jeff walked back into her townhouse. As soon as they were out of sight of the two on the patio Jeff took her into his arms and smiled at her.

"You are such a matchmaker, my Darling. How did you manage that?"

"Whatever do you mean, Jeff? I just invited my neighbor over for a glass of wine. I had nothing to do with what's happening out there on the patio." She smiled up into his eyes and thought to herself, maybe now John will have a reason to stick around.

Jeff pulled her close and kissed her lips. When he finally finished there he licked her bottom lip with his tongue, settling on the edge of her mouth pressing butterfly kisses there. He worked his way over her eyelids and across her cheekbones with small kisses, on down to her throat. He leaned her over backward slightly as she lifted her chin for more access for him. He slid his strong hands along her back, holding her in place. Then he returned his lips to hers as he lifted her into his arms. He walked over to the nearest chair and sat down, placing her on his lap.

Jeff placed his palm across the back of her head and pulled her tighter to him. Slowly Tina lifted her hands so she could sweep her fingers through his soft clean hair. She loved the feel of it and that he wore it a little longer than most men who were CEO's of corporations. She liked it that he was not one to follow fashion, but to wear his hair in his own style.

Jeff felt his heart going out to her, as it did each time he kissed her. He could feel her love wrapping up his heart and claiming it as her own, and he relished it. When the kiss ended he drew back, releasing her head to slide his hand down her spine to caress her back. He loved the feel of her back, the little indentations and the softness of her. He felt as though he couldn't get enough of her.

"I suspect John might not be in such a rush to go back now," she said to him softly.

Jeff laughed! "You may be right there, Sweetheart. I suspect he not only wanted to find the peace that he spoke of, but happiness as well. As did I, My Love."

"And tell me, my handsome love, have you found what you needed?"

"Ah, My Love, I have, and so much more!"

THE END

Bibliography

History of aspirin – Wikipedia, the free encyclopedia

About th

Writi
somet
to d
wrote
her g
her t
enoug
atten

Class learning much about ob
required investigations on ma
vehicle accidents, she was able
of findings and putting the in
to make it easier for the reader
at the scene. She decided to ta
began to write in earnest. W
shelf and several children's st
write to share the joy of findi
women's dreams. There is myst
paranormal in many of her sto
for everyone, with lots of possil

Bibliography

History of aspirin – Wikipedia, the free encyclopedia

About the Author

Writing seemed to have been something she had always wanted to do. In her school years she wrote romance and mysteries for her girlfriends. They encouraged her to write more, but there wasn't enough time. During college she attended a Police Report Writing Class learning much about observations. Since her profession required investigations on many subjects including those on vehicle accidents, she was able to enjoy the writing, (typing) of findings and putting the information in such a way so as to make it easier for the reader to picture what had transpired at the scene. She decided to take an early retirement and she began to write in earnest. With a dozen romances on the shelf and several children's stories as well, she continues to write to share the joy of finding that perfect half for many women's dreams. There is mystery and fiction, with a touch of paranormal in many of her stories too, so there is something for everyone, with lots of possibilities.